S.T.

THE GHOSTMASTER

A microsecond later, a gleaming figure appeared in the doorway. Will recognized it at once. *Il Fantasma* . . . And now it was here, in this room, barely ten metres from him. . . . Brilliant, and deadly.

S.T.O.R.M.
THE GHOSTMASTER

E. L. YOUNG

MACMILLAN CHILDREN'S BOOKS

First published 2007 by Macmillan Children's Books
a division of Macmillan Publishers Limited
20 New Wharf Road, London N1 9RR
Basingstoke and Oxford

www.panmacmillan.com

Associated companies throughout the world

ISBN: 978-0-330-44641-9

3 5 7 9 8 6 4 2

A CIP catalogue record for this book is available from
the British Library.

Typeset by Intype Libra Limited
Printed and bound in Great Britain by Mackays of Chatham plc, Kent

For Clare, James, Joy, Peter and Alastair

Prologue

Venice, Italy. 8 April. 02.26

'Lights!'

At once the dungeon blazed with white.

At last, thought the figure that stood trembling on the glass floor, with a pounding heart and staring eyes.

He trembled from excitement, not fear.

Hanging from an iron stave driven into one of the damp-streaked walls was an LED screen. It showed the contents of another room: the metallic glint of an ancient mirror, a stuffed bird, one dusty wing askew. A sagging leather armchair. A sculpture of an Ethiopian warrior. And there, inside a spindle-legged display cabinet beneath a leaded window, a square, ebony box inlaid with pearl.

'Cameras!' he commanded.

His pulse soared. Tonight, he would strike the slumbering city of Venice.

'You are ready, Master?' came a reedy voice from behind a red velvet curtain.

The figure took a deep breath. His lungs tingled. His senses seemed electrified. Through the fifteenth-century walls, he fancied he could hear fish swimming in the dank waters of the lagoon. The lights of the dungeon sizzled his retina. He could taste wealth. Knowledge. *Revenge.*

'I am ready. Activate the connection,' he whispered. 'And . . . *action*!'

Venice, Italy. 8 April. 02.28

In her frescoed bedroom in her parents' imposing palace on the Grand Canal, Cristina Maria della Corte di Castello Bianco sat up. Her black hair streamed around her shoulders, silvered in the moonlight. She pushed it back. Listened hard. She'd heard something; she was sure of it.

Silently, she slipped into the hallway. Saw hand-woven carpets, painted ceilings, cherubs smiling on masses of golden clouds. Nothing moved. But *something* had woken her. And before she'd opened her eyes she'd heard an odd *slithering*.

Surely it couldn't be her brother, whose room was down the hall but who was impossible to wake. Her parents were in Rome. The only other person in the house that night was Adriano, the butler. But what would he be doing, sneaking around the fourth floor at half past two in the morning? Had she imagined it . . . ?

No. There it was again! And it was coming from next door – from her father's museum. It *had* to be her brother or Adriano, Cristina reasoned, with some relief. No thief would know the code to switch off the thermal alarms active in each unused part of the forty-roomed palace.

Annoyed now at being woken, Cristina threw open the door to the museum.

'*Porca vacca!*' She clasped a hand to her mouth.

She wanted to cry out.

Could not.

Something was inside the museum. It was by the leather armchair, beside the open window, its back towards her. But what a back. It was hazy. Insubstantial. Grey. No, pink. The colours were shifting. Was it human? *No!*

'What—' she started. But her red mouth hung open, useless. Her eyes were streaming back data that her brain struggled to comprehend.

No, she thought. *No.* Yet realization was running in prickling shudders up Cristina's straight-talking spine to her astonished brain: what she was seeing was – *had to be* – a *ghost*.

The *ghost* was moving. It was stepping up to the broad window ledge. A soft breeze swept into the room.

'*No!*' Cristina cried, her vocal chords responding at last.

But before her legs would do the same, the figure twisted and fell, catching its foot on the sill. Its hazy body vanished into the night.

Cristina dashed to the window. Her bronzed hands pressed against the frame, her ears ringing with the thermal alarm *she* had activated, she thrust her head into the damp air. Saw nothing. The palace fronted directly on to the canal and this side was in shadows.

Cristina ran from the study. Along the hall, down the broad, marble-chipped staircase and to the worn stone steps outside the front door.

She peered hard to the left and to the right.

Nothing.

The canal looked peaceful. Moored wooden motor-boats bobbed up and down. An orange beam from an artificial light jagged across the moss-black water. Showed only ripples.

Cristina shook her head. What had just happened? What had she just seen?

Half an hour later, she still had no answers. But she'd realized two things.

One: the square ebony box was gone.

Two: underneath the open window, on a rug that had once belonged to a Shah of Iran, was a tiny pile of something very strange.

1

STASIS HQ, Sutton Hall, Oxfordshire. 14 April, Good Friday. 02.00

For one hour, the stately home had been silent.

Will Knight could time that to the second. Because for the past three and a half hours, he'd lain awake in his room. He'd listened, ears straining, as lab doors were slammed shut, as lights were switched off.

Now, he thought.

Will crossed to the trestle table desk. It supported a small black rucksack, a penknife and an angle-poise lamp. Will yanked the hot head of the lamp towards him. He flicked out the smaller of the knife blades. And he bared his forearm.

There it was. Translucent, a couple of millimetres across, stuck to his flesh with timed glue.

This glue was formulated to last 120 hours. The tracking dot would fall off in the morning, Shute Barrington had promised him. But Will needed his freedom tonight.

Holding his breath, Will pushed the tip of the blade underneath the rim of the dot. Then he lifted it. Pulled. Pain flared through his skin. But there was no blood. His skin – minus a few hairs – was intact.

There was no time to waste. Will shoved the tracker underneath his pillow and grabbed the rucksack. He opened the door. Saw no one. Lightly, he ran along the corridor and made a hard right down the narrow back staircase to the rear exit. Will hesitated. He'd have to use his pass key to swipe his way out. The swipe would be logged. But by the time anyone checked those logs, it would all be over.

His pulse starting to speed, Will held his pass to the automatic reader. A click. And he emerged into the black spring night. No moon. No stars. From his rucksack, he pulled a narrow-beam torch. It picked out jagged branches and bluebells, which lined the muddy track that skirted the wood. This track would take him right to his destination.

He glanced back. No lights. Nothing moved.

No one had seen him.

Two minutes later, and Will had cleared the wood. His breathing was coming fast. Behind him, shadowy elms and oaks creaked in the darkness. Concealed beyond was Sutton Hall, an E-shaped Elizabethan mansion, and the headquarters of the Science and Technology Arm of the Secret Intelligence Service – home to the men and women who, under the lead of Shute Barrington, created 'support technologies' and provided scientific advice to Britain's foreign intelligence service, MI6.

Here, Will had spent the past five days. And those days had been used well, he thought, as he made for the lakeside storage shed. Will tore off his jacket and jeans. Underneath, he wore a breathable dry-suit, 'borrowed' earlier from the primary store.

From the mess of equipment piled on the shelves, Will collected a pair of fins, a buoyancy control vest and a re-breather, and he pulled his new device from his rucksack.

The helmet fitted tightly. Running from the back were twin waterproof cables which connected to a strip of orange plastic and to a simple control panel that Will strapped around his wrist. Will pressed the plastic strip to his tongue. The sleeve of his suit felt loose. It was too big, but it would protect him from the worst of the cold.

And it would be cold. Will was sure about that. He fixed his gaze on the black water.

Research Lake 2.

It was circular, with a diameter of eighty metres. Connected by sluice gates to the larger Lake 1, which was invisible behind a line of silver birch trees.

Will knew all about Lake 2. He'd heard about it the previous day. It had a maximum depth of seven metres. There was a patch of slippery weed in the north-west corner. An underwater obstacle course, constructed from touch-sensitive plastic hoops, metal-framed tunnels and concrete boulders. And, somewhere in those dark waters, was the reason for Will's covert expedition.

A metal box. Contents unknown.

Barrington had told Will he couldn't have it. Tonight, Will would prove him wrong.

Will shut off his torch. And the world vanished. His retinas were stunned, rod cells demanding something – *anything*. But it was useless. No moon. No stars. No light.

Will bit down on the mouthpiece of the re-breather. The miniature canister would provide him with just seven minutes of air. Much less than a scuba tank, but a scuba tank would be far too large and unwieldy. This canister would have to be enough.

Ready. Will activated his helmet-mounted equipment.

Set. He pulled on his fins.

And he dived, plunging into the glassy water.

Cold rushed. It poured into the suit, scoring goosebumps across his skin. But Will barely noticed it. His brain was concentrating on the crackling patterns that were firing against his tongue.

His helmet was fitted with miniaturized sonar equipment. It emitted radio waves. When they hit something, they bounced back, and those returning signals were reported in the firing pattern of the one hundred and forty-four electrodes integrated into the strip of plastic stuck across Will's tongue.

After a little practice, his brain had learned to understand. It could use those tongue signals to build up a picture of the world around him. With this kit, Will could 'see' underwater. In the dark.

Now, Will focused. He knew the target box was somewhere in the south-west corner, among the touch-sensitive apparatus of the obstacle course. Last night, three of STASIS's finest research officers had used their experimental night vision kit to try to find the target. But their systems provided too narrow a field of view. They'd set off the alarms built into the inside edges of the hoops and frames before they'd had a chance to get close to the box. They'd all failed. Barrington had prevented Will from trying.

'You're fourteen years old, Will. I can't let you.'

The words burned in Will's brain.

As he descended now into the blackness, Will per-formed the valsalva manoeuvre. By pinching his nose and trying to exhale through it, he raised the pressure in his throat. This sent air through his Eustachian tubes into his middle ears, equalizing the pressure in his ears and in the water, and preventing his eardrums from bursting.

Will felt the pressure of the water increase against his body. A descent to ten metres would double the pressure, compared with the surface. Will was close to six.

And he hesitated. The sonar signals told him he was approaching a solid, circular-shaped object. A *hoop*. Instantly, they picked up something else. And Will's spine twitched. *Concentrate*, he told himself. It was soft. Waving. Anchored. *Weed.* Only weed.

Very slowly, moving his head to the left and the right, Will passed through the hoop, taking care to keep his arms tight along his sides. He probed the underwater landscape, and he made out the entrance to a tunnel formed from four ladder-like frames of metal. Scanning his head to the right, he 'saw' that it right-angled after ten metres. Was it the tunnel that had caught the others out?

Kicking gently, Will arched his body, easing himself inside. One touch, he knew, and the alarms would go off. But if he swam too slowly, he'd lose momentum, and so control. He had to judge his pace precisely. Shimmying, feeling more like a fish than a human, Will reached the kink. Instantly, he bent at the hip, angling himself around the bend. *What was that?*

There – underneath a gap in the rungs of the frame. Will could sense the outline of something oblong. He must be close to the lake bed, he realized. And this object was roughly the right size – twenty centimetres by thirty. Almost holding his breath, waving his fins just enough to keep him in position, Will reached out, through the gap. Touched slime. *A little to the left.*

His fingers hit metal. Instantly, he felt around the edge of the object. A box. Will grinned in the darkness. Ordering his hand not to tremble, he grasped the box, and millimetre by slow millimetre, lifted it inside the tunnel. At once, Will clasped it to his chest, and he shimmied forward, and out of the end, almost into open water. Will twisted his body, exultation making his heart race. He was ready to kick for the surface.

And he froze.

New signals were rushing against his tongue.

He had never felt anything like this before. But he knew at once what they meant.

Something was approaching. Not something. *Somethings*. And they were approaching *fast*.

'Sir!'

The screen beside Shute Barrington's bed burst into life. It showed the time: 2.15 a.m. And it showed the chalk-white face of Charlie Spicer, his deputy.

'*Spicer?*'

'Sir! Will Knight is in Lake 2. The sluice gates are open!'

Barrington's temperature instantly fell five degrees. '*What the hell is he doing there?*' But, even as he spoke, Barrington knew the answer.

'The interior tunnel alarm just sounded! I was in the Lake 1 lab. I've got the controls. I can see his clothes on the bank! I'm going for the launch.'

'The *devices?*'

'I'm on them, sir!'

'*You can make them listen to you, Spicer?*'

Spicer's mouth jerked. Nervous tension. 'Yes. Sir.'

'They'd damn well better!' Barrington hissed. He leapt out of bed, grabbed his leather jacket. And he ran.

Impact. It hit Will in the right thigh and sent him rushing backwards until his back collided with something hard. Fear rushed through him in pounding waves. His breathing was shallow and fast. But at least he still had the mouthpiece. At least he was still breathing.

He reached out. His hand clasped metal. The frame tunnel.

Instantly, Will arched his body and he slipped inside the frame. Perhaps it would give him some protection. But from *what*? He pressed a button on his watch. The face showed the time, air pressure, that bugging devices were absent from Will's vicinity – all sorts of facts that were irrelevant at this moment. But it also revealed one vital piece of information: he had forty-five seconds of oxygen left.

Will adjusted his helmet. He turned his head just as the second impact hit. The entire frame shook. Will gripped the bars with one hand, feeling his stomach lurch. And his other hand flailed. Will cursed, as he felt the box slip out of his fingers, into the blackness.

Triumph had vanished. He was seven metres under water. It was the middle of the night. He didn't know what was attacking him. He had ten seconds of oxygen left. No one knew he was here.

The negatives out of the way, what were the positives? Will racked his brain.

Nothing.

The sonar told him three objects were circling him. He had to do something and he tried to take one last, deep breath. *No response.* An ache gripped his lungs. He was out of air. Carbon dioxide was building up. He had no choice. He had to get out of that frame. He had to try to make it to the surface.

Will spat out the mouthpiece. He let go of the metal, and he kicked. Once more. The sonar told him he was out of the tunnel and he told his brain not to listen, kicking harder and harder still, ignoring the signals searing from his lungs. At last, he gasped as he broke the surface.

Instantly, Will's muscles turned to stone. Something invisible rammed into his shoulder sending him spinning and coughing. Eyes staring, Will peered desperately round. And he saw a light. A face. Felt the water churn.

Charlie Spicer. In a *motorboat,* the propeller close. Spicer's thick arm was reaching for his shoulder.

'Grab my hand!'

Spicer's fingers wrapped around Will's arm, digging into the flesh. Will felt himself pulled out of the water. Hauled into the boat. He was flat on his back, wires dangling from his head, shoulder throbbing.

'Are you OK?' Spicer looked like Will felt. *'Will?'*

For a moment, Will could not speak. He looked up.

Above him, the sky stretched black across Oxfordshire. Will's limbs tingled. His shoulder felt numb now. But nothing *really* hurt. He met Spicer's gaze.

And then, bursting through the miniature speaker slotted into Spicer's ear, he heard the voice of Shute Barrington: 'Spicer, I'm on the shore. Do you have Will? *Is he alive?*'

Will couldn't hear the engine of the anonymous Ford Transit SWB. Or the wheels of the van, as they headed for London. Only Barrington's voice in his head.

Will watched the countryside flash by, and then the outskirts of London and the headlights of lorries on the M25.

In the driver's seat beside him, Shute Barrington glared blue thunder at the road.

Barrington. Half an hour ago, he had been furious.

'That tracker was for your own safety!' he'd yelled, back at STASIS HQ. 'You're a fourteen-year-old intern, Will. You're our guest. I told you not to go in the lake *for your own safety*. If something happened to you, what the hell would I tell your mother? She'd fry me.'

Will had tried to explain.

All he'd wanted was to test his technology. Barrington should understand, Will thought. After all, Will made things. That was the reason he'd been invited to Sutton Hall.

Will had met Shute Barrington four months ago, in St Petersburg, with Andrew and Gaia, on the first official mission for STORM. 'Science and Technology to Over-Rule Misery' – or so Andrew had named them at the time. They had been on the trail of a dangerous new weapon. And STORM had beaten Barrington to it.

Will was STORM's inventor. Or 'the Maker' as Andrew sometimes called him, to Will's irritation. Impressed by Will in St Petersburg, Barrington had asked him to spend the first week of the Easter holiday out at the Oxfordshire base. Will's mother, a professor of astrophysics at Imperial College, had been a consultant to STASIS in the past. She knew the territory, and she'd let Will go on one condition: that Barrington guaranteed her son's safety.

The first day, Will had walked around in slack-jawed wonder. He didn't have clearance for exposure to every project. But he hadn't been disappointed.

Barrington had showed him a prototype hand-gun that automatically transmitted its precise geographical location when it was shot. In a conservatory converted into a lab, Will had tried out a hand-held device that could record and play back smells. Later, from behind toughened glass, Will had watched as Barrington demonstrated a way to explode silicon chips. The aim of the project was to create laptops that could be ordered to self-destruct if they were stolen.

For the next four days and nights, Will had helped to develop kit for underwater use. He'd brought his own ideas. Pet projects that he hadn't quite got around to completing. And he had concentrated on the sonar 'vision'. All he'd wanted was to test it. To pit himself against the prototype underwater vision devices developed by the STASIS techies. To prove that his idea was the best. Barrington had forbidden it.

'If you're going to work with us, you'll have to learn to listen to my orders!' Barrington had fumed, while Will dripped Lake 2 water on to the grass.

Barrington had been wearing only a pair of white boxer shorts under his customary black leather jacket. But his voice was steel. His blue eyes had been flaming. It was impossible not to respect him.

Will had taken Barrington's fury and returned it in kind. 'And you'll have to learn to take me seriously!'

But by the time the van pulled up outside the terrace in Bloomsbury, both Will and Barrington had calmed down.

Will glanced across the road at his closed front door, black in the monochrome darkness. And up, at his mother's bedroom, blinds shut. She wasn't expecting him back until lunchtime.

'. . . I got the box.' Will said.

Barrington dropped his hands to his knees. Leather creaked. 'Yeah. I know.'

'I dropped it when I was *attacked*.' Will whispered the last word.

Barrington's face clouded. 'I can't tell you what they were, Will. You understand? Not won't. *Can't*. You're smart. You get the difference.' Then Barrington pulled a black hold-all from the back seat. 'Your projects. I'm going on holiday. When I get back, you can impress me.'

Will nodded, relieved. He realized he'd been afraid that Barrington might decide to sever all links with STORM. With him.

At the front door, Will turned and called: 'I had a good week.'

Shute Barrington nodded. His expression still deadly serious, he replied: 'You did well . . . Don't work too hard. Eat chocolate eggs. You still look like you need them.'

Then the tyres screeched, and the van sped away.

3

Three trills. And a series of loud judders. Will's mobile was vibrating its way across his desk.

Will opened his eyes. Was confused for a moment. Then registered his things.

The oak desk, built five years ago by his mother, pushed up against the wall. The cricket ball that Eric Hollies used to bowl the legendary Donald Bradman out. This had been a present from Will's father, the Christmas before he died – before he was killed in action somewhere in eastern China, on a mission for MI6.

Now the ball was blackened. It had been scorched in an explosion in St Petersburg.

Sleepily, Will reached out a hand. A text message. From Andrew:

'URGENT. You must be back by now. If so come at once. Or call me!'

Will squinted. 1.30 p.m. He noticed a cup of coffee on the floor. Touched it. Cold. His mother must have noticed the closed door and crept into his room to welcome him back. He'd heard nothing. Will chucked the phone on his bed.

Five minutes later, just as he was falling asleep again, his duvet vibrated.

Five words.

'I mean it, Will. Now.'

Two o'clock, and afternoon spring sunshine lit the streets of Bloomsbury.

Pale green leaves looked unnaturally bright. The air itself seemed to gleam.

A school trip hustled past, flashing cameras and white, foreign smiles. Cars and cabs streamed by. Heading north, to Kings Cross and Camden. South, towards the jugglers and opera singers of Covent Garden and, beyond, to the River Thames.

Will walked quickly. His right leg and shoulder had been bruised in Lake 2 and they ached a little. But otherwise he was unscathed.

'Are you limping? What has happened?' his mother had called from the garden, when Will had finally made it down. A blue headscarf had covered her black hair, accentuating her Russian features. Will had her cheekbones, and her even gaze.

'It's nothing,' he'd replied.

Shears hung motionless. 'And coming back in the middle of the night – that too is nothing?'

'. . . I was awake. Shute had to come to London. He took me early.'

Lies. He didn't like them. But he didn't want to tell her the truth. She wouldn't let him go back.

Now, Will rubbed his leg as he walked. It took, he knew, just six minutes to cross the single square and make the two left turns that separated his house from Andrew's.

Geographically they were close. Architecturally, a world away. Will and his mother lived in a rented narrow terrace with dry rot and boxy rooms. As Will now turned the second corner, he glimpsed familiar spires, Georgian windows, twin chimneys and gables.

It was, Will realized, four months almost to the day since his first visit to the house.

In December, Will's father had been dead three months. His Russian mother had gone AWOL. Will had been living with one of her friends. He'd never felt so low.

Then Gaia, a girl from school, had led him to Andrew's back door and into another world. She had promised Will that STORM would change his life.

She'd been right.

STORM was Andrew's idea. Andrew Minkel. A multi-millionaire software tycoon, worth more than 100 million sterling by his fourteenth birthday. He'd decided to set up an organization of brilliant kids, with the optimistic aim of solving the world's problems. *Naive*, Will had thought at the time.

Andrew knew all about computers. Gaia was happy in the kitchen – so long as she was cooking up chemicals, and preferably explosives. Will was the inventor. And Caspian . . . Four days before Christmas, Caspian had been locked up in a secure psychiatric hospital. And so there were three.

Now, Will pushed open the wooden gate. From here, a neat path twisted around a spreading oak to the door, with its intercom. And Will smiled.

Andrew loved gimmicks. He'd talked about upgrading the biometric access system. On a yellow sticker, Will now read the word '*Smell*'.

Beside the intercom a metal suction cup rested on a hook. From the base of the cup sprang a cable that fed into the wall. At once, Will guessed what this was.

Grabbing the cup, he pressed it to his neck. Warm air gently heated his skin. Concealed inside the wall, a computer chip analyzed the odour molecules released from Will's body.

Evidently it was satisfied. Two words flashed up on the intercom display: '*Will Knight*'.

And then: '*Welcome to STORM*'.

Automatically, the front door jerked open. From the speaker came Andrew's voice, taut with urgency:

'Will! At last! We're in the basement!'

The steps to the basement were in the kitchen, at the end of the long hall. A tall girl was standing at the stairless steel fridge. Gaia. She was collecting bottles of water. Her brown curly hair was tied back. Bright brown eyes flashed a smile.

'Hello. Andrew was worried you were still with Shute.'

'I got back a few hours ago.'

Gaia kicked the fridge shut. Will looked tired, she thought. Or maybe just preoccupied. His eyes gave little away. It was sometimes difficult to tell what he was thinking. 'How did it go?'

Will hesitated.

She pulled a face. 'Don't tell me: classified.'

'I wasn't going to say that. I'll tell you. Later.'

Because Andrew's voice was echoing up the steps: 'Gaia! Is that Will? Come down! Hurry up!'

'Will! Welcome back!'

A small, skinny figure waved from a makeshift stage at the far end of the black-painted basement. Behind thick glasses, Andrew's blue eyes were serious. He was wearing his favourite red trousers and a purple T-shirt embossed with a representation of the caffeine molecule. His heavy gold watch gleamed in the dim light.

'Hello, Andrew,' Will waved back.

And he noticed that little had changed since his last visit two weeks ago. Metre-wide LED screens hung on the wall. Boxes of unopened kit were piled in the corner. The antique dining table that held the laptops was still strewn with papers. Only the steel bench, with its DNA sequencer, spectroscopic analyzer and other bits of specialised gadgetry looked untouched.

'Will, Gaia, please take a seat. I haven't had time,' Andrew was saying, 'to prepare a proper presentation. But I think that once you've heard what I have to say, you'll agree with me: we must act. And we must act at once.'

Will glanced at Gaia, surprised. Andrew hadn't asked about STASIS, hadn't said a word about Barrington. He looked utterly focused on whatever was occupying his impressive brain. But if Gaia was aware of Will's glance, she didn't react.

She pulled two dining chairs towards the stage. Andrew waved a hand. At once the main lights dimmed. A white curtain held by a rail to the back wall extended itself and flattened. Made from woven conductive plastic fibres, the curtain was a flexible computer display. Will knew the patent well.

'Watch closely,' Andrew whispered.

A video segment kicked in. It was fuzzy. But it showed a 120 degree view of a grand room. Will could make out a leather armchair and a sofa, a gilt-framed mirror against a dark green wall, a stuffed bird, the edge of an oil painting, and a series of glass-topped wooden display cases. It seemed to be some sort of museum.

'This,' Andrew said, 'is an MPEG taken seven days ago by security cameras in a palazzo in Venice.'

Will frowned. 'What are we looking at?'

'Wait. Watch the space above the sofa.'

Will waited. Nothing happened.

He was about to ask Andrew to fast forward when something moved. Beside him, Gaia had been shuffling in her chair. She froze.

Instead of watching the video, Andrew anxiously observed his friends' faces. He'd seen the footage perhaps twenty times. It still made no sense. Especially after what he'd learned that morning . . .

Will stared at the screen. From behind the sofa, *something* was moving.

What was it?

It had human form.

But *was it human*?

It had arms, a head, a neck, a torso. Yet its skin was grey. Opaque. The flesh seemed to ripple. Its ear sparkled. Its arm was glistening. Then, abruptly, it vanished from view.

'*Keep watching,*' Andrew insisted.

A moment later, a girl shot into the scene. Instantly, an alarm sounded, a siren wailing. Her back was to the camera. But from the angle of her elbow, Will could tell she had her hand to her mouth. For two long seconds, she did not move. The clip ended.

Andrew clicked his fingers to raise the lights. '. . . What do you think?'

Gaia stared at Andrew. 'What is this? Where did you get it?'

'That girl in the picture – her name is Cristina. I met

her in a secure chat room in February. You remember, when people were asking about St Petersburg – I took some questions.' And he coloured.

Will nodded. He remembered, all right. Andrew had been so excited about STORM's success, he'd nearly spilled all the details of their mission.

'What was that alarm?' Gaia said. 'Why didn't it go off when the . . . *thing* was there?'

'Well, exactly,' Andrew said. 'Cristina says the palace is fitted with thermal alarms. So whatever it was, it wasn't emitting significant heat.' He bit his lip. 'Cristina sent this seven days ago. I've been busy. I only watched it last night. And she said if she didn't hear from me, she'd investigate for herself. Anyway, in her email, she said, and I quote: "This MPEG shows a ghost stealing my family's most valuable possession. I saw the ghost leap out of the window. Then it vanished."'

'It's a hoax,' Will said.

Andrew didn't look put out. 'That's what I suspected at first.'

Gaia nodded. 'She created it. It's a fake.'

'Like I said, that's what I *thought*. But don't either of you watch the news?'

Andrew clicked his fingers. Once more, the basement lights dimmed. 'Watch,' he said. 'This appeared on BBC World *yesterday*. I saw it on their site this morning.'

A female news anchor was sitting at a desk, shuffling

papers. 'Now we cross to Sirena Smith in Venice. Sirena, tell us more about these *ghostly* goings-on.'

A young woman in a white shirt nodded seriously. 'I'm standing outside the Galleria d'Arte Moderna. This is one of Venice's most important galleries. It's home to works by Matisse, Rodin and Henry Moore. Needless to say, security is extremely tight. Yet last night, some-one – or *something* – managed to defeat the security systems and make off with the priceless *Salome* by Gustav Klimt. Now, one of the guards has told local newspaper, *Lo Stivale*, that the security footage does catch the thief in the act. But, the guard says, and I'll translate: "This was no man. I swear. It moved like a man. But the skin gleamed. It had no eyes. This was a ghost."'

The anchor nodded. 'So is he making this up – or are we talking perhaps about a corruption of the security footage?'

'Well, the footage hasn't been released, and the director of the gallery is remaining very tight-lipped. But here in Venice, the news is really causing quite a stir. Local media have already nicknamed the thief *"Il Fantasma"* – the ghost.'

The clip ended.

Will focused on Andrew as the lights went up. 'What are you saying? There's a ghost in Venice and you want STORM to investigate?'

'Do you believe in ghosts?'

Will hesitated. 'No.' And something sparked in his

memory. Something to do with Venice, and ghosts. But he couldn't quite make a fix.

'Gaia?'

'I don't know, Andrew. Do you?'

'I don't believe in ghosts per se,' he said. 'But I do believe something unusual is going on.'

'If it is, what's it got to do with us?' Gaia said.

Andrew took a deep breath. 'Well, if it can be subjected to scientific scrutiny, it's to do with us. And let's say for the sake of argument, it is what people call a ghost – that it is some kind of *anomaly* – then that is for science to investigate. And Cristina said she found a powder on the floor beneath the window. This suggests our ghost leaves a tangible trail.'

'And what do you think's more likely?' Will asked, one eyebrow raised. 'That it's dried ectoplasm or dust missed by the cleaner?'

Andrew nodded. 'I expected scepticism. That's as it should be. But imagine if this *is* a "*ghost*". If we could really get a handle on what people think they've been seeing for millennia. And,' and now Andrew's expression became more troubled, 'there's another reason we should go. I've been trying to get hold of Cristina since last night. She gave me her mobile number. She isn't answering it. Or her email. I think that's odd. And she said if she didn't hear from me, she'd investigate. Cristina put her trust in me. *Seven days ago.*'

Suddenly, the delicate cogs of Will's memory clicked. '. . . I read something recently about ghosts. A few months ago – I think a body of a boy washed up on an island in Venice. The article was talking about ghosts.'

'That ghosts killed him?' Gaia said, incredulous.

'No. But I can't remember exactly.' Will looked at Andrew. 'You really want to go?'

Andrew nodded. 'Cristina gave me her address. She invited me – all of us – to stay. Obviously she wants our help to find out exactly what's going on.'

'Though as far as I know, ghosts aren't known for burglary,' Will said. 'More for dragging chains and wailing.'

'Exactly, Will!' Andrew looked pleased.

Will shook his head, irritated. He hadn't meant that in support of Andrew's plan. Surely this was a person somehow masquerading as a ghost. Should that really interest STORM? Even if this thief had somehow managed to beat the thermal sensors. 'Would Cristina really go and investigate?' Will said. 'Surely she'd let the police handle it.'

'Her family's *most treasured possession.*'

'Then maybe *her parents* are already out there looking for it.'

'They're in Rome, she said. It's something to do with business. They can't come back, or they won't. For whatever reason, Cristina said she'd feel obliged to at least look for the missing item.' Andrew pushed his glasses back up along his nose. 'Look. It's only Venice. And it's Friday. We could give it the weekend. If it looks like nothing, we'll be back for Monday. Two days. In a palazzo in Venice . . . in spring . . . It's not like I want to drag us on a dilapidated train through the middle of the Russian winter.' And he flashed a smile at Will.

Will glanced at Gaia, who shrugged slightly. And he considered Andrew's arguments. He was sceptical, certainly. But he couldn't help being curious. *If* this wasn't a hoax, it was interesting, no matter what it truly was. Two days in Venice. The alternative was an Easter lunch at the house of his mother's friend, Natalia. Then what? Work on his STASIS projects. And he could take them with him. 'All right,' Will said.

Andrew beamed. 'Gaia?'

'. . . All right,' she said, though with more caution.

Andrew ignored it. 'Then I'll sort out the tickets and I'll call Sean to bring the car and see you back in here in twenty minutes. And don't forget your passports!'

Outside, Will plunged his hands in his pockets. Gaia lived in the opposite direction, in a flat above an estate agent in Charlotte Street, with her father.

'I didn't expect that,' Will said.

Gaia nodded. 'I think this girl will turn out to be crazy.'

'Yeah. Girls. Usually are.'

She smiled.

'So are you going to take the explosive this time, or make it as you need it?' he said.

'I'm not sure exactly what you need to blow up a ghost. I'll have to do a little research.'

Will's turn to smile.

'. . . Dad's from near Venice,' she said. 'A place called Padua.' Gaia focused suddenly on the flat, grey pavement.

And it struck Will that he'd have to explain to his mother he had to go away. Perhaps he'd do it from Andrew's car. It was all right for Andrew. His parents, who were mostly overseas, had gone on a six-month tour of South America. His father wanted to investigate traditional psychiatric practices, Andrew had said. Andrew got on well with his parents – from a distance. Gaia and her father were different.

'Are you going to tell your dad you're going ghost-hunting?' he said.

She shrugged, and was silent. He should say something. But he knew the situation. What could he say?

'. . . I'll see you back here,' he said awkwardly, and he turned to walk home.

'Will!'

He was ten metres away. He turned.

Gaia hesitated. She shook her head. Smiled. Waved.

Will nodded. And was gone, behind a rushing coach-load of tourists.

I missed you this week, she'd wanted to say.

Sotopartego e Calle Corner, Venice. 15 hours earlier.

Cristina della Corte shivered. It was dark in this narrow dead-end passage, off a street lined with closed shops. The stone walls of the alley crumbled. A single white light attached to the ancient wooden beams that formed the roof illuminated graffiti, red and dull green. *Forza Roma.* Football slogans. *No studente.*

At the far end, the passage opened directly on to a back canal. The only eerie sound was of mooring ropes creaking. The boats were covered for the night, blue tarpaulins tied around outboard engines. Cristina could smell rotting wood, and the stench of the green-black water.

Cristina turned away to the light, to glance once more at her watch. Diamonds glinted. And she cursed herself. She should have left it behind.

Yet she'd had little time to prepare, or to plan. Only three hours earlier, she'd heard from a boy who identi-fied himself as Dino. She'd found him in a chat room the day before, when she'd been doing a little *probing*.

He'd said nine o'clock. Now where was he?

In her pocket, she felt for her mobile. She scrolled through her contacts. Perhaps she should try Andrew Minkel one last time. Tell him all she had learned. All she knew about the *ghosts*. And the rest. The rumours.

'Cristina?'

The dull rasp cut through her spine. Cristina spun around. A boy had emerged from the shadows near the main street. He blocked the exit from the alleyway. Behind her, ropes strained.

Cristina took a deep breath. She nodded.

He stepped forwards, into the white light. The boy was a few years older, she realized. Sixteen or seventeen. She saw lank hair. White hands. A gaunt face, with black eyes, bright as olives. They bored into her.

'You won't need that,' the boy said. He pointed to her phone.

'. . . No?' And Cristina was ashamed to feel her heart thud against her ribcage.

The boy shook his head. Held out his hand for the phone. '*No*. You won't need anything that belongs to this unhappy world, Cristina. You will have *us*.'

4

Will's mother was out. She'd left a note on the kitchen table.

Will wrote a note in return. Andrew had asked him to go to Venice, to visit a friend. He would be back on Monday. He'd spend the rest of the holiday at home.

Will told himself he'd call later. He was still fourteen years old. He was still her son. But in the past few months, he'd grown up. Last September, his mother had vanished, leaving him to make his own decisions, and just because she was back he wasn't going to return to the old way of things. Will was determined to set the course of his own life. Even if he didn't explicitly recognize it, STORM was critically important to him. And so, right at this moment, was the mission to Venice.

Will didn't pack much. His passport, toothbrush, some clothes. He bundled the lot into the side pocket of the black hold-all. Perhaps his new devices might come in useful in Venice. In St Petersburg, his gadgets had certainly been invaluable. The toothphones from the Russian trip were on his desk, and Will threw them in.

Before heading for the front door, he made one last stop. In the kitchen, underneath the sash window, was a large metal cage. Inside this cage, curled up on a bed of wood shavings, was a rat.

No ordinary rat. A friend of his grandmother's had given Ratty to Will in St Petersburg.

In Russia, wires had poked from Ratty's head. Electrodes, surgically implanted into his brain, allowed Ratty to be remote-controlled.

One night earlier that spring, a professor of veterinary surgery at Imperial College London – and a friend of Will's mother – had conducted an operation to internalize the electrodes. Now, Ratty almost looked normal. Until his head-mounted miniature video camera and microphone were attached, that is. And his new foot pads.

In Russia, Ratty had been STORM's reconnaissance eyes and their ears. Perhaps, in Venice, he would be again.

As Will now collected his high-tech pet from his cage, he inspected the surgical scars. The hair had grown back well. Satisfied, Will patted the rat's head before slipping him into his jacket pocket. 'Good job,' he murmured.

Six minutes later, he found Gaia waiting outside Andrew's house. She carried a small black rucksack and a pair of sunglasses.

'Sean's on his way!' The shout came from around the back. A moment later, Andrew appeared, dragging a suitcase behind him. He'd changed his clothes. Now he was wearing a pair of outdoor moisture-wicking trousers with multiple zip pockets. His eyes fixed on Will's hold-all. He couldn't help wondering whether the latest devices were inside.

But Gaia was raising an eyebrow at Andrew's case. 'What have you got in there?'

Andrew took in her small rucksack. 'Is that all you're taking?' He looked incredulous.

'*Two days*, Andrew,' she said. 'At least, that's what you *said*.'

'It's not just clothes. Kit. You know.'

Will and Gaia exchanged glances. 'What sort of kit?' Will said.

'A torch. Waterproof matches. You know.' And Andrew coloured.

But he was saved by the deep-throat growl of an unmistakable engine. He knew what was coming, even before the monster tyres and the gleaming black bullet-proof chassis hurtled around the corner.

Andrew smiled. 'Here's Sean.'

Sean was Andrew's driver. He was a huge man with broad sloping shoulders which stretched the fabric of his green military jacket. As he leapt out of the SmarTruck, Will caught a glimpse of his surprisingly friendly brown eyes. Though that impression was offset slightly by the rest of the face. A white scar carved its way across his chin. Then there was his forehead. Sean had his own personal battering ram.

If Sean was surprised by the luggage, he said nothing. Silently, he lifted the case, the rucksack and the hold-all into the back of the SmarTruck. Mark III.

A 4.5-litre, V6 turbo engine. Forty-two inch tyres on twenty-inch rims. Up to sixteen inches of ground clearance. Maximum speed: eighty-five miles per hour.

Built for third world war zones or border patrols. There was space for a surveillance module, with a 360-degree camera and laser range finder, to be fitted to the back. If configured with a weapons station, a remote-controlled 50-calibre machine gun could blast a pursuer to bits.

'Still no weapons module,' Will observed, as the truck pulled away.

'It's on order, lad,' came the voice from in front.

Andrew rolled his eyes.

'Has to be hand-made by Mongolian eunuchs in Ulan Batar, doesn't it, Mr Minkel?'

'Indeed,' Andrew replied. 'And they're rather hard to find these days.'

'I have my contacts,' Sean said.

Will couldn't help smiling.

They shot down Shaftesbury Avenue, through the traffic, on to Monmouth Street and then St Martin's Lane. Suddenly the car slowed to a halt. Nothing was moving. Will wound down the window and stuck out his head.

Gaia tried to see past him. 'What's going on?'

'It looks like a demonstration.' Will could see people ahead, placards raised. A man in a green jumper was blowing a whistle. 'Something's probably happening in Trafalgar Square.'

'If only we had the reconnaissance drone, eh, Sean?' Andrew said, and he frowned at his watch. He leaned forwards, to peer through the windscreen.

And a wave of people swept on to St Martin's Lane. A few at the front had megaphones, but it was hard to make out what they were saying. The placards swivelled, and came closer.

No to Terrorism.

No war.

No Hate. G8.

Another bore the words: *48 – how many more?*

'Forty-eight – what do they mean?' Gaia said.

Andrew turned. 'You haven't heard?'

'Heard what?'

'I meant to say – but then I was thinking about *Il Fantasma*. There was a bomb in Paris this morning.'

'Forty-eight dead,' came Sean's voice from the front.

'The Group of Eight countries are planning some kind of terrorism summit here next week,' Andrew said. 'I imagine that's what the G8 thing is about.'

At last, the crowd reached the SmarTruck. Will could see the anger on the demonstrators' faces. He hadn't heard about the bomb. But he'd been asleep, and then with Andrew. And he remembered something that Thor, a STASIS techie he'd met in St Petersburg, had said at lunch the previous day. Will had taken a seat next to Thor in the canteen.

'This meeting will be critical,' Thor was saying. 'If this deal isn't done—' and then he'd noticed Will and shut up.

After five days, Will had got used to it. His security clearance took him only so far. Had Thor been talking about the G8 summit? Perhaps. But it could have been about anything. A STASIS meeting on new vending machines for the table-football room, for all Will knew. Everyone complained about the warm chocolate and the green Japanese 'snacks'. Were they made from processed seaweed? Were they actually *food*?

'All clear,' Sean announced.

Will was back in the present. The tail-end of the march had passed them, four police officers on chest-nut horses bringing up the rear. Ahead, the traffic started to move off.

And Will remembered something else: his father, on the village cricket green near their old home in Dorset, teaching Will physics as he taught him to bowl. Explaining that he worked for MI6 because he wanted to make the world a safer place. Now Will's father was dead. And, today, forty-eight others. For the past two weeks, newspapers had been talking about the prospect of another war. And he was going to Venice on the trail of a ghost.

But what could he do? He was fourteen years old. You can only do what you can, his father had told him once. Don't feel bitter for not achieving what you *can't*. Cold comfort, Will decided.

Venice. Good Friday. 15.00

Cristina was being led through an echoing castle.

The previous night, Dino had taken her directly to a damp room with a camp bed. It was like a cell. Ancient mould and rotting insects had tormented her delicate nostrils. Cristina had lain awake, eyes on the weak moonlight that slanted like a snail's trail through her slit window. And she had wondered if she'd done the right thing.

A ghost, or what appeared to be a ghost, had taken her family's box. She was well aware of the rumours about a ghost cult on this haunted island, the Isola delle Fantasme. One of the sons of a Dutch diplomat friend of her father's had vanished two months ago. It was the boy's disappearance that had finally triggered the raid here, no more than fifteen minutes by fast motorboat from St Mark's Square, the pigeon-ridden heart of Venice.

The police had found only Rudolfo, the reclusive owner of the miserable island. But the police had not used the internet to investigate, Cristina decided. It hadn't taken long for her to discover wild claims and strange stories. And to find Dino. And when she had mentioned the theft, Dino had not denied that the cult was involved. He hadn't exactly conceded it either. But he had invited her to meet him, his only insistence that she come alone.

This was risky, certainly. But Cristina trusted herself and her abilities. She would not become brainwashed. She would discover if the cult really existed, if it had committed the thefts, and how – and she would escape back home, succeeding where the police had failed. Everyone would fête her. Perhaps even her parents. Even STORM.

But lying on a sagging bed for hours had not been a part of the triumph she had envisaged.

All morning, Cristina had waited for a knock. She had shouted out. No one had answered. She'd heard nothing, apart from the gentle wash of lagoon water against the castle wall.

Then, at last, a sound! The olive-eyed Dino had arrived with a risotto broth, telling her to eat it quickly if she wanted to be in time for the meeting.

Now, as she followed him – as she experienced the *reality* of the castle – Cristina's feet did not drag. She had to find out where the ghost had come from, *if* it was really a ghost – *if* it could have come from here. And she had to find out who had stolen her family's most precious possession, and if she could get it back . . .

The winged lion. Symbol of St Mark. Symbol of Venice.

This particular lion was crafted in the sixteenth century. It had a body of twenty-two carat Spanish gold, blood-red rubies for eyes, and rare yellow diamonds, the colour of sunflowers, encrusting its soaring wings. But the object's true value did not lie in the metals and jewels. This lion had been presented to a great ancestor of Cristina's mother on his admittance to Venice's ancient and secretive governing body, the Council of Ten. According to family tradition, the lion was passed down the female line. It symbolized her family's glory and its antiquity. And, by rights, it would be hers.

If she could, she would retrieve it.

From here? From this castle on the Island of the Ghosts?

Once, this place might have been luxurious, she thought. But any comforts were long gone. The walls were bare, bar occasional antique portraits of grim-looking women in jet cloaks and tight strings of tarnished pearls.

Cristina's trainers thudded on the Istrian limestone. Wrought-iron chandeliers hung, black and ominous, above her head.

Cristina glanced down at her clothes. She was glad that at least she'd worn something plain. Jeans, a T-shirt and a white hooded top, with sleeves long enough to conceal her diamond-studded watch. Her long hair was loose.

Dino wore a grimy white shirt and dirty jeans. Everything about him was grimy, she decided. Even his voice.

Dino glanced back. Cristina did her best to wipe the apprehension from her face.

'Not far, Cristina,' he whispered.

And she stopped. She'd felt something. She turned suddenly. Saw only the passageway stretching. But she had felt it. A cold that had passed into her body, instantly spreading. Alarm made her heart race.

To her surprise, Dino gave a laugh. 'You feel it?' he asked darkly. And he jogged a few steps further on, to jab a bony finger at a portrait. It showed an elderly woman wearing a velvet mask. 'You see her – our Contessa – she haunts this passage. And there are others like her. You wonder why my patron's castle is known as the most haunted in Venice? This place, that once was the asylum for lunatics?' He laughed again. 'I warn you: never wander alone. Our ghosts are known for materializing. If they *touch* you, truly, you never forget it!' Dino's intensity seemed to stream from his eyes, charging the very air.

Cristina blinked at him. Here, in the gloomy darkness, surrounded by dead faces, *feeling* what she had felt – that cold that had swept through her like an illness – did she believe in these ghosts? Perhaps . . . Yes.

'Come on,' Dino said.

He started to stride away. Cristina hurried to follow

him. Around two further corners and into a wider passage, and Dino stopped at what appeared to be a dead end. A red velvet curtain barred the way. The air smelt decayed. Moisture glistened on the stone walls.

Dino smiled again, baring discoloured teeth. 'Now, you will see the Master,' he whispered. 'Now, you belong with *us*.'

'Good morning, ladies and gentleman. And welcome to this British Airways flight to Venice.'

At the rear of the club class cabin of the Boeing 737, Gaia and Andrew were settled in soft leather. Will was across the aisle. The cabin was mostly empty. There were only two other passengers: an Italian businessman with an attaché case and a young blonde woman glittering with gold. They were sitting a couple of rows up towards the cockpit.

Will leaned over to the window. He could see fields. Neat trees, tamed hedges. England. Disappearing. And he found his mind occupied with the demonstration. And the bomb. *Forty-eight* people dead. He hadn't even known. But he had to concentrate on the task in hand. And that was Venice and Cristina and her ghost.

He turned to Andrew, across the aisle. 'How much do you know about Cristina?'

Andrew had been showing Gaia the notes he was entering into his smart phone. Now he dropped it into his lap. 'Not a great deal. She goes to the Accademia del Genio. It's for gifted pupils. When I talked to her, she said she was working on cryptography. Jason Patel – someone I met at the Science Olympiad last year – he introduced us. He mentioned to her that I'd been to St Petersburg and got caught up in something quite important. It was Jason who set up that online meeting.'

'Cristina speaks English?' Will said.

Andrew nodded. 'Though I understand she's from an old Italian family. But that's really all I know.' He paused. His eyes flicked to the overhead locker. He was itching to know what was in Will's black hold-all.

As the SmarTruck had approached the airport, Andrew had turned to Will. 'I don't know exactly what's in your bag, but have you thought about how you're going to get it on to the plane?'

'. . . It should be all right.'

'A bomb's just gone off. Security will be tight. Are you sure they'll really let it all through?'

Will had hesitated.

'Sean knows people, don't you, Sean?' Andrew had said. 'He can help. Maybe we can say we're going to a science fair . . .'

Andrew's idea had worked. The security officer had taken Sean and Will into an inspection room. When he'd finished, he'd even wished Will good luck in the competition.

'So are you going to tell us exactly what you managed to get on-board?' Andrew said now, his gaze jerking up.

Beside him, Gaia turned expectantly. 'And you were going to tell us how things went with Shute.'

Will hesitated. He'd signed secrecy papers. But he was allowed to take projects away from Sutton Hall. And surely he was allowed to talk to Andrew and Gaia about his work. It was partly for the benefit of STORM, after all.

So he told them about the tongue sensor. Research Lake 2. The *attack*.

'Excuse me, sir, would you like something to drink?'

An air stewardess had appeared. She carried a tray with glasses of champagne and orange juice. Her red lips were set in a polite smile.

'No, thank you,' Andrew said quickly, without taking his eyes off Will.

If she was offended at her off-hand dismissal, the stewardess didn't show it. She only moved on, towards the blonde woman.

Gaia's eyes were wide. 'You don't know what they were?'

'It's *sonar*,' Will said. 'I can make out shapes. I can't tell for sure what things are. I can't even tell if they're living or not. Shute wouldn't tell me. He said they're classified.'

'Sounds very fishy,' she said.

'Was that a *joke*?'

And Gaia frowned. 'Your pocket just moved.'

It was unzipped an inch. Will jerked the zip right down. He reached inside.

Andrew grinned. 'Ratty! You brought him!'

Will lifted the animal's paws. The week before his assignment with STASIS, he had created detachable pads, inspired by gecko's feet. Millions of tiny hairs protruding from the pad could provide incredible adhesion to almost any surface.

Will had removed the animal's tiny camera and mike before going through security. Ratty had stayed very still in his pocket, almost as though he knew it wasn't safe even to twitch.

'I'd better not let him out here,' Will said.

Gaia glanced at the young female passenger, who was accepting a glass of champagne. 'You might get a bit of a reaction.'

'You might get him confiscated,' Andrew said seriously. 'Does he have a pet passport? Did you show him to security?'

Will screwed up his face. 'What do you think?' Gently, he patted Ratty's head and slipped him back inside his pocket.

Andrew's eyes rose again to the moulded plastic lockers. He pushed his glasses back up the bridge of his nose. 'And what did you show security?'

The stewardess was now heading towards the rear of the cabin, minus her tray of drinks. Will waited for her to pass behind the curtain, then, without a word, he rose and pulled down his bag.

'Is it safe to show us here?' Gaia said. Her voice was low, her eyes shining.

'If I can't use them in a public place, they're not much use,' Will replied. Now, as he eased back the zip he frowned. He hadn't put that there . . .

Resting on top of the sonar helmet was a small black box. Very gently, Will removed the lid. And heat rushed into his cheeks.

'What is it?' Andrew said.

Will angled the box towards him. Gaia leaned over for a closer look.

'You're going to have to explain,' Gaia said.

Will picked up one of the thin circles of film. 'These are tracking dots.' Tucked down the side of the box was a slip of paper. Will dropped the dot back into the tin, lifted out the paper. He read: 'To make sure you have plenty for next time. 120 hours each. No more. *NO LESS.*'

'I've heard about these,' Andrew said.

'I didn't invent them,' Will said. 'I had to use them while I was at STASIS. They monitor you twenty-four hours a day. Supposedly to sound an alarm if anyone walks into a test location – in case it's dangerous. They transmit a radio frequency signal.'

'But what do you use to pick up the signal?' Andrew asked.

'. . . You could use this.' Will reached into the bag and brought out a black jacket. He shook it out and handed it to Andrew.

'What's this?' Andrew patted the pocket. Felt something hard.

'There's a hard drive in there,' Will said. 'Solid state. Put it on.' He waited until Andrew had pulled off his heavy jumper and slipped on the jacket. 'Now feel in your inner pocket. Pull it out.'

Andrew retrieved a slender, silver-coloured head strap. Attached to it was a single moulded black eye-piece. 'You wear this?'

Will nodded.

Andrew took off his glasses and blinked. He fixed the patch into position. 'I hope this isn't pirated technology, Will.' He grinned.

Will shook his head. 'Your jokes are as bad as Gaia's . . . You don't have to use the eyepiece. The lining fabric is the same stuff as your display curtain – it'll work as a screen. There are ten ring-shaped sensors in your pocket. Put them on and you can pretend to type on your knee. The system will recognize what you're trying to enter.'

'A wearable computer,' Gaia said.

Andrew was fiddling with the eye-patch. And he beamed. 'This is amazing. I've seen virtual displays before. But the clarity is fantastic. Even with my eyes.' He lifted the patch. 'This is great, Will – you'll be able to do all sorts with it.'

'I made it for you.'

Andrew looked stunned. And then doubtful. Was Will joking?

'I got the parts from STASIS – Shute knows about it. He gave me half the stuff,' Will said quietly.

'Don't you want it?' Andrew said, in amazement.

Will coloured slightly. 'You're the computer genius.'

For a moment, Andrew didn't know what to say.
'. . . Thank you.' His blue eyes radiated his pleasure.

And Will looked down, uncomfortable. Out of one corner of his eye, he saw Andrew turn to Gaia and grin. Out of another corner, he saw the stewardess handing a menu to the businessman with the case. She glanced towards the rear of the cabin. And her smile flickered as her gaze passed Andrew's forehead, and the eye-patch. What did it matter, Will thought. They'd been through security. She could think what she liked. But he waited for her to reach them and distribute their menus before returning to his hold-all.

Torn between watching Will and reading the menu, Andrew sneaked a glance at the list. There was a choice of beef tenderloin with salad or a quail's egg omelette. Gaia peered over.

'*Quail's eggs,*' she said, disgusted by the vegetarian option.

'They're delicious, Gaia,' Andrew said. 'My aunt used to serve them soft-boiled . . . I wonder what they're having in economy.' And Andrew turned, aware Will was watching him.

'. . . We could try to find out,' Will said. But he hesitated. He'd said his inventions were no good if they couldn't be used in a public place. In large part, this was true. But there was no getting away from the trepidation he felt at getting out the second device in a busy, contained environment, like a plane. If it was spotted – and he had to face the fact that the risk was high – there was no way he could grab it and make a getaway.

No excuses. He had to try.

Will lifted a small cardboard box from the bag. Inside, on a bed of woodchips, was the device that had kept him up until three o' clock in the morning on his first night at STASIS HQ. Shute Barrington had been busy. But Charlie Spicer had helped him assemble the final components.

Now Will took Ratty's remote control from his pocket and flicked through the touch screens. He lifted the device on to his lap and hit 'Activate'.

At once, the eight extendable tentacles responded. To Andrew and Gaia's amazement, they started to uncurl from the tubular body of the robot. These tentacles were prehensile. They had artificial muscles for strength. And they were dextrous. Using the two miniature cameras slotted into the ends of the first pair of arms, Will knew he could use them to pick up something as slender as a sheet of paper with ease.

'An octopus?' Andrew's voice was a hoarse whisper.

Will nodded. '*Inspired* by an octopus. But I didn't copy the movement exactly – it's too awkward.'

Now, with a quick glance to make sure the stewardesses were occupied, Will set the robot on the carpet of the gangway. Curled up, it was ten centi-metres long. But each of its telescopic arms could extend up to thirty centimetres. Will grabbed the viewing screen from Andrew, selected the third option for input. And he instructed the robot to scuttle on six of its eight arms, under the curtain that separated club from economy.

'Will it be OK?' Gaia said, her voice awed.

Will didn't reply. He was too busy concentrating on the remote control and the images that were streaming back to his screen. Andrew leaned over to look. He watched with Will as the octopus robot stuck close to the wall.

Then, very slowly, Will inched it forwards. He instructed the camera arms to wave, like the tentacles of a sea anemone, searching for a discarded menu for Grabber to pick up. He could see none. But the cameras did show that one man across the aisle already had a plate. A 'special meal', Will guessed. It would have to do.

Will sent the robot scurrying forwards, and, as the man turned to look out of the window, a camera-equipped arm shot up and out. At once, Will retracted the arm and he whirled the robot around. But not before he got a shot of a young boy, eyes wide.

Silently, Will cursed. He brought the robot back to his seat and snatched it up.

Gaia held out her hand for the screen. Will passed it over and she clasped it to her chest.

Trying not to smile, she pretended to inspect the image.

'Blinis with caviar!' she exclaimed. 'Cornichons!'

Will smiled now as he recognized two of Andrew's favourite foods.

'And we only have beef and quail's eggs . . .'

Andrew shook his head at her. And he extended his grin to Will. 'It's fantastic,' he said, pointing to the robot, which was now safely back in its box.

Gaia put down the screen. 'Does it have a name?'

'. . . *Grabber*,' Will said.

'Excuse me?'

Will looked up sharply.

The stewardess. 'The beef or the omelette, sir?'

After she had noted down their orders and moved on, Will reached back into his bag.

'You've got something *else*?' Gaia said.

'A few things,' Will said. 'Apart from the toothphones. And the tongue kit. I can't really show you this –' and he inched out a section of rope – 'but it's self-hardening – if you throw it out it becomes stiff. I call it Hard Choice. Then there's this.'

This was the one device that security should have taken from him. Except that Will had designed it with disguise in mind. MI6 field officers sometimes needed gadgets that looked innocent, and were anything but.

From a black silk bag, Will shook a cylindrical metal object.

'A torch?' Andrew said.

'No,' Will said quickly. 'It looks like a torch. Actually, it is supposed to be an infrared torch. I was thinking it could be useful to send signals in Morse code at night. Only someone wearing an infrared night vision kit would be able to see them. The airport security guy thought it was a good idea . . .'

'So what do you mean, it's *supposed* to be a torch,' Gaia said.

'I haven't got the infrared working properly yet.' Will paused. 'And there's something else inside . . .' Deftly, he unscrewed the head of the torch. Inside were two fat batteries – which the security officer had inspected. Quickly, Will shook them out. He pressed two fingers hard against the inside of the battery casing, and tugged at it. At last, the casing gave way under the pressure. It fell into his lap, and along with it came a narrow metal cylinder with a single red button. The cylinder fitted neatly into his palm.

'This is the real device?' Andrew whispered.

Will nodded. 'I call it Blind Spot. This button activates a laser. It'll dazzle someone. They won't be able to see for a few minutes. But it won't blind them. Not unless it's at really close range.'

'A *weapon*,' Andrew said. 'And you managed to get it through!'

'The guy thought this was a torch. And I'm fourteen years old. And Sean was vouching for me. And I had all this other stuff—'

'Can I see?' Gaia was holding out her hand.

Will passed her the baton. She gripped it and

instantly a beam of light split through the cabin. Red seared Gaia's retina.

'*What are you doing*?' Will's voice. Angry.

Gaia opened her eyes. Saw Andrew's horrified expression. Will's face. She *could* see them, she thought with relief. She wasn't blind. And she scanned the cabin. The stewardess was talking to the businessman. No one else seemed to have seen the flash.

'Sorry,' Gaia whispered. She glanced at Will, whose face was black. Gingerly, she passed over the weapon.

'You're lucky it wasn't pointing in your face,' Will hissed.

'You're lucky it wasn't pointing at yours!'

'All right!' Andrew said. 'It was an accident.' He pulled down his eyepatch, nudged the computer into life, and connected to the plane's wireless network. 'I think I'll see if there's been any more activity on the part of *Il Fantasma* . . .'

Aware that Gaia had shifted in her seat to stare hard out of the window and Will had turned away, Andrew focused on the virtual image, which appeared to be a good twenty centimetres in front of his face.

He found the BBC website. And hit an icon for the latest streaming news.

The anchorwoman was talking about rising fuel costs. Platinum prices had fallen for the fourth time in a row.

'*And now back to our main story. A bomb has exploded in a market in Paris. The tally of dead has risen to fifty-nine, and another eighty are reported injured. No group has yet claimed responsibility. The meeting of G8 ministers in London on Wednesday will now focus on proposals for new anti-terror measures . . .'*

Updates followed on demonstrations in Santiago, a fuel spill in Alaska and the birth of a celebrity baby. Nothing about ghosts.

Andrew frowned. He'd placed his faith in Cristina. Where was she? he wondered. And he whispered to himself: *'I hope you were telling me the truth . . . I hope you're all right.'*

One thousand kilometres away, and closing, Cristina della Corte was staring.

It was all she could do.

The velvet curtain had concealed a door. Dino had ushered her through it. He had instructed her to wait and he had vanished.

Cristina had remained frozen. *Staring.*

She was at the edge of what might once have been a dining hall. The high, vaulted ceiling arched into darkness. At the far end was a stone balcony, at first floor height. On either side, twin lion heads were mounted on pale oak, manes dusty. Crossed spears decorated the two long walls. Their polished blades reflected flames that licked around black logs in the marble-edged grate. By these flames, Cristina counted at least thirty figures, dressed in white.

They wore cloaks with hoods. None were adults, she realized. They were talking in low voices, and Cristina caught flashes of different languages: English, French, Spanish, Italian.

'They come from all over.' Dino's voice in her ear. She jumped. 'The reputation of the Master is spreading. They hear about his powers. They want to be with him. With him, they can be with their dead . . .'

Dino's voice paralysed her. The awful words kept coming.

'There – the boy with the glasses. Last year, his brother died. Last night, the Master contacted him.'

'Contacted his brother?' Cristina managed.

'Through the Master, they talked. For the first time in a year. The Master can reach the other world. He can communicate with ghosts . . .'

'The Master owns this castle?' she forced herself to say.

'The castle belongs to a relation. Rudolfo. He also works for the Master.'

'And is it true?' she stumbled. Her words fluttered through her mouth like moths. 'The Master can send you to the other side . . . and bring you back?'

No response.

Cristina didn't dare to turn around. Had Dino vanished again? But then she felt his breath hot on her ear. She heard his words, slightly slurred.

'If you are chosen. And you must earn that, Cristina. You must earn his love.'

'How?' she whispered.

'You will see.'

Suddenly, Dino raised his grimy arm. He pointed to the balcony. 'The Master is coming!'

Silence electrified the room. Thirty figures turned as one, like filaments snapped into line by a magnet.

Cristina watched as a tall man in a dark red cloak stepped out on to the balcony. She saw slit-like eyes, a wide, thin mouth. It was as though his features had been sliced with a knife.

'Rudolfo,' came the whisper in her ear.

And then, the chanting began. It wasn't Italian. She strained to make out the words. Was it Latin?

The figures in white chanted together, in a low, powerful voice. Three words, over and over. *Adoremus in aeternum.* She didn't know what it meant.

Rudolfo stepped aside. Apprehension twining around her heart, Cristina watched as the Master strode out past Rudolfo.

The Master was dressed in black. The garment resembled a monk's cowl. He wore the hood down low, over his head. When he raised it, Cristina shivered. He had no face.

No. He had a face. Behind a black gossamer veil.

Cristina saw patches of red where his eyes should be. Another patch of red for his mouth, which spread now, like a pool of blood, as he opened his lips to speak.

Heat-sensitive fabric, she realized.

'My friends,' the Master said. His voice was deep with power. It echoed through the room, seeming to rustle the cloaks, to fan the flames in the grate. 'Tonight, my friends, *I* need *you*.'

6

'This way!' Andrew shouted. 'Hurry up! Follow me!'

Andrew raced out of Marco Polo airport, along a covered walkway, to a dock and a line of motorboats. They were identical. Sleek, white-hulled, with elegant wooden interiors. Beyond, lights glittered across the expanse of the dark lagoon. Will stared, taking in the soda orange of channel markers, the white Vs of wake. Beyond, hidden in the night, were the palaces and the domes of crumbling Venice.

And Will felt a thrill in his blood. The same thrill he'd felt on the train on the way to St Petersburg. He couldn't imagine what lay ahead. And that was the point. It would be *unexpected*. Real life.

Around them, tourists dragging cases were struggling towards the boats. 'We're going by water?' Will asked.

Andrew grinned. 'Water taxi. The only way to travel.' To the nearest driver, he said in slow English: 'Grand Canal? Eighty euro?'

Andrew had travelled to Venice a year ago, he'd said,

for a conference on operating systems. He'd been introduced then to the water taxis.

Gaia's father was Italian, but this was her first time
on his soil, though she spoke Italian fluently – along
with French, Mandarin, and rudimentary Arabic and
Spanish. But then Will had seen her learn Arabic. She
only had to read a word to remember it. The wonders
of eidetic – or photographic – memory.

Now Will watched as, with Gaia's linguistic help,
Andrew clinched his deal with the driver. And he felt in
his pocket. Ratty twitched. He was OK. There in the
pocket next to Ratty was his mobile. Will had called his
mother while Andrew waited for his case to emerge on
to the baggage carousel – and while he had tried
Cristina yet again, without luck.

The conversation hadn't lasted long. His mother had
sounded concerned.

'You know these people in Venice?' she'd said.

'. . . No.'

'. . . You will be careful?'

'Yes,' Will had said.

And now he heard Gaia's voice in his head. She'd
been standing next to him.

'Why didn't you just tell her the truth?' she'd said.
'She knows about STORM.'

Will had hesitated. 'She wouldn't like it if she knew,'
he'd replied. 'So I must be a coward. But then she'd
rather not know. So I think that's cowardly too.'

He'd spoken quietly. Now, in the boat, Will wondered what his father would have thought. What would he have made of STORM?

Sometimes, Will tried to imagine conversations between them. But already, his father's face was fading. His voice was distorting, so Will couldn't be sure if the voice he heard in his head was really his father's any more.

He focused on the lagoon around him, on motor boats and vaporettos – water buses transporting people across to the islands, to the red-brick glass works of Murano, the multi-coloured houses of lace-making Burano.

Gaia was beside him, Andrew in the front, trying to talk to their driver.

Will dragged his eyes from the lagoon. Wind tossed his hair around his face.

'Did you tell your Dad where you were going?' he said.

Gaia didn't respond. When Will had decided she was pretending not to have heard, she turned suddenly and said: 'He isn't very well.'

But then Andrew was yelling from the front. 'Look!' he cried. 'That's the entrance to the Grand Canal!'

A church rose, its moon-coloured dome gleaming, trifoil white lights illuminating the stone steps. Suddenly, they were in the carotid artery of the city. Palaces veered high, edging the black glossy water. Will gazed up. Through Moorish windows he saw flashes of vast oil paintings and chandeliers glittering in lofty rooms.

Candles flickered on an open stucco balcony. Signs of exalted lives.

This was more grand than Will could have imagined. Something from a fantasy, alien to his world.

'See – that palace with the flag!' Andrew said, excitedly, from the front passenger seat. 'That's where the ghost of a murdered artist once painted the windows red!'

'How do you know that?' Will asked.

Andrew grinned. 'I did some background research this morning. *Know your enemy*. It's an old saying.'

'Know when you're talking rubbish and be quiet,' Will said. 'That should be another.'

Will glanced at Gaia. She was staring at the palaces, at the vaporetto stops, people crowding, waiting to hop on. He could see she was impressed.

Andrew turned. 'It looks beautiful, but the lagoon is badly polluted. In 2004, the National Society for Oncological Medicine identified Venice as Italy's top location for tumours.'

'Nice,' Gaia said.

'It's all the petrochemical waste,' Andrew continued. And he turned back to the driver, who was now speaking in a stream of rapid Italian. Andrew glanced back. Raised his eyebrow at Gaia.

'He says: "Look. We are here,"' she said.

'That's all?' Andrew said, surprised.

But the taxi had stopped, answering his question. In

front of them were five stone steps, leading to the towering columned entrance to a grey-fronted palace.

And there, mounted beside the door, was a brass bell.

'No intercom,' Will said to Andrew, as they jumped out of the boat and up to the steps. 'No smell recognition technology. No wonder they got burgled.'

'Your jokes are worse than Gaia's,' Andrew said, but he was smiling good-humouredly. As the driver hauled out the bags and sped away, he pressed the bell.

Moments passed. Will took in the full-length windows of each storey and the patinated walls, the stone discoloured by black pollution on one side, bone white on the other. A sharp smell filled the air. From the weed sliming the bottom step, Will thought.

'*Buon giorno*,' Andrew said brightly.

The front door was ajar. There, in the gap, was a tall, angular man, dressed in a dark three-piece suit. Thinning hair was combed straight back over his egg-shaped head. No trace of a smile on his narrow mouth. No trace of any expression.

Gaia stepped forwards. In Italian, she explained who they were and why they had come. 'Cristina invited us to stay,' she said again.

'. . . You had better speak to Signor Angelo,' the man answered at last, in accented English.

'Angelo?' Gaia whispered to Andrew, as the door was thrown back and they stepped into an expansive entrance hall. Through stone arches, staircases disappeared up to the left and to the right.

As they followed the butler across the polished mosaic floor, Gaia noticed a black sign pushed into the shadows. It bore the word: '*Bienvenuto.*' Welcome.

The butler was already opening another carved door ahead, to the right of the atrium. 'You take visitors?' Gaia called.

The man paused. 'The museum is open to the public on the first Tuesday of every month,' he replied. 'Come. This way.'

And he showed them into a room more sumptuous than even Andrew had ever seen. Gilt-framed oils hung on the richly papered walls, alongside marble reliefs showing heroes smiting their enemies. Miniature shelves held sculpted busts. Sofas were upholstered in dark green silk.

'If Signor Angelo is still awake, I will inform him that you are here,' the butler said, and he vanished.

'Look at this place,' Gaia breathed.

Will was crossing to the lead-paned windows, which overlooked the canal. Outside, he could see the lights of the palace opposite – more dramatic paintings, and more colossal chandeliers. Beside him, porcelain sheep arranged on a velvet-draped table stared blankly into space.

The door was opening.

'Good evening,' came a cool, rich voice. 'My name is Angelo. Cristina is my sister.'

For a moment, no one spoke. Angelo seemed a figure from another world. He was dressed in a midnight-blue silk dressing gown, with matching slippers. His curly black hair was smoothed back over his scalp. Bronzed skin shone. He looked like a young 1940s movie star.

Slowly, Angelo's glittering gaze took in first Andrew, and then Will, and Gaia. It paused on Gaia, on her rich skin and her dark eyes.

Will noticed. He bristled.

But Gaia was the first to recover her voice. She explained about Cristina's email, and her request for them to investigate, and to stay.

'My sister is not here,' Angelo said.

'I've tried to call her,' Andrew broke in. 'She isn't answering her mobile. Or her email. Do you know where she is?'

Angelo shrugged. 'Abroad? Down the coast? My sister and I might be twins, but we are not Siamese, you understand? We have our freedom here. You say you are STORM? She mentioned something . . . 'And a flicker of a smile crossed Angelo's full lips. 'What is the square root of 5,642?'

'*What?*' Will said.

'You say you are STORM. You are supposed to be brilliant scientists – my sister told me. If you are, tell me what is the square root of 7,856.'

'. . . Eighty-eight. And a bit,' Andrew said flatly, after a moment.

Angelo nodded. *As though he knows the answer,* Will thought.

'What is the fourth element from the right in the periodic table?'

'Which row?' Gaia said.

Angelo hesitated. 'Eleventh.'

'There are only nine rows!'

'Then fourth!'

'*Arsenic,*' she said darkly.

Will narrowed his eyes. They could do without Angelo.

'Look – we really are who we say we are,' Andrew said, his instinctive dislike of Angelo increasing by the moment. 'Otherwise how would we know about the box? Or your sister? Does Cristina often disappear?'

Angelo shrugged his broad shoulders. 'I like to have parties. I like to watch TV. To see my friends. Cristina is so serious. She always has projects. She goes away, she does her work, her investigations – I don't know.'

'But the box,' Will said. 'It was stolen.'

'It has *gone,*' Angelo conceded. 'Cristina claims she saw a ghost.' He raised an eyebrow. 'For myself, I think she took it. How else could the thermal alarms be beaten?'

'*Cristina took it?*' Andrew sounded offended. Angelo ignored him.

'And your parents are still in Rome?' Gaia said. 'Aren't they worried? They've been burgled.'

To her surprise, Angelo gave a brief laugh. 'My father is engaged in finalizing a business deal worth at least one thousand times the contents of that box. What do you expect will be his priority? The police have made their investigations. What more can be done?'

'They saw the footage?' Andrew asked. 'They saw the figure?'

Angelo sighed. 'If you ask me, they think Cristina herself fabricated this "footage".'

'But the modern art gallery,' Andrew said. 'The papers are saying a *ghost* stole a valuable painting.'

Angelo rolled his handsome eyes. Clearly he was uninterested in this discussion. 'I am telling you the facts. Believe what you will. Now – if you wish, you may stay a few days. Perhaps Cristina will return. It is up to you.'

Andrew glanced at Will, and at Gaia. They nodded.

'Thank you,' Andrew said, doing his best to sound pleasant. 'We'll stay. By the way –' And Angelo was forced to meet Andrew's blue eyes. 'What was in the box?'

'Ah.' A curious expression crept over Angelo's face. 'You really want to know . . . ? Then follow me.'

'First, I will show you where – and where not – you can go,' Angelo said.

He was leading them back into the entrance hall, towards the left-hand staircase.

'In each of the rooms of our house there is a thermal alarm. It detects body heat.' He indicated a keypad mounted on the wall. 'This is for the atrium. For security reasons, only my family and the butler can know the codes. I am forbidden from telling anybody else – even guests. You can go into the bedrooms I will show you, and the bathroom and the kitchen – but without me, that is all. Even our garage, it has alarms.'

'Garage?' Will said. The palace was right on the canal.

A thin smile twitched Angelo's lips. 'I will show you a glimpse. If you wish.'

Now Andrew's rare anger burned. This was a rich boy who liked to condescend. He enjoyed showing off. And he hadn't even earned his wealth. He'd inherited it. What right had Angelo to feel superior?

Still tingling with dislike, Andrew followed the others through a heavy wooden door in the stone wall. He found himself on a limestone landing stage, in a vast room, whose ceiling flickered with reflected light. A roller door formed the far wall.

Andrew's pulse kicked up a notch. 'This is your *garage*?'

'This is Venice,' Angelo said, faintly amused at the reaction of his guests. 'Here we like to travel by boat.'

Beside Andrew, Will stared. He'd never seen anything like it. Bobbing in the water were six power boats. He recognized two: a Hinckley push-button convertible, with a skin of Kevlar and glass. Beside it was a luxurious Azimut, teak decking almost alive in the half-light.

But now he followed Andrew, who'd made his way along the balcony to inspect the king of them all.

Twenty-four feet long, shaped like a narrow arrowhead and gleaming a mean black with a single gold stripe, this boat was like nothing Will had ever seen. Pure power was condensed into the whip-line hull. Will could almost sense it straining. The interior was decked out in black leather and black composite fibre, trimmed with gold.

'What *is* that?' Will said.

'It is mine,' said Angelo. 'Custom made by a venerated company in Como to my own specifications. She is propelled by a jet of water ejected out of the back, and she is capable of sixty-five knots. That is eighteen carats. *Solid.*' He pointed to the jetstick, used, Will guessed, like a joystick to control the machine.

'Sixty-five knots – what's that? – seventy-five miles an hour?' Andrew said. 'I thought the speed limit in the lagoon was about fifteen.' And he coloured at Angelo's scornful glance.

Angelo addressed Gaia: 'I call her *Venus*. She is the goddess of the lagoon. Perhaps I could give you a ride in her sometime.'

'Perhaps,' she said coolly.

And Angelo's handsome forehead knotted. He was surprised at her non-committal response, Will thought. Instantly, Angelo affected to be bored. 'Come,' he said briskly.

As they left the garage, Will couldn't resist one final

glance. The *Venus* shone in the darkness, her hull seeming to ripple like the flank of a racehorse. It was, Will thought, the most beautiful machine he had ever seen . . .

Angelo led Will, Andrew and Gaia up the staircase, past the first landing, with its shadowy passage and unlit chandeliers, past the second, and then the third. At the fourth, he stopped. He was pointing to the left. Will saw four doors, painted white, with gold-plated handles.

'Those first two are your bedrooms,' Angelo said. 'You will find your bags.' He turned to the right, past another white door, and he stopped. Cupping his hand around the keypad to prevent anyone from seeing, he entered a sequence of numbers. After a moment, Angelo pushed open the door.

'This,' he said, 'is my father's museum.'

The scene was familiar. Will recognized it at once from the footage in Andrew's basement. Now, he saw that the oil painting depicted an armed knight astride a horse. The wallpaper was flocked. The bird was some kind of parrot.

'The box was in there?' Will said. He pointed to the furthest cabinet.

Angelo nodded.

At once, Will crossed to the spot. His eyes darted to the richly patterned rug, and to the patch of floor below the window. Cristina had told Andrew she'd found powder on the rug. There was no sign she'd left any behind. As Will glanced back, he saw that Angelo was showing Gaia a gemstone chess set and, by the sofa, Andrew appeared to be tying a shoelace.

'This is turquoise,' came Angelo's voice, as he inched closer to Gaia.

Andrew put a finger to his lips, securing Will's attention. Suddenly, Andrew reached out underneath the sofa, and he grabbed something. Angelo started to turn, to raise a translucent pink rook to the chandelier, and Andrew flushed.

'What's this?' Will said quickly, drawing Angelo's gaze to him, and giving Andrew time to shove into his pocket whatever it was he had found.

Will was pointing to the rug.

'A *carpet,*' Angelo said, in a tone that suggested Will must be stupid.

'So – what was in the box?' Gaia said, taking her chance to edge away from Angelo, towards Andrew, at the sofa.

Angelo faced her. 'A gold lion. Jewelled. It has special significance for my mother. For *Cristina.* My father displayed it because he felt obliged to, not because he loved it. Now I will take you to your rooms.'

As he led the way out of the museum, Andrew caught Will's eye. He pointed to his pocket, and he winked.

7

'It's a *PDA*.'

Will was sitting on the edge of a majestic single bed. It was forged from gilded iron, the head and foot a mass of swirling, ornamental gold. 'And?' he said impatiently.

'The memory's been wiped.' Andrew fiddled with the PDA. 'You can switch it on all right, but there's nothing there.'

'So?' Gaia said. 'Does it have anything to do with Cristina's ghost?'

'I'm not sure,' Andrew said. 'But it's certainly *odd*.'

'I don't see that it tells us anything,' Will said. 'It could belong to Cristina's father. Or Cristina. Maybe she dropped it when she rushed in.'

'That wouldn't wipe the memory,' Andrew protested.

Will shook his head. 'I think we have to ignore the PDA for now. It doesn't help.'

Andrew took off his glasses, and started to polish them with the sleeve of his jumper. 'Then we need to establish priorities. We agree, I imagine, that our first priority is to find Cristina. Whatever the ghost is, something is going on, and if she's gone after a thief, she is at risk. Especially as she isn't answering her phone. Or her email. And if Angelo doesn't know where she is, we need to find clues somewhere else.'

'Like?' Will said.

'Her computer. Maybe she emailed someone to tell them where she was going. Maybe she keeps a diary. Though we can't get into her bedroom without the code,' Andrew observed.

'We could ask Angelo,' Gaia said. 'If we explain why, he'll let us in.'

'Perhaps,' Will said. And he looked pointedly at Andrew. 'But I've got all this kit with me – do we really need Angelo?'

Andrew smiled slightly. 'I can't see how we'd need Angelo when we have *the Maker*. And it would be important, wouldn't it, to test the devices in a genuine field situation?' He looked at Gaia, who raised an eyebrow.

'It would be quicker to ask Angelo,' she said.

'Not necessarily,' Will said.

'We don't even know where her bedroom is!' Gaia protested.

'In her email, she told me that when she heard the noise she ran "next door",' Andrew said. 'Now if you remember, the museum was the last room on this side of the corridor. So her bedroom must be . . . ?'

'Through there,' Will said, pointing at the wall behind Andrew.

Will mentally scanned the contents of his black hold-all. Did he have anything that they could use? Perhaps.

'Can Grabber take out thermal cameras?' Andrew said.

'Not without sounding the alarm.'

'. . . Could we use Ratty somehow?' Gaia said, with a little reluctance.

Andrew shook his head. 'He'd trigger the thermal sensors.'

'But if they have CCTV, they'll see Ratty – and they won't care.'

'He can't turn on a computer,' Andrew protested. 'And if the alarms go off, no matter what we might hope, someone *will* smell a rat.'

Andrew's gaze shot to Will, who was poking his head into the fireplace, peering up, the dazzle gun in his hand.

Will shot a flash up through the chimney. Relaxed. The chimney was clear.

'What are you doing?' Gaia said, exchanging a glance with Andrew.

Will turned to her. 'We send in Ratty so far – up the chimney, and down the next pot, into Cristina's fire-place.'

'Up a chimney?' Andrew's voice rose an octave. Then realization dawned. 'The gecko foot pads.'

'Yeah.'

'You're not going to let Ratty all the way down into the grate?'

Will shook his head.

'You're going to . . .' But here Andrew's thinking ran out.

'You're going to use Grabber!' Gaia exclaimed.

Will nodded. He threw the dazzle gun back on to the bed. Gently he removed Ratty from his pocket. He used the remote to instruct Grabber to uncurl two tentacles and wrap them firmly around Ratty's belly.

'Will he be too heavy?' Gaia said.

'Grabber doesn't weigh much. Rats are strong.'

'I still don't really see—' Andrew started.

'We use Ratty to take Grabber down the chimney in Cristina's room – but not so far down that he triggers the sensors,' Will said. 'Grabber disengages into the fire-place, crosses to the computer. We use the remote to get him to use a tentacle to switch on the computer. One of the cameras in his arms can feed back the image from the screen, and Andrew, you use his arms to make entries on the keyboard. That way we won't activate the sensors.'

Andrew grinned. The neatness of the plan impressed him. 'I feel like we need one of those handshakes. You know, like American ball-players – *Go STORM!*'

'No handshakes,' Will said. 'At least not until we find your Italian friend . . . Are you ready?'

He threw Andrew the remote for Grabber, along with the screen that would display the camera feed. With a quick parting pat, Will deposited Ratty into the fire-place. And he hesitated. 'Of course if we don't find anything on her computer, we'll be wasting time.'

Andrew's eyes widened. 'What other options do we have?'

'It seems odd that Angelo doesn't know *anything*. She told him about us. Maybe Cristina said something else before she left that would mean something to us, even if it doesn't to him. And while we check out Cristina's computer, it would be good to keep him occupied.'

'So what do you suggest?' Andrew said.

'You'll be busy. I have to watch Ratty.' Will turned to Gaia. Saw her tense. He didn't particularly like it, but what could he do?

'Why would he want to talk to me?' she protested.

Andrew and Will exchanged glances.

'You mean – because I'm a girl.'

Andrew met her flaring gaze. 'The rules of biology are as strict as the rules of physics, Gaia,' he said simply. 'You know that as well as me.'

The last thing she wanted, Gaia decided, was to spend time with Angelo.

He was handsome, undoubtedly. But he was also arrogant, and it left her cold. How different he was to Andrew. To Will . . . Gaia wasn't in the mood to deal with a boy like Angelo. She had other things on her mind.

Two days ago, her father had been admitted to St Thomas's Hospital. His half-sister, Amelia, had travelled down from Edinburgh to 'look after' Gaia. She was a tight-lipped, over-exercised, elastic band of a woman, who had disliked Gaia's mother. And yet Gaia had been obliged to comfort her, as Amelia feared for her brother – as Gaia feared for her father, *despite everything*. When Gaia had packed up her rucksack and announced she was leaving London for a few days, Amelia, eyes blazing, had agreed to call if there was any change. So far, nothing.

Gaia reached the ground floor. She would have to put thoughts of her father and her aunt to one side, she decided. Even though she was here, in Venice, barely twenty kilometres from her father's own birthplace. She had heard him in voices at the airport. She had seen his face in the blur of men rushing to greet relatives.

And she found herself hoping Angelo might have gone to bed. But as she approached the garage she saw a green LED on the keypad, indicating the thermal alarm was deactivated.

Inside, Gaia found him sitting pensively in the black and gold boat, a book in his elegant hands. A novel? Italian poetry? Somehow she doubted it.

'Hello.'

He looked up. Brightened. 'Your friends are not with you?'

'Unpacking.'

'Then come – let me show you in more detail. *Venus*

is my newest and most treasured possession.' A genuine smile lit Angelo's perfect features. He waved her forwards.

Reluctantly, Gaia approached the boat. The hull shimmered in the light reflected from the green water. She saw now that the book was a user manual.

As she came closer, Angelo's cologne filled her nostrils. Musky and sweet, merging with the rotting stench of the weed in the canal. Her stomach clenched. Gaia concentrated on the gold fittings and the flawless leather seats.

'So Cristina didn't say anything about where she was going?'

Angelo's smile faded slightly. 'I told you – no. After the police came and said they had no clues, she said to me she had contacted a boy in London who worked with an organization called STORM. She said you were brilliant scientists. Three days later, she went. But I told you: she goes away often. I am not her keeper. So—' Angelo's black eyes narrowed. 'How exactly are you brilliant? What sorts of things does this STORM do?'

Come upstairs, Gaia thought. *You might be surprised.*

'Damn!'

Through Grabber's left-hand camera, Andrew saw that Cristina had employed high level encryption to protect access to her email. Using Grabber was preferable to asking Angelo for assistance, but it was still hard going manipulating the robot arms to tap the keys. It had taken a full six minutes to get this far. And now he was at a dead end.

'Can you break the encryption?' Will asked.

Andrew didn't look up. 'This is her field of expertise.'

'So now what?'

Andrew dug into his pocket. 'I could check deleted files.'

'How?'

'I should be able to get software from the internet to reconstruct the file allocation table.'

'English?'

'It'll tell me where deleted files are.'

Will nodded. He'd dispatched Ratty to wait on the red roof of the palace until Grabber finished. Now he too could do little but wait.

He let his eyes wander over the bookshelves that lined the far alcove of the guest bedroom.

There, in front of a blue-bound set of histories of the Roman Empire, was a photograph in a polished silver frame. Will picked it up. It was quite recent, judging by Angelo's appearance. Smooth-skinned, hair slicked back, he was broodily eyeing the camera, one arm around the waist of what Will guessed had to be his mother, the other around the shoulder of a slender girl. Black hair hung glossily over her shoulders. She had large, almond-shaped eyes, smoky with kohl. A red mouth, parted in a brilliant smile. Cristina. It should have been obvious, even from behind. She was beautiful.

And Will's eyes were caught by something else. An antique volume in English, entitled *How to Build your own Steam Engine*. Will flicked through the pages. It was a step-by-step guide. If only he'd had this in Dorset. Quickly, he became engrossed. Minutes passed. Every so often, he heard Andrew scribbling something on a notepad. Then the door opened suddenly, and Will almost started.

Gaia. 'I told Angelo I had to go to bed! Haven't you finished yet?'

And Andrew's head shot round, an excited look in his blue eyes. 'Yes. We can bring Grabber back now. I've found something.'

8

'I think I know where Cristina has gone.' Andrew said, as Will gently unwrapped Grabber's arms from Ratty's belly. 'I managed to get up some deleted notes. There's all kinds of stuff. Ghost stories. Newspaper reports. And in the last entry, she wrote: "The Master, Isola delle Fantasme".'

Gaia blinked at Andrew. 'Isola delle Fantasme – *Island of the Ghosts . . .*'

He nodded.

'Is that a real place?' Will asked.

'It's a real nickname. I Googled it. There are about forty islands in the lagoon. Some are privately owned – like this one. All that stands on it is a fifteenth-century castle, which once upon a time was a mental hospital for women. Before the castle, there was a hospice for pilgrims coming back from the Middle East. It's supposed to be the most haunted place in Venice. Two months ago, the police raided the castle. Some children had gone missing. One of them, the son of a local businessman, had told a friend they were going to the Isola delle Fantasme to join a ghost cult.'

'A *cult*?' Gaia said.

Andrew nodded. 'I did some more digging. Cults have been in the news a lot here – especially satanic cults. Quite recently, the leaders of one of these cults went to jail for burying a woman alive. Anyway, apparently whoever was supposed to be running this ghost cult on the Isola delle Fantasme was claiming he could talk to the "other side". He targeted children who'd lost family.'

Will glanced at Gaia. Andrew's words left him cold. He'd lost his father. She'd lost her mother. If she felt his gaze, she didn't meet it. 'So hasn't anyone shut this cult down?'

'They tried,' Andrew said. 'Two months ago, I think, a body washed up on the next island. According to the news reports, it was badly disfigured. It couldn't even be identified with DNA.'

'I read about that,' Will said. That was the story. And – yes – the news report *had* talked about a ghost cult. Though it hadn't mentioned the Isola delle Fantasme.

'You mean no one reported this kid missing?' Gaia said. 'What do you mean *disfigured*?'

'I don't know. I was using a translation engine. Maybe it wasn't accurate. You should read the reports. Anyway, according to this paper the police raided the island and found nothing. Only the guy who owns the place.'

'So is there a cult?' Gaia said.

Andrew shrugged. 'According to the police – no.'

'But you're sure Cristina's gone there?' Will said.

'Why not? She thinks she might be after a ghost. And she wrote "the Master" – which was supposed to be the name of the cult leader.'

'So what now?' Gaia said cautiously.

'I don't think we have a choice,' Andrew said. His voice was low.

'But if there is a cult—' she started. 'Maybe we should go to the police. We can tell them we think Cristina's gone to the island.'

'I doubt they'll raid it again,' Andrew said.

'They might – if they didn't find anything the first time.'

'And risk further embarrassment? For what – because we say we think she's there and she might be in trouble? Her own brother wouldn't back us up.'

'We could try.'

Andrew shook his head. 'Angelo will say she often goes away and doesn't get in touch. And the police will say give her forty-eight hours, then come back – whatever the standard line is. Meanwhile, if this island has anything to do with the ghost thief, and if there really is a cult, she could be in trouble. I move that we go and investigate. Will?'

Will hesitated. Andrew had made a decision, that much was clear. Gaia looked far less certain. The details of the newspaper article evaded him. So he switched his focus to Andrew. Nodded.

Andrew looked relieved. 'Gaia?'

It seemed as though she had little choice. '. . . Where is it?'

Andrew grinned. 'I downloaded a map.' He pulled down his eye patch. An image of the lagoon materialised. 'It's not far from here – maybe fifteen minutes by water.'

'So how do we get there?' Gaia said.

'We could get a water taxi. Or . . .' And a gleam crept into Andrew's blue eye.

At once, Gaia guessed what he was thinking. '*No way*,' she said.

At the mahogany desk in his father's old study, Rudolfo smiled. If you could call it a smile. His slit-like mouth twitched up at the edges. His heavy eyelids descended.

Rudolfo replaced the receiver of his black telephone and scrawled two numbers on a sheet of plain paper: $1 million. $10 million.

$1 million for the winged lion. $10 million for the Klimt. That was more than enough. The Master would surely be pleased.

He would order the new equipment at once. If it was dispatched tonight, it could be here on the island by the morning. Perhaps the Master would indeed achieve his goal, though time was running out . . .

And, perhaps then, the Master would leave.

An *uncharitable* thought, Rudolfo reprimanded himself. The Master was family, after all.

But he couldn't deny that the Master's arrival and *unusual* activities had interfered greatly with his life. Did he like the Master? No. Did he respect him? Yes. Revere him? No. For he knew the Master for what he truly was. An obsessive. A liar. A manipulator.

Rudolfo did not particularly like children. Still, he had been upset by some of the outcomes of the *experiments*. Though they volunteered of their own free will. They trusted the Master. More fool them.

And Rudolfo's mind shot to the session barely two hours ago, when his unpleasant relation had spotted the new girl. The beautiful young girl with long, black hair.

Rudolfo threw his gaze around the room. The familiar contents of his study reassured him. The infrasound generator. The books by William James, Arthur Koestler and Robert Morris. ESP cards, with their wavy lines, stars and circles, used to test extrasensory perception. Rudolfo had trained as a parapsychologist – an investigator of strange and supernatural phenomena.

Now, Rudolfo dragged open the top drawer of his desk. Inside were the original plans for the castle, plans that the Master had insisted on studying, and which he had once used so successfully to evade the police. Lying on top was a sheet of paper bearing the telephone number for the Institute of Quantum Physics.

Rudolfo hesitated. He picked up the receiver and dialled one of the castle's internal numbers.

Two sets of rings. Three. Four. Five . . .

'*What?*' The Master sounded furious.

'I – I' And Rudolfo blushed at his own nervousness. It was his castle, after all! 'Master, the lion has sold for one million dollars, the painting for ten!'

There was a pause. 'That is good news.'

Relief flushed through Rudolfo's body.

'Yes, Master. I will order the equipment right away.'

'Tell them it is urgent. You know when the meeting starts!'

'Yes, Master, I will tell them it's urgent. It will be here for the meeting. I'm sure they will fly it—'

'I don't care how it gets here!' the Master screamed. 'Just get off the phone and order it!'

Rudolfo shook. For a few moments, he listened to the dull tone of the cut connection. His hand trembling, he replaced the receiver. *Yes, Master,* he whispered.

Still shaking, he dialled the number for the institute, which was in Switzerland, not far from the Italian border.

'This is Rudolfo. We have the funds. Dispatch at once for urgent experiments.'

Two words came: 'Six hours.' Then, once more, Rudolfo found himself listening to a dead line.

The Master had sworn that as soon as his mission was accomplished, he would vanish. No one would track him down. And now they had the money, and the final equipment was en route. They would be ready.

Tomorrow, the Master would complete his plan. Then he would leave. Life would return to normal.

Rudolfo's throat throbbed. *Stress*, he thought. He needed something to drink. He kicked the door open and he strode out into the passage, towards the kitchen.

He did not notice a figure hiding in the shadows behind his door.

A beautiful girl, with long, black hair.

'*Hurry up!*'

Gaia was peering through the slimmest of narrow cracks, into the airy darkness of the entrance hall.

Behind her, in the garage, Will waited impatiently. Gaia's black rucksack was on his shoulder. He'd emptied her clothes and shoved the devices from the hold-all inside. On the stone floor beside him was a second rucksack. Andrew's. Taken from his case, and packed quickly with 'kit' Andrew had said might come in handy.

Andrew was in the *Venus*. His entire concentration was fixed on the virtual display. '*Come on,*' he breathed.

'You know this is stealing,' Gaia whispered, almost surprised at Andrew, who was usually so ethical. Though Andrew could talk about the importance of every person reducing their 'ecological footprint' while still keeping a monster SmarTruck in the garage. Maybe he was as human as anyone else.

'Borrowing,' Andrew corrected.

'If we're going to borrow, why don't we just take one of the boats with keys!'

Andrew and Will exchanged a quick glance. Wasn't the answer obvious?

'You're sure you can break into its computer?' Will whispered.

'I told you I could,' Andrew murmured. 'It just takes a little time.'

'Well, hurry up,' Gaia said. 'Angelo loves his boat. He could be back any minute!'

Andrew waved the voices away. The wireless hack was going well. Any boat – or car, for that matter – that relied purely on wireless security exposed itself to trouble. But the decryption process took a little time. A few more moments . . .

And the engine growled. Andrew beamed.

Instantly, Gaia ran to the boat, leaping into the back, on to soft black hide. Will tossed Andrew's bag to her, then his. He loosed the mooring sheet and jumped behind the jetstick.

Andrew raised his eye patch to his forehead. Replaced his glasses. 'Seriously, can you drive this?'

'Let's see,' Will said, and he grinned. He'd never even driven a car. But he had once taken the controls of his father's old Cessna T-37, flying high over Dorset. *Jet-stick*, he thought. Just like playing a game. How difficult can it be? He eased the stick into reverse. The *Venus* responded at once, gliding backwards.

'How do we get out?' Andrew said urgently.

And his head shot round. A shout.

Angelo. He was on the stone landing stage.

'Hey!' Words tumbled out in rapid Italian.

'How do we get out?' Andrew hissed.

Gaia's eyes were searching for an answer. 'There!'

Angelo was now dashing around the edge of the stage, to a spot where he might throw himself upon the *Venus*. 'Gaia! No. This is stealing! My *Venus*! What are you doing?' His voice curdled with disbelief and fury.

'Borrowing,' Will shouted. 'It's for your own good. Believe us. There!' He jabbed his finger in the air, and then towards Gaia.

On the wall near the garage door, about four feet up, was a circular black box pierced through with a green button. As Will spun the boat, Gaia half-stood, and she reached for the button. Slammed it. She didn't turn. She didn't want to look at Angelo.

With a soft creak, the metal barrier glided upwards, clear of the canal. Orange light jagged into the garage.

'No! Wait!' Angelo. Livid.

And Gaia held tight to her seat, as Will slung the *Venus* out into a side canal, then on to the Grand Canal itself. Night-soaked palaces shimmered. She could hear Angelo, echoing in her ears, as though he was being tortured. '*No!*'

Instantly, Will shot the *Venus* into position, nose pointing towards St Mark's Square. She responded at once, shooting out a steam of water. And Will grinned.

They were in Venice. In a futuristic jet boat. On the trail of a missing girl and mysterious ghosts.

The *Venus* was supremely responsive. Will only had to touch the jetstick to provoke a response. Which made it easy to make a mistake. As they passed the Guggenheim, he caught the rear of the boat on a candystripe mooring post.

'Will!' Andrew's voice, raised in alarm. Maybe he should be driving. He conceded too much to Will sometimes. 'I think you crunched it!'

Will scowled. His head shot round. 'Gaia – what's the damage?' The *Venus* was still going OK.

Gaia was gripping her leather seat, leaning out to try to check, hair flying back across her face. 'We look fine!' she called.

And Will grinned.

'Just be careful. This is *borrowed*,' Andrew said, and he straightened his glasses.

'Will!' Gaia's voice. Louder this time. 'Will – it's Angelo! Go faster!'

Will glanced round.

'Just go faster!' she yelled. 'I can see him. He's in that wooden boat!'

Will took a deep breath.

'You know the limit here is eight knots,' Andrew said. 'If the police see you—'

'—They won't be able to catch me,' Will finished. 'Hold on!' He gripped the jetstick, shoved it forwards.

At once, the *Venus* blasted through the canal, a cloud

of water erupting behind them. The speed was almost surreal. Will only had to touch the jetstick to nudge her along the curve of the canal, between the vaporettos carrying late-night tourists, who started to point and stare.

At last, Will saw the glittering lights of the terrace of the Gritti Palace hotel. They were almost there. Almost in open water. Ahead to the left, the Campanile tower of St Mark's Square loomed. 'Where's Angelo?' he yelled.

Andrew's head was skewed, blinking, focused on Gaia. 'Gaia?'

She glanced back. 'He was there. Now I can't see him. There was a vaporetto—'

Despite himself, Andrew smiled. 'Go for it,' he shouted to Will. 'If Gaia can't see him, there's no way Angelo can catch us.'

And they were out! The Grand Canal and all its glories were behind them. Ahead was a huge expanse of black water, dotted with the lights of channel marker posts and boats. Will no longer held back. He pushed the jetstick as hard as it would go, and he heard Gaia whoop as she slid back into her seat, as they rocketed across the lagoon.

'Do you think anyone's seen us?'

Andrew spoke softly. The *Venus* was in still water, on

the far side of the Island of the Ghosts, on a beeline for the shore.

Two minutes earlier, Andrew had pointed it out. He'd double-checked the map. Past Murano, heading west, then a slingshot around an uninhabited outcrop of marshy land, and there it was: a hump-backed island, topped with an eerie silhouette.

The castle was reaching for the heavens. A Gothic eruption from the rock.

Will glanced at Andrew, then the forbidding walls of the castle, slashed with high slit windows oozing yellow light. 'We have to hope not,' he whispered.

Here, the castle blotted out the moonlight. Will's eyes and his nerves felt tense. He had just navigated a semi-circle of sand banks. The jet boat could cope with shallow water, but here the sand almost penetrated the surface. He could just about see the banks, absolutely black beneath the glossy surface.

Will turned, to Gaia, and beyond. No other boats. No sign of Angelo. They'd taken his fastest. He'd had no chance.

And as Will turned back, Gaia felt her heart thud.

Safe in the palazzo on the Grand Canal, she'd agreed to go along with the plan. But what if there was a cult? What if there really were – what if there really were *ghosts*? Did she believe in ghosts? She'd told Andrew she didn't know. In the blackness of a foreign night, as she felt the soft crunch of the composite hull against sand and vegetation, she felt less certain.

The island was dense here with shrubs and stringy bushes, roots reaching right to the water's edge. The slope of the land hid them from the castle. Still, as Will got out, he started to gather strands of creeper to cover at least the windscreen of the *Venus*. Mud caked his trainers. The island stank.

Pinching her nose, Gaia stepped out on to the bank. 'It smells bad.'

'Could be rotting leaves,' Andrew whispered. 'Or sewage.'

She pulled a face.

'I'm just being factual.' He looked at the mooring line, which Will had secured around the twisted trunk of a bush. 'You think the boat will be all right? What if someone finds it?'

'Then they'll take it and we'll be trapped forever,' Will whispered back. 'Or we'll use our brains to find a way out. We've done that before.' He surveyed his camouflage efforts. 'That'll have to be enough.' And he listened. Heard nothing. The island was silent. If someone had noticed their arrival, they were lying in wait, rather than dispatching a welcoming party. 'Are you ready?'

Andrew glanced at Gaia. He could see only the whites of her eyes. 'Would you rather wait here?'

'On my *own*?'

'I just thought—'

'No,' she said.

And she followed Will, who was starting to make his

way through the bushes, up the slope. As the bushes thinned out, he stopped suddenly. Reached into his rucksack, felt for the silk bag. He retrieved Blind Spot, and he held it out to Gaia.

'Take this,' he said. 'If you get in trouble, shine it in their eyes.'

She took it. '. . . But you might need it.'

'You hold on to it.'

'What do I get?' Andrew said, hitching his bag further up his back, and gripping his torch. He hadn't switched it on. But it felt good to hold it, in case of emergencies.

The torch had been a good idea, Will realized. For all his high tech kit, he'd neglected to pack the basics. And he was leading the way. In theory, he'd need it first. 'Pass me the torch.'

Trustingly, Andrew held it out.

Will dug around for Barrington's box. 'I think we should wear the tracker dots. Just in case we get split up.' He passed one to Gaia, who nodded and pressed it to her stomach.

Andrew took his. 'I was hoping more for a weapon,' he whispered.

'The dazzle gun's all I've got,' Will whispered back. 'Stay close to Gaia – she can protect you!'

Will resumed his ascent of the slope. Andrew sighed. Sometimes, he should really make a firmer stand against Will, he thought. But he held his tongue. He and Will were getting on better these days. He wanted to keep things that way.

Will was crouching low now, as they emerged from the vegetation and on to a clear patch of long grass. From here, they had a good view to the castle. It was barely twenty metres away. Solid. Stained black. The scene was motionless. At least no one seemed to be patrolling.

Again, Will reached into his bag. He found the small fuse box he'd shoved down the side. Carefully, he withdrew the first of four devices.

'Put it on—'

'I know,' Andrew said, taking his toothphone, 'the back molar.'

Will nodded. 'And remember – talk quietly.'

'Will, roger,' Andrew said.

And Will felt a slightly uncomfortable sensation as the tiny hammer in the toothphone transmitted Andrew's voice up through his jaw to his inner ear, while the words simultaneously vibrated their way to him through the air. *Tooth-talk*. It would allow them to keep in touch if they got separated.

'If we do get in trouble,' Will whispered, 'don't head straight for the boat – it might have been spotted. Meet back here, behind the trees – OK?'

Gaia nodded. 'So what now?' she whispered. Tension strangled her words. Suddenly it seemed hard to speak.

Will met her gaze. He understood how she felt.

Though he didn't share her trepidation. Or, if he did, he welcomed it. He wanted to feel the way he had in St Petersburg. Doing something that mattered. Taking risks. Doing all he *could*. Normal life was nothing next to this. He took a deep breath, fixed his eyes on the castle. 'We go in.'

STASIS HQ, Oxfordshire, England. Easter Saturday. 01.00

The C-17 Globemaster transport plane was waiting. Four Pratt & Whitney engines ripped through the darkness. Charlie Spicer jogged towards the open cargo hold, feeling his shoes squelch and his wet trousers chafe his legs. But, all things considered, the transfer had gone well.

Spicer himself had gone out with the team in the launch. He'd looked on anxiously as the cargo was carefully manoevred into slings. These slings were dragged behind the launch to the shore. Then, using the helicopter's hook and winch, they were lifted into two steel transport crates. Those crates were now safely stashed in the C-17.

Waving from the hold was Thor, one of STASIS's most recent recruits. Physically, Thor (short for Thorium – his code-name, taken from the Periodic Table of Elements) was an unimpressive specimen. He erred on the giraffe side of lanky and his over-large, sky-blue eyes gave him a permanent look of surprise. Two distinctive bumps on his long nasal bone promised to tell violent tales. The fights hadn't been his fault. That was all he would say.

Academically, though, he was much harder to beat. A first from Cambridge University. Three times winner of the Royal Institute of Engineers' Brunel medal. He had seen field action only once so far, in St Petersburg. And he had acquitted himself well.

Thor's long blond eyelashes blinked now, as he watched Spicer approach.

'We're all set,' he shouted above the noise of the engines.

Spicer nodded. 'Good. And remember—'

'Don't sign them over to anyone except Mr Barrington. I know, sir.'

Spicer nodded again. 'Wait—'

'—For the democratic intelligence and security service and Mr Barrington. I'll make sure of it, sir.'

'You have the controls?'

Thor patted his pocket. 'Yes, sir.'

And Spicer felt waves of pride and anxiety. They left him feeling sea-sick. This would be the first active duty for his new creations. They were ready. Still, he couldn't help wishing he had more fingers to cross. Ten didn't seem quite enough.

'Safe journey,' Spicer said.

Thor grinned. Mock-saluted. Then Spicer backed away, head down. From the shore of Lake 1, he watched as the C-17 took off and veered away into the night. The aircraft did not carry weapons but even if it had been a Tornado GR4 armed to the gills, Spicer would have found it hard to decide which was more dangerous: the plane, or the cargo inside.

Will checked his watch. 2.05 a.m., local time. The evening breeze rustled the leaves of the bushes behind them. From here, he guessed, it would take a good thirty seconds to make the run to the castle. The looming front door faced them, wind-ravaged gargoyles glaring out with dead eyes from the lintel. But it might as well have been bricked up. They'd have to find a less obvious way in.

'So we're clear,' Will whispered. 'We try to find out if this place has anything to do with the 'ghosts'. We try to find Cristina. We leave.'

Andrew nodded quickly. He pushed his glasses along the bridge of his nose. Will read the gesture. Andrew was nervous. He had reason to be.

'You and Gaia take the left. I'll take the right. There might be a back entrance.'

'I don't think we should split up,' Andrew whispered.

'It's OK,' Will said. 'Gaia will be with you.'

'I didn't mean—' Andrew started, colouring.

But Will raised a hand. 'We've got the toothphones, so we might as well use them. Let me know when you find something.'

'*If*, you mean,' Andrew said. And he lifted his rucksack to his shoulder.

Andrew had been secretive. Stuff, he'd said. Torches and things. What else is in there, Will wondered.

And then he ran.

The ground was scrubby. Thin grass and soft mud. He covered it quickly, listening to the sound of his breathing. It reminded him of his dip in Research Lake 2. He'd heard nothing else, just the bubbles produced by the bellows action of his lungs. Seen nothing. *Felt* those things. His right leg still ached. He had to ignore it.

Will reached the wall, turned his back to the stone. He glimpsed Andrew and Gaia disappearing around the far side of the castle. The lagoon stretched into the distance, Venice hidden from sight.

Here, in the shadows, Will felt safe.

The feeling didn't last long.

One hundred metres from Will, on a small beach out of sight of the *Venus*, Dino completed his task.

The vehicles were stored in a neat wooden hut. They were in fine working order, Dino made sure of that. There were three. One each for him and the two other cult members charged with protection and surveillance.

Mostly, they had very little to do. The island had a

reputation as the most haunted spot in Venice and there were few locals steely enough to head for its shores. The small, dark-sand beaches held no interest for tourists. Who else would come? The police? They had tried, once. But Rudolfo had a cousin, in the Venezia station. The Master paid well for advance notice of unwanted incursions.

Now Dino made his way up to the gravel path, which led to the castle.

He froze.

Something had moved.

Dino reached into his pocket, yanked out a torch. The beam flickered across the wall. And it settled.

Dino stared.

Blinking in the sharp white light, a boy a little younger than him was glaring back. The stranger's eyes flashed anger.

'*Hey!*' Dino started to run.

'This is impenetrable,' Andrew said, pulling out his toothphone.

Gaia did the same. 'There must be a way in.'

'There is. The front door. Look at it – it's a castle. It's built to keep people out.'

'So we just give up and head back to the boat?'

Andrew hesitated. A small part of him did in fact want to say yes. Then he thought of Cristina. In the chatroom, she had seemed so intelligent. She had asked such probing questions. She had sounded so *charming*. And if he could find some sort of scientific explanation for what were commonly known as ghosts . . . 'No.'

'Right,' Gaia whispered. She slotted the toothphone back over her molar. And she overtook Andrew to lead the way along the grey wall.

Starlight shone weakly above. Gaia moved slowly. The ground was uneven and it was difficult to see. Suddenly, her eyes opened wide.

Andrew heard it too. A voice, through his jawbone.

'My name is Will. I came because I heard about the Master.'

'The Master?' Dino's eyes narrowed. This was most unexpected. A new boy. Caught at the castle. Unexpected and alarming. 'What do you mean?' he demanded. 'How did you get here?'

Will blinked. Dino was training the torch right on his eyes. Running had been an impossibility. He'd had to stand there, against the wall, while Dino approached him, torch raised like a weapon.

'I heard that the Master lives here,' Will stammered. 'I got a water taxi. It dropped me off. I want to meet him.'

Will was trying his best to look scared. He was nervous, certainly. But it had to appear more than that. He had to look terrified, and needy. Whoever this boy was, he was evidence that someone besides the owner of the castle lived here. And this was a *boy*. If there was one, were they more? Could there really be a cult?

If there wasn't, mentioning the Master couldn't hurt.

If there was, the fate of their entire mission to Venice could rest on this boy believing him.

'Why do you want to meet the Master?' Dino rasped.

And Will felt his pulse race. So the Master was real. He did exist! Cristina had been right – and Andrew had been right to trust her note. At least, there was a Master. Will had to stop himself there. Stick to what you *know*, he told himself.

'I heard – I heard he speaks to ghosts.'

'And why should that interest you?'

Why should that interest you? '. . . I lost someone,' Will said at last. His expression faltered. And he let it reflect some of the pain that still ate into him. Conflicting emotions charged through his body. Anger, at being discovered by Dino. Guilt, at mentioning his father now, even indirectly, in this way. Misery, at his loss.

Pain and misery won.

Dino lowered his torch. Jerked his head. 'My name is Dino. Come with me.'

Again, Will caught his breath. It had worked. *He'd been believed.*

Around the other side of the castle, Andrew and Gaia were staring at each other in something close to horror.

'Will, be careful,' Andrew whispered.

Gaia held a finger to her lips.

But Will could not have replied. He was inches

behind Dino's back, watching as the boy's grimy fingers flicked a key to unlock a low, wooden door in the grey wall. Dino had to bend to pass through. Will followed. He emerged into a damp stone passageway, which instantly forked into two. At once, Will turned and slammed the door shut.

Dino nodded. He set off, leading the way along the left-hand passage, and Will quickly reached behind him. Lifted the latch.

'That's a useful side door,' Will said, as he caught up with Dino.

The boy frowned. But of course the remark had not been directed at him. Rather to Will's toothphone – to Andrew and Gaia.

'So I will get to meet the Master?' Will asked.

'The Master is very busy.'

'Where are we going now?' he said.

Dino stopped suddenly. 'You have a phone?'

Will tried to register confusion. 'Why?'

'If you have a phone you must give it to me.' Dino's eyes drifted to Will's rucksack. 'Is it in there?'

'I brought a few clothes,' Will said quickly, afraid Dino would search his bag. 'My phone's in my pocket.' He reached into his jacket. Touched warm fur. Ratty. His fingers fumbled for plastic. 'What if I need to call someone?'

Dino's lips parted in an unpleasant smile. 'Who would you want to call? You are here. Free from the misery of the world. You are with us.'

'Us – so there are many?'

Dino scowled. 'Even if you keep this phone, you will not be able to use it. The Master insists. The castle is fitted with signal blockers.'

'So why take it?'

But Dino did not seem impressed with Will's argument. 'Hand it over.'

Reluctantly, Will produced his smart phone. Either this Master was illogical, or Dino was stealing goods from new recruits, to make money on the side. Will watched Dino's eyes run greedily over the device and decided it was the latter.

Now Dino set off again, his trainers squeaking.

The atmosphere in the passage was oppressive. Musty air settled in Will's lungs. 'Where are we going?' he said again.

Dino shook his head. All he said was: 'You'll see.'

'It could be worse,' Gaia said.

She was skirting around the back of the castle. Andrew was following her, stepping gingerly. '*How?*'

'At least Will's in. It sounds like there *is* a cult. So if Cristina's here, he should find her.'

'Exactly.' The word shuddered through her jaw. It was bizarre, having a three-way conversation, when one of the people involved in that conversation wasn't physically present.

Inside the castle, Dino stopped, turned.

'Nothing. I was just thinking,' Will said.

Back outside, Andrew pointed ahead. 'Look!'

There it was. A low, wooden door. An iron hoop for a handle. Gaia glanced up. Clouds passed and revealed a crescent moon. Andrew's face was as pale.

'Ready?' she whispered. And it wasn't lost on her that Andrew, for all his brave talk back at the palace, was now the one who needed encouragement. But she understood Andrew. And she trusted him. He might sound scared, but he would never crumble.

Andrew nodded.

She pushed. Led the way in.

With the door closed behind them, the silence was absolute. A bare white bulb on a shrivelled cord dangled dangerously from the ceiling a couple of metres along the passageway. And then another. Gaia shivered. The rough-hewn walls were wet, she noticed. Moisture glistened, like something living.

'I wish we had Ratty,' Andrew whispered.

'Which way?' Gaia said, hoping a practical question would pull him back on track.

Andrew regarded their options uncertainly. 'We could ask Will which way he went.'

Silence. Perhaps Dino was talking, and it was awkward for him to speak.

'. . . OK,' Andrew said. 'Let's try right.'

The passage was narrow. Gaia stayed hard up behind Andrew, partly to urge him on, partly to pretend to herself that she wasn't afraid. She could see the tool marks in the huge stone blocks that made up the walls. Gouges, chisel hacks, and scrapes, like something made by finger nails.

After ten metres, the wall right-angled. Andrew stopped.

'Go on,' she whispered.

He peered around the corner. Waved her on.

Here, the passage widened. It seemed easier to breathe. But Gaia found herself colliding with Andrew. She peered around him. 'What's wrong?'

'Look,' he said. Unlike the others, the right-hand wall was not bare. Ahead was a series of oil paintings in oval dirt-stained frames.

First came a portrait of a pinched-cheeked young woman with a powdered face and a vast wig topped with purple flowers, strands of glossy pearls strung like rope around her neck. The paint was flaking and cracked.

Slowly, Andrew walked the gallery, inspecting the faces. They were related, he decided. He saw the same wide mouth and identical slit-black eyes in old women, young men and even a child with black curls clustering around her scrawny shoulders.

Gaia followed him. She hesitated by a portrait of a woman in a flowing black cloak and an embroidered mask which covered her eyes. This portrait bore an inscription, etched into a gold plaque. *La Contessa di Grimaldi*. What sort of person had their portrait painted with a mask, she found herself wondering. What did they have to hide?

And Gaia turned. She'd felt something. A chill. She saw nothing. Only an iron chandelier, and a bulb, casting its wasted light.

It was nothing, she told herself. A Gothic castle and gloomy paintings. Tricks of her own imagination.

And she froze. *Again!* This time, her stomach was gripped. She felt fingers closing around her guts. And nausea swelled. There was no mistaking this! This wasn't in her mind. *'Andrew!'*

Ahead, Andrew turned very slowly. He registered the fear in her eyes. 'Yeah,' he said quietly. 'I know.'

'You feel it?' Gaia realized she was shivering. The grip on her guts was released and she glanced back once more, and saw something move. *A grey shadow.* It flickered across her eyes, evading her pupils, vanishing into nothing. She ran to Andrew, grabbed his arm. 'There's something here! Did you see that!' Gaia swivelled her head, eyes desperately searching, fixing on nothing except a series of static frames.

The bulb. The walls. The paintings. *La Contessa*, in her black velvet mask.

Gaia's breathing was coming fast. *Something is here*, she thought. And: *Ghosts do not exist.* But her brain refused to believe it. The uneasiness was spreading through her body. Why had they come to the island? Why hadn't they gone to the police? This girl Cristina was missing. Had she been here? Had she seen these things? And Gaia blinked as once more something grey flitted at the edge of her vision. An apparition. Cold iced her spine in freezing waves. 'Andrew,' she hissed urgently. 'I think we should get out of here.'

But Andrew had dropped his rucksack to the ground. With trembling fingers, he pulled at the zip.

Gaia dropped to a crouch. 'I *mean* it,' she said urgently. 'I don't like it.'

'Wait,' he said. 'Just a second.'

'What are you *doing*?'

Andrew was setting a small instrument on the ground beside his bag. He plugged in a microphone. Held it up. Fiddled with a switch. Waved the mike. Squinted at the reading.

'Oh my God.' He sounded stunned.

Now tension erupted from Gaia. '*What?*' Her voice had been loud. She didn't care.

Andrew held up the instrument. Showed her the digital read-out. 'Look.'

'I don't know what I'm looking at!'

His eyes were bright. 'The infrasound readings are off the scale!'

'*Infrasound?*' Gaia stared at him. What was he talking about?

She watched in consternation as Andrew dropped the mike and ran his fingers along the stone blocks of the wall. Something shifted. One of the blocks was loose. Andrew tried to get a good hold. No good. It was too tightly jammed to move without the aid of a tool.

'I bet you anything there's an infrasound generator behind there.'

'Andrew, what are you talking about!' she pleaded.

'This is where the reading is strongest,' he said quietly. And he looked up at her. 'There is a science to ghost-busting, you know.'

Gaia's eyes widened.

Andrew stood and dusted off his trousers. 'I brought this stuff on purpose. I thought maybe I'd use it in the museum at Cristina's palace. I didn't feel anything there. But this is classic. Even if we don't find any *ghosts*, I'll write this up and get invited to every parapsychology conference going.'

'Andrew – What. Are. You. Talking. About?' Her cheeks were red.

He blinked. 'Really, Gaia, you shouldn't get so upset. It's all right. Lots of work has been done on this. There was an engineer at Coventry University who thought his lab was haunted and he wasn't the only one. People went in there and they felt uneasy. They reported seeing something grey. Anyway, this engineer found that an extractor fan in the lab was generating an infrasound of 0.56 Herz.'

'*And?*'

'Basic biology. Our bodies don't like infrasound much. It can make you feel ill. You get problems with balance. Low frequency sounds can vibrate your eyeballs and distort your vision. They can make you *see* things.'

Andrew eased his infrasound detector back into his bag. 'There's another researcher in Hertfordshire. He investigated reports of apparitions and phantom footsteps in some underground streets in Edinburgh. He sent in groups of people to four different spots, only he didn't tell them that only two actually had a reputation for being haunted. More than eighty per cent of those people reported spooky sensations in the most haunted site. They thought they'd been touched. Some said they saw apparitions of people and animals. But less than half felt anything at the sites that didn't have a reputation for ghosts.'

'And he found infrasound generators?'

'In that most haunted site there was an infrasound rumble, caused by traffic overhead. And the two haunted sites were less humid, so they felt colder. Other research has shown odd breezes can encourage people to think they're in the presence of ghosts.'

Gaia stared at him. Slowly, his confident explanation was thawing her fear. 'How do you know all this?'

'I told you. I did some research. And Dad's a psychiatrist, remember. He had a patient once who thought he was possessed by a spirit.'

'That wasn't down to infrasound?' Gaia said doubtfully.

'No, unfortunately, he had something called a disconnection syndrome . . . To do with his brain. Anyway, what I'm saying is that *someone* here is trying to make people think there are ghosts. They're trying to make this castle feel haunted. '

Gaia nodded. The odd tugging at her guts was still there, but at least now her brain had a semi-reasonable explanation. 'But what about Cristina's ghost? That wasn't a grey flash – we *saw* it, if it wasn't a fake. And why would someone want to make this place seem haunted?'

'If we really do have a ghost cult, recruits will be expecting this place to feel haunted. They have to believe in ghosts – or a ghost cult wouldn't exactly work.'

Gaia searched for a hole in Andrew's explanation. Couldn't find one. Infrasound, she told herself. Infrasound and breezes. Smoke and mirrors. 'You could have told me all this earlier.'

'I—' And he hesitated, then packed up his mike. 'I didn't know that this is what we'd find. And, yes, you're right, this ghost thief is still a mystery. And the answers aren't in this passage. Though if you ask me what I really think about all this, I think you have to steer clear of convictions. Anyone who thinks current science can explain *everything* is totally wrong.'

Gaia was surprised. 'But not in this case.'

He gave her a quick smile. 'In this case, we've shown there is an alternative explanation.'

Andrew stood up, slung the rucksack on his back. 'We haven't heard anything from Will for a while.'

'No,' Gaia said. 'Where do you think he is?'

11

'A friend told me about this place,' Will ventured. 'She said she was coming to join you, and I should come too. That was a few days ago. Her name's Cristina. Did she really come?'

Dino glowered at Will, who forced his expression to remain hopeful.

'Is she here now?' Will said.

Dino didn't reply. He was pulling back a red curtain.

This wasn't going to work, Will decided. Dino would tell him nothing. Perhaps he was afraid of the 'Master'. Perhaps Cristina had already gone snooping in search of light-fingered ghosts, and had been discovered. It had been a risk to mention her. A risk Will had felt he'd had to take.

Now Dino ushered Will into the dining hall.

'Wait here,' he said. And he vanished.

Will stared. So it was *true*. If he needed further proof of a cult, here it was: a small huddle of figures in white hooded cloaks, warming themselves by glowing logs.

Kids. In this castle, on this island. So why hadn't the police found them? And could Cristina be among them?

Will wondered something else: did no one here sleep?

He strained to hear their conversation. Made out nothing. He couldn't even tell how many were male, how many female. He knew what Cristina looked like bare-headed and smiling in the sun. With these cloaks, it wouldn't be so easy.

Will edged into the shadows towards the back of the room. A few heads turned briefly. They showed surprisingly little interest in the new recruit, Will thought. The feeling was not mutual.

In his pocket, Will felt for Ratty. He crouched, as though resting, and he lowered Ratty to the floor. Next, he connected an earpiece to the display screen. Glancing down at the remote, which he held close to his thigh, Will switched Ratty to 'active'. He instructed the animal to run around the perimeter of the room, staying in darkness.

Fifteen seconds later, Ratty approached the fireplace. A wide wicker log basket provided perfect cover. Will pulled out his toothphone – it was impossible to listen to Andrew and Gaia while also focusing on Ratty's quiet audio. He ratcheted the volume up to maximum and he heard:

'They haven't come back.' A girl's voice.

'Are you sure?' Another girl.

'Why would they volunteer and leave? It doesn't make sense.'

'Then where are they?' A boy. 'What if—' Will fiddled with his earpiece, and he missed a second '—the other side.'

'They stayed there?' The first girl. Disbelieving. 'Can you do that?'

And they stopped talking. A door close to Will had opened. Other figures in white started to stream in. Some rushed to the fire. This was dangerous – for Ratty.

Quickly, Will retrieved him, switched him to 'standby' and slipped him back into his pocket. He tried to make sense of what he had overheard. But there was insufficient information. Volunteered for what? And 'the other side'. Did they mean the world of ghosts? Of the *dead*?

Will glanced towards the open door. No one else was entering. Dino was still absent. He needed some answers. He had to take his chance.

Will strode rapidly from the dining hall. The passage was silent. No footsteps, apart from his. No movement, only the flickering of the dim overhead bulbs on the worn flagstones and the twitch of Ratty in his pocket.

Will didn't know what he was really looking for, or where to start. So why not here – at this, the first wooden door.

The handle was of heavy iron. Freezing to the touch.

Will held his breath as he waited for a creak that did not come. Did not come, because the door was locked – with a new steel mechanism, he noticed. Will cursed.

Quickly, Will made his way further along the passage, to a second door. He grasped the handle. It turned half way. And held. Locked. But this, at least, was an old-fashioned lock. If the door was built like the one through which he had followed Dino into the castle, there was a simple latch on the other side. A good five millimetre gap separated the door from the wall. Will couldn't reach through that. Neither could Ratty. But he had something else that might.

One eye on the look-out for white-clad cult members or – worse – Dino, Will rifled through his rucksack. The stiff cardboard box was right at the bottom. He pulled the control screen from his pocket and he activated Grabber.

At once, the robot's slender arms began to unfurl. Would they be slim enough to reach through the gap and dextrous enough to lift the latch? There was only one way to find out.

Using the touch screen, Will extended Grabber's first tentacle to its maximum length. He had thirty centimetres of carbon fibre to work with. But only the last ten centimetres were skinny enough to fit through the gap.

Carefully, Will inserted Grabber's arm. The tiny camera in the end swirled and twitched. It wasn't easy to get it to curl back on itself. But at last, Will looked at the imaging screen with relief. There it was.

A latch.

Three seconds later, Grabber had lifted it.

Will slipped inside. Shut himself into blackness. His eyes waited for light that did not come. He saw only green stars, triggered by cells firing in his confused retina. Apart from a skinny rectangle of dim light around the door, the room was black.

Mentally thanking Andrew, Will retrieved the torch from his pocket, fumbled for the switch and blinked. First, he focused on the walls. Saw a bookcase crammed with leather volumes and four immense oil portraits. Narrow eyes, lace collars, pearl jewellery slung in long strands across taut chests.

A carved Egyptian screen zigzagged across the far right corner. Angled away from the wall was a brown leather sofa. On a table beside it, Will noticed a nineteenth-century ceramic phrenologist's head. It showed the cranial bumps supposedly associated with personality traits. *Secretiveness. Combativeness. Self-esteem. Destructiveness.*

Will switched the beam to the right. Found a desk. It was piled with magazines, a dead plant in a Chinese pot and an old-fashioned black telephone. Then the torch showed a series of drawers, with a bright brass key.

Curious, Will crossed to the desk. He left Grabber beside the plant and he twisted the key, opening the first drawer.

The first thing he saw was a piece of paper, scrawled with a telephone number. The code was +41. International. Somewhere in Europe.

Underneath, he found something much more interesting.

Facsimiles of architect's drawings. They seemed to have been made in the 1800s. Will clamped his teeth around the torch and flicked through them. *A castle*. This castle. At least, it seemed to be. Yet the rooms were marked with words like sanitorium, electro-therapy, water treatment . . . Andrew had said the castle had been a psychiatric hospital in a former life. Whatever it had been, the fundamental architecture was unlikely to have changed. And these plans could at least show him where, in theory, he might find clues to the ghosts – or Cristina.

Will eased Ratty from his pocket. Gripping him gently by his belly, he directed the animal's camera towards the first of the plans. He could record the drawings and play them back when he was somewhere safer, to reconstruct the layout. Will scanned Ratty's head across each of the sheets of paper. Then, as he was concentrating on the last, he stiffened.

Someone was at the door. They were inserting a key. Still holding tight to Ratty, Will dashed behind the leather sofa and flicked off the torch.

He listened to his breathing. And he controlled it. Softly in. Softly out. Like smoke from a chimney. As his father had taught him.

A male voice uttered an exclamation of annoyance. Perhaps because the door had been left unlocked. Will could see nothing. He could only crouch, as the overhead light flicked on and the room was lit by two bulbs. Suddenly, sparks flew from his spine. *Grabber.*

Will inched towards the edge of the sofa. A tall man in a dark red cloak was sitting at the desk. He had his back to Will. And he was picking up the telephone. *Now*, Will thought.

There was no way he could retrieve Grabber under his own power. The robot's legs would make too much noise on the stone floor. Will needed something stealthier. Something cunning. And silent.

Carefully, Will set Ratty on the ground. Gripping the remote, he sent the animal scurrying to the desk and up the leg. The man was grunting to himself, completely unaware that inches from his back a small remote-controlled rat with a video camera attached to its head was closing in on a robotic octopus.

'Hello?' The man rose from his chair, receiver in his large hand.

Will ordered Ratty to freeze.

'Tell him I must speak to him immediately!'

And the man slumped back down in his chair.

Will prepared to activate Grabber and instruct him to uncurl his legs, in preparation for attachment to Ratty's belly, when something totally unexpected happened.

Ratty opened his mouth. And he clamped down on Grabber's body. Will stared at Ratty's video feed.

122

Without further instructions, Ratty scurried back down the leg and behind the sofa.

His heart thudding, Will took Grabber from Ratty's narrow mouth. He looked into his pet's beady black eyes. Ratty was remote-controlled. There was no doubt about that. But Will knew he couldn't totally over-ride the animal's natural behaviour. And he also knew that rats were smart.

Had Ratty somehow guessed what he wanted? No. That was presuming too much. It had been an accident. Ratty liked to bite things. He bit Grabber . . . That had to be it. Will stroked the rat's head. 'Good job,' he mouthed.

'You said six hours,' came the angry voice from the desk. 'We have a meeting! The equipment must be here sooner! The Master demands three – he will double your price!'

And Will heard the man rise and stamp out of the room, slamming the door closed, and turning the lock.

For two minutes, Will waited. He timed himself, forcing his limbs to remain still. Thinking about what he had just heard. What equipment, he wondered. And what meeting?

Will was about to get up when he noticed another door. It had been concealed by the carved Egyptian *mashrabiyya* screen. But from this angle, down behind the sofa, he could make out the handle. Will flicked on Andrew's torch. No key.

He ran to it. It creaked open. Holding his breath, Will stepped into another dark room.

Immediately, he noticed two more doors, one off to the right, another in the opposite wall beside a hefty wooden dresser carved with bull's heads. Will tracked the beam. And his attention was drawn by a metal lab desk.

Quickly, he darted the light over an unusual combination of objects. A 3D printer. A desk lamp. A set of micro forceps. Beside the printer was a plastic box. Will lifted the lid and found grey granules. At that instant, he noticed something else.

The floor was not of stone. It was transparent. Will crouched. Rapped it gently. Glass. Or Perspex. Beneath this material, small metal mountings were arranged in a regular pattern on the real stone floor below. It was impossible to guess what they were for.

Will flicked the beam across the glass to the walls and he found further mountings, driven in at intervals. Two of the mountings held something. *Miniature cameras.*

His brain churning, fixing on nothing, Will got up. And his thoughts blanked. A noise.

Instantly, he flicked off the torch. Someone was opening the door to the right. He couldn't hide underneath the desk. They'd see him at once. He had little choice. Will pressed his back to the freezing wall and hunched against the black wood of the dresser.

His ears seemed to flinch. The person had stepped inside the room. And he waited. This person wasn't moving. So what were they doing? Will could hear their breathing. It sounded delicate. He could see nothing. In this room, there was no light. His vision, which he took for granted, was as utterly useless as it had been in the depths of Research Lake 2.

And then the main light burst into life, a floodlight that plunged the world into white. Will squeezed his eyes shut. They hurt, burning red. When he opened them, he saw that someone was watching him, uncertainty written all over her features.

125

Will opened his mouth. Words did not come.

He watched thoughts flash through her black eyes, making them sparkle.

And Cristina noticed the carbon-fibre head of Grabber, sticking out of the top of Will's jacket pocket. She frowned. Surely it couldn't be . . .

'. . . Andrew Minkel?' she whispered, half in disbelief.

Will blinked at her. *Cristina*. He should have recognized her.

It seemed strange to hear Andrew's name on her red lips. But she was here! Cristina della Corte. Black hair shone. The photograph hadn't really done her justice. There was something almost supernaturally vivid about the caramel colour of her skin, the quartzy glint of her eyes.

'My name is Will Knight. I . . .work with Andrew.'

'You belong to STORM?' she said excitedly.

Will tried to re-order his mind. He nodded.

And she flashed white teeth. 'So you came! I am Cristina! Is Andrew here?'

'Somewhere,' Will said.

'You are not together? But it is not safe . . . Things are happening here. I contacted Andrew days ago. I thought he had dismissed me.'

'He's been trying to call you,' Will said. 'Last night and this morning.'

'They took my phone! But how did you find me? When did you come?'

'We just got here,' Will said, ignoring the first part of the question. Andrew could explain his computer intrusion for himself.

'So you have seen this room? Look – there are cameras. I don't know what for. And here—' Cristina was carrying a black bag in her right hand. With her left, she lifted the box from the desk and opened the lid. 'You see this? I found powder like this in my father's museum. On the rug – where the ghost vanished. Did Andrew tell you?'

Will nodded. He recalled their discussion. Dust left by the cleaner, or so he'd said.

'This is your powder?'

'Mine? No! I found it here – here in this room. The dust in my home, it came from here. It is identical.'

Will held out his hand for a closer look. Cristina handed him the box. She opened the black bag and produced a microscope. 'I came here to hide this for later – to look at the dust.'

'It's antique,' Will said. It was brass, the words *Carl Zeiss Jena* inscribed in cursive letters on the barrel.

'But it is all I could find. But you are here! And what conclusions have you made? What do you think of the Master?'

'I haven't seen him,' Will said. 'What do you know about him? Do you know who he is – do you know his name?'

Cristina's beautiful mouth stiffened. Her black eyes glittered. 'No. It is always "the Master". But something serious is going on here. This cult is not what it seems. They tell us the castle is haunted, but I think that is to make us afraid, to stop us exploring, and to make us love this Master, to believe in him even more. I think they *make* the ghosts here somehow – I don't know how. And something else is happening. The Master asks for volunteers. He tells us he can take us to the other side. Yesterday, two went with the Master and Rudolfo – the Master's relation. They have not come back.

'Others have vanished,' she continued. 'But the people here, they don't like to talk. They say only: wait, you will see. But I don't want to see. I want to find my property, find out what they are doing, and leave.'

'What do you think they're doing?' Will asked.

Cristina's delicate brow knotted. 'I don't know what they volunteer for. But the Master used this ghost to steal my lion. It is of gold, it has jewels – that is its value. If he is stealing things, is he after money? Only money? Or money for something? Because why have a cult? Why have volunteers? I don't know.'

'Did you hear about the gallery of modern art?' Will asked. 'A "ghost" made off with a Klimt yesterday. It was all over the news.'

'The Galleria! Yes!' Cristina's eyes widened. 'And the police still have not come!' She shook her head. 'So the ghosts are stealing valuable things – is that the only reason? For wealth?'

But Will had no answer. And how could the ghosts be 'made'? Did the thefts have anything to do with the 'equipment' the tall man had mentioned?

Cristina glanced at her watch, diamonds sparkling. She must have kept that well-hidden from Dino, Will thought. 'I think now we should go straight to the hall. A meeting is about to start. If I am late, they will wonder where I am. Then we can come back and investigate this powder properly together. You are in hiding?'

'A boy called Dino knows I'm here,' Will said. 'He thinks I want to join the cult. I told him I know you. I had to – I was trying to find out if you really were here. He doesn't know about Andrew and Gaia.'

'Gaia?'

'The other member of STORM. There are three of us.'

'Ah, yes, I heard there was a girl . . . But if Dino knows you are here, you should come with me. He will notice if you are missing. Come to the hall. You will see what the Master is like. Then we will come back here. We will look at the powder. And STORM and I, we will find out what is happening!'

At the precise moment that Will found Cristina, Andrew and Gaia made a discovery of their own.

The castle contained a warren of passages, it was clear. Back past the unnerving portrait of the masked Contessa and away towards the east they had found a slippery, spiral stone staircase that led down to another set of passageways, forking off to the north, south-east and west.

'We're going to get lost,' Andrew said.

'I can remember the way.'

'You're sure?'

'Ask me what's on page one hundred and twelve of your father's book about the Bismarck Archipelago.'

Andrew smiled. 'With a photographic memory, your mind must be very full.'

'Not as full as yours,' she said generously.

Andrew's smile broadened. 'Shall we carry on down here?'

'Maybe we should try Will again. Will. Hello? *Will?*'

No response.

A trace of anxiety swept across Andrew's face. 'Do you think he's all right?'

Gaia nodded quickly.

'. . . Of course,' Andrew breathed.

Gaia stopped. Ahead, a door was standing open. Cautiously, Gaia approached and peered in, expecting it to be empty like the succession of others they had passed. But the light from the passage showed what looked like an old hospital trolley, and a bench with Perspex beakers. In one corner a fume cupboard gleamed dully.

Curious, she went in.

The trolley was sinister. Aquamarine paint was peeling, revealing raw rusting iron underneath. Looped around the foot rails were two old leather ankle restraints, worn thin. Warily, Andrew peered at the leather straps. Was this a remnant of the castle's use as a lunatic asylum, he wondered. And he shivered, imagining the state and the fate of the patients that had once used this bed. 'This looks like something from the eighteen hundreds,' he whispered.

Gaia hadn't heard. She was concentrating on the bench.

Chemistry was *her* subject. Gaia recognized all the tools of the trade. Among those tools was a small canister, marked 'Plastised RDX'. Gaia peeled open the lid. There was a strip of the stuff, stuck in the bottom. 'Explosive,' she murmured.

On the front of another white plastic canister, *Al* was printed. *Aluminium.* Gaia read the contents label. This pack had contained an extraordinarily fine powder of the metal, the spheres just thirty nanometres – thirty millionths of a millimetre – in diameter.

'What is it?' Andrew whispered as he crossed to her, trying not to glance back at that bed.

'I'm not sure exactly.'

She picked up one of the beakers. In the bottom was a gel-like residue. She sniffed.

'Well?' Andrew said.

'I don't know.'

'What do you think's in there?'

Andrew was pointing underneath the desk. Gaia backed up. She saw a small silver-coloured box with a heavy door.

'It's a safe,' she said.

'A safe,' Andrew nodded. 'A perfect place for secrets.' He bent down and scrutinized it.

'What are you going to do? Pick it?'

He glanced up. 'You did say "explosive" a moment ago, didn't you? I was rather hoping you might be able to offer a quicker alternative.'

Gaia considered. She was familiar with plastised RDX, and she could make a fair guess about the size of the chunk required to blast open that safe door.

'I don't have a—' fuse, she had been going to say, but before the word was even out she remembered something. 'You know back in London you said you had useful kit – a torch, *waterproof matches*?'

Andrew nodded.

'You have those matches?'

'Somewhere,' he said. 'What are you going to do? *Light* it?'

Gaia held out her hand. 'Just give them to me.'

It took Andrew a few moments to dig out the match book from beneath the infrasound kit and the wind sensor, which in the end he'd decided hadn't been required. 'Here.' And he watched as Gaia carefully removed two matches, closed the book and inserted the base of one of the matches back into the side of the pack. The head stuck out at a right angle, bright red.

'If I stick this book to the explosive, when I light this match, we'll have a few seconds to get back before the whole book ignites,' she explained. 'We'll have a decent fuse.'

Andrew grinned. 'Something tells me you've done this before.'

'Once or twice.' And she remembered the over-blown 'horror' she'd caused when she'd spooked a particularly arrogant physics teacher at her previous school. Her father should have been furious but he hadn't even turned up to the exclusion meeting. She'd guessed where he was: at home, with one of the bottles he thought he hid from her in the back of his wardrobe.

Carefully, Gaia pulled the RDX from the canister and pressed it on to the front of the safe, just above the lock mechanism. She wedged the edge of the match book into the explosive.

'Ready?' she said. 'Can you close the door?'

Andrew nodded, and backed up. 'It won't be too loud? What if someone hears?'

'We haven't seen anyone, have we? And I'm not using much – just enough to blast the lock. Look at the door – it's solid. It should be OK.'

Quickly, Gaia struck the other match against the rough strip, and held the blazing head to her fuse. Excitement rushed through her as she dashed back to join Andrew at the rear of the room. She had control. Even if was only over explosive . . .

Two seconds later, there was a sudden flash of light and a muffled bang. No worse than an over-the-counter firework.

'You can open your eyes,' Gaia said. She ran forwards, waving away smoke, and saw that the explosive had worked perfectly. The door of the safe was standing open. Impatient, she reached inside.

'What have you got?' Andrew said.

'Only this . . .' She retrieved a sheet of paper, folded in half.

Andrew's eyes opened wide. He reached out, coughing a little, but Gaia held the paper close to her chest. In her own time, she unfolded it, and then scowled.

The top line was in Russian, a language she knew only slightly. Below, the letters RDX had been crossed through. Beneath was a chemical formula, with further notes in Russian. Gaia could not read the text, but she could read the formula, all right. That language was truly international. Her heart, already excited, began to race.

'What is it?' Andrew asked.

'RDX is an explosive,' she whispered.

'As I can bear witness. But it's been crossed out,' Andrew observed.

'Yeah, in favour of a gel compound of nano-sized aluminium and iron oxide!'

Andrew nodded. He knew enough chemistry to understand. Bring those two together and you could cause some serious damage. 'So this is a recipe for another explosive? With nano-sized particles?'

'It's new technology,' Gaia said. 'The smaller the size

of the reagents in your gel, the better you can predict and control the explosion.' Her face was pale.

'So someone here is making a high-powered bomb.'

'This Master?' she breathed.

'If he's keeping the recipe in a safe, I'd guess he's planning something serious! What's that – ?' Andrew took the paper from her. Scrawled in red at the bottom of the other side were four dense lines of maths. Step by step, Andrew worked through them.

'So what does it mean?' Gaia asked.

'I don't know – it seems to be some sort of algorithm for describing the positions of objects – millions of objects – I have no idea—'

And Andrew stiffened.

'What?' she said.

'Did you hear that?'

'. . . What?'

'Wait! Shh.' Andrew ran to the open door. Held a finger to his lips. He pointed towards the passage.

Then it came again.

This time they both heard it.

A strange murmuring. A fretting. Like something softly crying.

Cristina led the way. Her white hooded top blending in with the cloaks, she edged between the bodies assembled in the dining hall. Eyes turned to her. And Will scanned the crowd, searching for Dino. But if he was wearing a cloak, he'd be impossible to spot. Will caught only glimpses of anonymous shrouded faces, features exaggerated by the flames.

So he had found Cristina, he thought. And she was safe. One target down. But the others were proliferating. Could 'ghosts' be made? Was Cristina right – were they really kept or even created here? And why? What happened in that room with the cameras? And what was the powder? Questions ricocheted around Will's skull. Without answers, they had no way out.

But there was little time to think. Will had been moving with Cristina towards the fireplace, and now a white-clad arm beside him shot out in the direction of the balcony.

'The Master's coming!' a boy's voice called.

Voices rose together: *'Adoremus in aeternum. Adoremus in aeternum.'*

The low chanting had a visceral effect. Will's body seemed slowly to electrify. The words charged into his veins. He studied Latin, and he understood:

We will adore you forever.

Who? Will thought. *The Master?* Dead relatives? And he felt himself tense, ready to take flight or fight, as a tall man in a ripe-crimson cloak emerged on to the balcony with a flourish of his hands. Will made out a slit-like mouth and narrow eyes. The man from the study, who had talked about the 'equipment'. Gently, Will reached into his pocket. He lifted out Ratty's head, cupping it in his hand, and he activated the digital video transmitter. He needed footage of this.

'Silence!' Rudolfo commanded. Instantly, the voices ceased. How easy it was to control these children, he thought. What a contrast to the Master!

Rudolfo stepped aside. As he bowed his head respectfully, a figure in black strode out.

Now, the silence deepened. It hung, thick, in the air. Will felt his blood chill. His eyes could not resist the hideous, flowing mask. He stared as patches of red formed and spread, where the Master's flesh and breath came into contact with the cloth. Will could make out the brow ridge, the nose, the oozing red of the Master's parting lips.

'My friends!' the Master cried.

And Will felt his ears seize. The voice was oddly contorted. Muffled by the mask.

The Master raised his arms. He swayed slightly, as if in some sort of trance.

Will glanced at Cristina. She flashed him a look that said: 'Shh. Watch.'

'I sense spirits in the room,' the Master said at last, in a voice so low and strange Will almost shrunk towards the flames. 'I hear a man. He passed last year. A kindly man. Too long at his desk. A loving family. Too many demands. His voice is confused. I cannot hear his name. It begins with "L". Yes, with L!'

The audience was hanging on his every word. Gripping each other. Will noticed tears roll down the cheeks of a girl standing beside him. And he felt faintly sick. He knew what he believed. His father had loved him and now he was gone. But if he hadn't felt quite so sure of his beliefs, could he have been susceptible to these words – to all *this*? Perhaps.

This promise of the spiritual, without religion – it had appealed to Victorian scientists, seeking to free an after-life from Christianity, Islam, Judaism. But this cult wasn't about honestly held beliefs, Will found himself thinking. At least, as far as the Master was concerned, it wasn't. Something more sinister was going on.

'Lorenzo!' A boy shouted now. 'My father. Lorenzo!'

'I see him!' the Master replied. 'He wants to know if you are studying hard. He tells me there was a birthday that he missed, while he was still with us. He is sorry.'

'My birthday,' the boy shouted, his voice wavering. 'Last year. He was in America.'

And a curious restlessness swept through the crowd. They were like fish on a line, Will thought. This '*Master*' had them.

So he lured vulnerable children to the island, with the promise of communicating with their dead. Will could think of only one reason why: so they'd believe in him, be beholden to him, so they would volunteer – but for *what*? And what did volunteering have to do with the ghosts?

Now the Master exhaled heavily, the red patch staining half his face. 'Your father is still here. He can see you,' he breathed. 'He is pleased that you wish to con-

138

tact him. Your father wishes you to stay with friends. He wishes happiness for you. And a useful life. Free from the pressures of the world. Free from constraints. Free from ordinary life. Free from time itself.'

Will started. 'Free from time itself'. He had heard words like that somewhere before. Or if not those words, that sentiment. Once more, his memory skidded. He focused on the present. The Master was turning his head blindly, as though searching for something invisible. 'I see another spirit! A woman. She has a kindly face!'

Cristina looked back, her black eyes wide. 'We could slip out now,' she whispered. 'Dino's over there – look. He's seen us – he looked at me. If we leave now, he won't notice.'

Will followed the jerk of her head. He could make out a tall boy, hood half-way back along his skull. Dino. From behind, white figures were starting to push forwards. Two boys were clamouring for the Master's attention. The hall was filling with commotion. Will eased Ratty right back inside his pocket. And he nodded. He *had* to start finding some answers, instead of more questions.

The powder, he thought. He'd start there.

'Sir!'

Shute Barrington's head shot up.

A young Italian man in a neat, black suit was standing in the doorway of Barrington's temporary office, behind the security annexe.

Attached to this annexe was an extravagant summer villa, positioned smack in the centre of a small, circular island.

Barrington had arrived on Friday afternoon. He had been sped by police boat from Venice airport to the Isola delle Maschere. Island of the Masks. So-called because the ancient family that owned the villa had been famous not only for their political achievements, but also for their lavish Carnival masked balls.

In the dusty museum on the second floor, Barrington had inspected a series of antique masks. The white *larva*, from the Latin for 'shadow' or 'ghost', which had a sinister protruding nose. The *moreta*, formed from black velvet and kept in place with a mouthpiece, rendering the wearer silent. And perhaps most famous of all, the *pantelone* – the mask of a drooping-featured old man.

Barrington had found the display unpleasant. Even unnerving. But then his nerves were a little on edge. With good reason.

'Sir,' the young man said. 'A delivery has arrived. In a plane!'

Barrington nodded. The short airstrip was behind the palace. He didn't envy the pilot. The slightest mistake and you'd be in the lagoon. Barrington himself had opted for a scheduled flight to the civilian Marco Polo airport. 'Right.'

'They refuse to release this delivery, sir! They ask for you! Even Signor Calvino, he has asked – and they demand you!'

'All right. Understood. *On my way.*'

The young man nodded vigorously and vanished.

As soon as he had gone, Barrington's mouth twisted into a smile. 'Cane' Calvino wouldn't like that. He was in charge of security. Barrington had come along at the insistence of the British. It had been made clear to Calvino that he, Shute Barrington, was to be given free rein to deploy *any* technological security measures that he saw fit.

But no one liked sharing power, Barrington decided. Especially not 'The Dog'. Quite how the nickname had come about, Barrington wasn't sure. But Calvino did resemble a bloodhound, at least physically, with his drooping eyes, soft mouth and comfortable paunch. Calvino was over-weight. Over-weening. And over-promoted. As far as Barrington was concerned, Calvino should be deferring to him.

Slowly – all the better to irritate The Dog – Barrington made his way around the side of the villa. He passed the entrance to the ballroom, where the 'garden party', as it was code-named, would be held. Security was extraordinarily tight. No one could be admitted to the complex unless they passed a series of checks. And only Calvino and Shute Barrington held the list of people who would be permitted to try. With the exception only of Charlie Spicer and Thor, even his colleagues back at STASIS HQ thought Barrington was on holiday.

Safe on his Personal Digital Assistant, Barrington reflected, he had not only a list of the eminent – and highly secretive – guests, but also the layout of this sumptuous eighteenth-century pleasure villa, and details of precisely how it was to be protected.

Barrington stepped out into the night. He took in the irregular sight of the city in the distance. To the east, he saw the dark castle that dominated the Isola delle Fantasme. Island of the Ghosts. And 'The Ghost' – *Il Fantasma*, as it was called by the papers – was an irritating development for a man obsessed with understanding everything – and with security.

Though, Barrington reflected, while this villa was just ten minutes from downtown Venice, as far as any gate-crasher was concerned, it might as well be on the

Moon. Not only was the 'garden party' unprecedented, so was the security. Barrington was making sure of that.

As Barrington expected, The Dog was waiting for him at the airstrip.

'This man refuses to tell me the contents of the cargo!' Calvino fumed. His brown suit jacket was flapping in the wind from the plane, his longish hair whipping to one side, badly parted.

From the passenger seat, Thor waved. 'Hello, sir. Delivery, as requested, direct from Charlie Spicer.'

Barrington nodded. 'I'll get you some assistance, Thor. The holding tanks are round the back.'

'Very good, sir.'

Calvino's eyes bulged. 'And you are going to tell me what is in this cargo!'

Barrington flashed him a tense smile. 'I can do better than that, Cane. Give me half an hour and I will gladly show you.'

Less than one kilometre away, Will was trying to focus.

It wasn't easy.

For one thing, the ugly little seance was replaying through his mind. And Cristina's microscope was an antique, all right.

Then there had been their awkward exit from the dining hall. Cristina had collided with a blond boy, arriving late.

'Where are you going?' he'd demanded.

Will had regarded him with distaste. 'We have been sent by Dino,' he said tightly.

'Sent where?' the boy said, with a trace of uncertainty.

Will had raised an eyebrow. 'Disturb him if you like,' he said, glancing back into the hall. 'I'm sure he will thank you for it.'

It had been enough.

The boy had hesitated, then stepped aside. They really were afraid of Dino. And Will and Cristina walked free.

Now, Cristina was by the desk in the mysterious glass-floored room, watching him. Will had tilted the shade of the desk lamp so that light was cast across the 'stage' – the brass platform that would support his sample.

His palms damp, Will carefully poured a few granules of the powder on to a slide. He slipped the slide on to the stage. The brass was cold to his touch, smooth after more than a century of use. He had three magnifications to choose from. Will twisted the x150 lens into position and he peered down the dusty eyepiece. Now all he had to do was focus.

'What do you see?' Cristina said impatiently. She kept glancing at the door. Afraid, Will imagined, that they'd be discovered. Whether the 'spirits' hung around or not, her glossy black hair would soon be missed.

'Hold on,' he whispered.

He adjusted the brass fine-focus wheel. And at last,

the granules became clear. At least, their shape was resolved.

And Will tensed. He tapped the slide gently, sending the tiny balls rolling. His head jerked up.

'That ghost. Tell me: what did it look like?'

'You saw the security video?' she asked, surprised slightly at the strength of his tone. 'Then you saw it. It wasn't human, that is all I will swear. I thought it was a ghost. But I don't know . . .'

Once more, Will lowered his eyes to the barrel. He realized he'd been hoping that somehow in the space of those few seconds the sample would miraculously have changed. Because what he was looking at was barely believable. He held his breath. 'But I think I know what this is . . .' he murmured at last.

And he shook his head. These granules were supposed to be years away. *Five,* at least. He'd read about them. At least, he'd read about the theory, in a journal called the *Annals of Micro-Engineering.* That had been at Christmas, he realized. At *Andrew's house.*

Will lifted his head.

'What?' Cristina exclaimed.

Will barely heard her. He was taking in the cameras and the empty metal fittings underneath the glass floor. And he remembered something else: Angelo, holding up a pink crystal rook to the light in his father's museum, while Andrew retrieved a PDA *whose memory had been wiped.*

It had to be it. There was no other explanation that

accounted for all of the facts. The appearance of the granules. The camera fittings in this room. The glass floor. The PDA.

'*What?*' Cristina said, impatience boiling over. 'What can you see? What is it?'

Will took a deep breath. Without all the evidence, it would have seemed so unlikely he wouldn't have brought himself to say it.

But at last, here was something that made a kind of sense.

'Smart dust,' he said.

'*Smart dust?*' Cristina looked disbelieving.

'Self-organizing milli-scale robots.' Will sent his chair rolling backwards and pointed to one of the miniature cameras still attached to the wall. 'According to the *theory*, if you could take a three hundred and sixty degree image of someone or something, you could control a pile of this dust to organize itself to take on the form of that target, and to move as it moves. You would use a wireless network to control the tiny robots. The skin can change colour. They're designed to mimic anything.'

'Like a person,' Cristina whispered.

Will nodded.

'So this *dust* – *this* is what made up my ghost? Tiny *robots?*'

'It looks like it.'

And Will felt a certain amount of awe. This was an astonishing technology, no doubt about that. Hide a pile of dust somewhere in a room along with a wireless-enabled PDA, and later, from a remote location, it would be easy to use that wireless connection to give that dust form. To make it appear as a twenty-first century *ghost*.

Cristina's palace was open to visitors one day a month, Will recalled. A visitor could have left the necessary gadgetry behind then, after the deed was done, wiped the PDA's memory remotely.

Why had this Master stopped at a jewelled lion and a painting, Will wondered. Technology like this could be used to ransack the *world*.

Cristina raked a bronzed hand through her hair. 'So they really *are* making the ghosts.' Her violent-black eyes blinked at Will. 'You know, for a moment, I did doubt – at first, I thought maybe the ghosts could be *real*.' She bit her lip. 'But this is how they did it. We have the proof. Good. I knew it!'

Good? Will thought. Yes, at least there was an answer here. 'But this room doesn't look like it's been used recently,' he said. 'The cameras are mostly gone. And the gallery was robbed yesterday. Well, the day before yesterday, now. I'm going to get some footage of this place.' He produced Ratty from his pocket, and Cristina stared in open disgust.

'What is that?'

'What does it look like?' Will said, offended.

'It looks like a rat!'

'Surgically enhanced,' he said tightly, as he activated the video camera. 'Remote-controlled. Fitted with audio and video transmission equipment.'

'*Remote-controlled?*'

'That's what I said.' Will aimed Ratty's head at the rest of the powder in the box.

'In the old days, Venice used to send galleons to Egypt with the sole purpose of collecting wild cats to bring back to kill the rats! They were wise, my ancestors!' Then Cristina bit her lip. Will belonged to STORM. And – and nothing. Though he was good-looking in a pale English sort of way. 'But this one looks quite cute.'

Cute? Was Ratty cute? He was a working pet. Satisfied with his video, Will switched off the camera. He gave Ratty a quick stroke.

'I'm going to call Andrew and Gaia.' He had to talk it through with Andrew, he thought, to be *sure*.

'But phones—'

'We don't need a phone,' he said.

Cristina watched in surprise as Will pulled the toothphone from his pocket and slotted it over his molar. Surprise turned to amazement as she heard him whisper: 'Andrew – are you there?'

For nine minutes, Andrew had been kneeling beside a wooden door. The strange fretting sounds had come from behind here – they were sure of it. But so far there had been no response to Andrew's calls or his knocks.

Gaia had watched him in silence. She'd glanced repeatedly at her mobile. No reception. She didn't know about the blockers. But they were on an island. In a castle with walls a foot thick. Unable even to take a call from her aunt.

Her father was sick. She could do no good in London. But could she really do any good here? Suddenly she wasn't so sure. This place was oppressive, and it was giving her the creeps, infrasound or no infrasound. She was beginning to feel she'd had enough.

Think about the explosive, she told herself.

Sol-gel nanocomposites were extremely advanced, but they were relatively easy to make – or so she'd read. You could do most of the chemistry in an ordinary beaker.

'Hello? Can you hear me? . . . Gaia?'

Gaia forced herself back to the present.

'Can you try?'

'If there is anyone in there, surely they'd have answered you.'

'You heard the noise – someone has to be in there. Maybe they're scared – they could be injured. You're a girl. They might respond to you when they wouldn't to me.'

'I don't see why.'

Andrew sighed. Gaia wasn't being much help. In fact,

she was behaving a little oddly, he thought. He put it down to all the talk of ghosts.

Then, reluctantly, Gaia knelt down by the door. 'Hello?' she said. '*Hello?*'

No response. She shrugged.

Andrew sighed again. 'I'm going to give Will another try.' He rose and inserted his toothphone.

'Will, this is Andrew. Will do you read me . . . ?'

Nothing.

'. . . You forgot to say over.'

Andrew smiled. Good. She was all right. 'Will, do you read me? *Over.*'

Nothing.

'Will, hello, if you can't talk just say one word, OK?'

Gaia stood, slipping in her own toothphone.

'Will. Please.' And Andrew's voice vibrated through her jawbone.

Sighing again, Andrew picked up his rucksack.

'So what now?' Gaia said.

And instantly, they both heard it.

'Andrew, are you there?'

Will's voice.

'Will!' Andrew hissed. 'Where have you been?'

'I've found Cristina.'

'*Cristina?*'

'Don't sound so surprised. She is the reason we're here.'

'I meant—'

But Will interrupted: 'Have you found anything?'

'A recipe for a bomb,' Andrew said. 'And the fact that this place isn't actually haunted. At least, I don't think it is.'

'A *bomb*? OK. I've found out what the ghosts are. Come to me.'

'What are they?' Andrew exclaimed.

'I'll show you. *Come to me.*'

Gaia glanced at Andrew. 'How will we find you? I can get us back to the way into the castle –'

'No,' Will said impatiently. 'Use the tracker.'

And Gaia flushed. *Of course.*

At once, Andrew brought the wearable computer to life. He found the software. Hit the Tracking icon. On the virtual screen, a red dot appeared. Will was in his sights.

'I've got you,' he said. 'Over.'

And his heart was pounding. For a number of different reasons.

They had Cristina. Will said he knew what the ghosts were! And they'd been relatively safe, he realized, out here, alone, in these outer passages.

Andrew crouched suddenly. He put his mouth to the keyhole in the wooden door. 'If you can hear me, we are going to get help. All right . . . ?'

Now they'd go to Will. They'd discover the truth. Perhaps they'd find out who this Master was, and what he was doing. 'Are you ready?' he said to Gaia.

She hesitated. Shook her head. But she was thinking:

we have Cristina. We understand the ghosts. Now we can leave.

'It'll be OK,' Andrew said. 'You're with me.'

Will focused on Cristina's shining hair, which was curtaining her face. 'Will Dino be looking for us?'

She raised her eyes from the microscope. 'At first, when I slipped away, I was surprised. I was always looking behind my back. But the other cult people, they take no interest in me. Then there is only the Master, Rudolfo and Dino. And two others – boys who are supposed to protect the secrecy of the island.

'Dino is always sneaking around. I am supposed to meet him every few hours. I am supposed to learn more about the cult before I am initiated. But I think perhaps once you are in here, they don't worry. Dino told me there is a security system to sound the alarm if someone leaves the castle. Then you are on an island – how would you escape? And they talk about the ghosts. They tell us this place is haunted by different spirits. They tell us not to go in the passages for our own safety. And if you believed in evil spirits, would you walk around this castle?'

'You don't?'

'Don't believe? I wasn't sure. How can you be sure? But I told myself that, on balance, I believed there was a scientific explanation for the ghosts, not a supernatural one. Normal ghosts do not steal.'

Will smiled faintly. 'No, normal ghosts don't do that.'

'But a ghost has robbed La Galleria d'Arte Moderna,' she said. 'And the police have not come here still.'

'Why would they?' Will asked. 'How did you know to come *here*?'

'Talk to people on the internet, and it is not difficult to hear rumours about this place! But then I am fourteen. Dino told me to meet him in a very quiet street, and to come alone. Perhaps it was easy for him to believe that I was serious about the cult, and not a threat. The police are like oxen.'

'They found nothing last time,' Will said quietly.

'And yet here we are – and we know they are wrong,' she replied. 'So what happened? They were bribed? Or there are secret rooms, and the Master knew they were coming, and they hid? This is a castle. There will be chambers. Cells. Places the stupid police could not find.'

And her eyes shot to the door. Will had heard it too. Instantly, he flicked off the torch. Cristina turned off the lamp. Footsteps. In the passageway outside.

Will planted his back against the wall. His breathing seemed unnaturally loud.

Old hinges creaked.

'. . . Hello?'

Andrew. Of course. Will lifted the torch, flicking it on.

Andrew blinked. Whispered: '*Will?*'

Will dropped the beam. And he grinned at Andrew, and Gaia beside him. She was gripping Blind Spot.

Andrew glanced at her. 'I'm glad you weren't tempted to actually use that. Your aim isn't the best. You might have got me.'

'Your eyes don't work properly anyway,' she said.

'Gaia – I really—'

'– Cristina,' Will interrupted, and he swept the beam across her face and back, '– this is Andrew, and Gaia.'

'Hello,' Gaia said. She reached behind her, switched on the main light.

Andrew's blinking became manic. He took in Cristina's stunning features and bright, quartz eyes. He hadn't imagined her like this. Or maybe he had. But that had been *imagination*. Diamonds flashed from the dirty cuff of her white sleeve. He rubbed a hand, weighed down by his gold watch, against his trousers and nervously held it out to Cristina. '. . . Gaia, don't you think we should turn that off,' he said, jerking his head towards the light.

'It's all right,' Will said. 'I don't think anyone's used this room in a while.'

Andrew was still blinking. '. . . I'm glad we found you, Cristina,' he managed.

She took his hand. Nodded. And she smiled. White teeth. A red mouth.

Andrew couldn't help staring.

'Are you all right, Andrew? Maybe I did catch you with Blind Spot,' Gaia said, pretending to inspect it.

Andrew shot her a glance.

'Blind Spot?' Cristina said, as she took in Andrew's multi-zip action trousers, his canvas jacket and his purple T-shirt with what looked like a *molecule* on the front . . .

'Oh, it's nothing,' Andrew said quickly.

'Thanks,' Will said meaningfully.

Andrew coloured. 'I didn't mean it like that –' He looked around him. Noticed the miniature cameras. The microscope.

'You found a *bomb*?' Will asked.

Gaia explained about the gel. 'Though it doesn't necessarily mean it's a bomb. A standard mix of aluminium and iron oxide is used to ignite airbags and things. It's highly explosive – but it has other uses apart from blowing things up.' But it was kept in a safe, she thought. Why keep something innocent in a safe? 'And we heard something inside a locked room – it was like a crying,' she said. 'It sounded like a *person* . . .'

'A crying?' Cristina exclaimed. 'Yes, I have heard it!'

Andrew was kneeling down. Peering at the floor beneath the glass. Will gestured towards the microscope. 'Look at this,' he said. 'These are like the granules Cristina found by the window in the museum.'

Andrew made for the antique. He bent his head over the eyepiece, twisting the brass wheels until the sample was in focus. For a moment, he was silent. Then he looked up. Pale blue eyes expressed disbelief. Will realized Andrew had reached the same conclusion.

'This isn't actually possible. These are *years* away,' Andrew whispered. His eyes shot to the metal fixtures on the walls.

'What are?' Gaia said.

Quickly, Andrew explained. 'Self-organizing miniature machines! Three hundred and sixty degree cameras. An internet connection. This is *genius*. I should have thought of this. But I thought—'

'—It wasn't possible.' Will nodded. 'I know.'

'I read all about the theory—' Andrew started.

'In the *Annals of Micro-Engineering*,' Will finished. 'I read it at your house.'

'*What?*' Gaia exclaimed. 'What do you mean they can self-organize?'

Andrew blinked at her. 'These are millimetre-scale robots – "milli-bots". Each one contains a chip. They're self-contained. They can communicate, they can sense, they can move. They can even display a colour on their skin. And they can work together, like a network.'

Gaia still looked disbelieving. 'But how do they form a ghost? How do they move around? How do they stick together?'

'They could use magnetic forces to move around each other?' Will said.

Andrew nodded. 'Yes, at this scale, I'd say magnetism would be most likely. And if I look again –' he paused for a moment, to peer once more down the microscope '– no I can't see it, the resolution's terrible. I imagine there's some kind of nano-fibre for adhesion.' Andrew shook his head. 'But I can't imagine who has done this. Whoever this person is, they really are brilliant. I should know them. I should have heard of them!'

'I saw the Master,' Will said.

'*And?*' Gaia said.

'I don't know. He was wearing a cloak and a mask. It was modulating his voice.'

Andrew took a deep breath. 'We have to find out who he is.'

'*I* also have no idea of his identity,' Cristina said firmly, feeling a little left out. But at least this Gaia had obviously never heard of self-organizing milli-bots either.

Gaia glanced at her. She still felt on edge. Ghosts, the absence of phone contact, the bomb, the fretting noise . . . they hadn't known what to expect, but this was *serious*. And she wanted to hear from her aunt. Strange, she thought, that she should feel this so strongly now. Maybe it *was* the talk of ghosts.

Gaia faced Will. 'We've found Cristina. And we know how the ghosts are made. That's what we came for. And whoever's making that *noise* is locked up. They could be injured. We need help. We should use Ratty to take footage and go to the police.'

158

'I've got footage. But something else is going on here,' Will said. 'This Master is recruiting volunteers for something and we have no idea what. It can't be for making the ghosts. Not unless he wanted bodies to video, to use as models for the ghosts – but he could use his own. He wouldn't need a pool of willing kids.'

'We should let the police find out exactly what he's doing,' Gaia said. 'We've done enough.'

Will frowned. Gaia had to be curious. She *had* to be. Had the castle got to her? Something strange was going on, that much was clear. And if they left now, they might never discover what. The police were oxen. Cristina herself had said it.

'If someone is locked up and they're injured, maybe we can try to get them out. We can't leave yet,' Will said, at last.

'We've got Cristina – and this room, and the dust,' Gaia said, with frustration. 'With the video footage, we can go to the police. The police will come now. They'll have to. And they'll have the equipment to break down that door.'

'But the Master is planning something.' Cristina said. 'I heard Rudolfo talking about a meeting. He wants equipment for it. What equipment? What meeting?'

'Who cares what he's planning,' Gaia said. 'If it's here, we'll get the police to come. They'll stop it.'

'But if they don't come,' Cristina said.

Gaia's eyebrows shot up. 'When we tell them about *this*?'

Cristina shook her head. 'They came once before. They found nothing they could make sense of. What will this room tell police? They will not understand!'

Gaia glanced at Will. 'But we've got video – they'll have to come. Or we'll go to the papers. We can tell them all about *Il Fantasma*!'

There was a pause. Then Cristina's voice rang out distinctly: 'I say we try to find out about what else is going on.'

So, Gaia thought, here is a girl who is used to getting her own way.

Not this time.

'*No*,' she said.

Her body stiffening, Cristina faced Andrew. 'You have come all this way! Imagine, if this Master can do this –' and she swept her arms around the room – 'what else is he planning? It is more advanced even than this? And who is he, this Master, who hides behind his mask?' She took a step towards Will. 'If this meeting, whatever it is, happens in the next hour, what then? What might it mean? The police will be too late!'

Gaia waited for Andrew and then Will to rebut her. And waited.

Silence.

Very slowly, Andrew removed his glasses. He polished the lenses with the sleeve of his jacket. Gaia knew what that meant. And she flushed with anger.

They would support Cristina over her.

'I'm not staying,' Gaia said, her cheeks burning.

Andrew looked up at her. 'Gaia, we are, quite literally, in the same boat. We must leave together.' His voice was gentle.

'Then come *now*!'

Andrew glanced once more at Will. And Gaia was aware that Cristina's eager black eyes were also fixed on Will. Gaia did not want to look at him.

So she did not see the expression on Will's face as he said: 'I think we have to stay.' He didn't like this. They were a team. He wanted Gaia to agree with him. His idea of a team.

Gaia turned away. So. It was decided.

'Just until we find out what's happening to these volunteers,' Will continued, remembering the conversation he'd overheard in the dining hall just after he'd arrived. And then the newspaper article about the boy, who had washed up on a neighbouring island, disfigured. Had he been a *volunteer* . . . ? 'If this Master has created a cult to provide himself with subjects, we owe it to everyone trapped here to find out why, and what he's doing,' Will said quietly. 'And if the ghosts aren't part of that, what are they for? Is he using them to get money to buy something he needs, for experiments?'

Cristina nodded. Her eyes shot once more to her diamond-studded watch. 'I have to meet Dino. It is arranged. I am already late, and he will be suspicious if I do not come. But those crying noises . . .'

'I might be able to use Grabber to unlock the door,'

161

Will said. He turned to Cristina: 'So we'll check it out and meet you there?'

Gaia barely heard. Her jaws were clamped so tight she could feel the pressure sparking pain up through her temples. At last, she forced herself to look at Will. And she saw only resolution. Like a hot stove, it burned her gaze instantly away.

'Gaia?' Andrew said softly.

'What am I supposed to say?' she whispered.

'Say you'll stay with us.'

She turned to him. And she scowled. *'Niente di buono,'* she murmured. *Nothing good will come of this.*

Shute Barrington rested his arms on the cold steel of the holding tank. He was satisfied. The cargo appeared to have tolerated the journey well. The weapons had been attached and in a few minutes, he would demonstrate the technology to 'Cane' Calvino, who would accept that STASIS knew one or two things about defence and protection.

Well, actually, he wouldn't.

Or rather, he would accept it, but he'd pretend not to.

Barrington sighed. He hated power politics.

'Sir!'

Thor was jogging across the tarmac. Behind the officer's head, the crescent moon cut a silver slit through the night.

'Let me guess,' Barrington said, as Thor reached him. 'Calvino's busy.'

'No, sir, he's coming.' Thor peered uncertainly into the floodlit holding tank. He reached into his pocket. Pulled out a PDA with a pink case. Read a text.

'Thor, is that yours?'

Thor flushed. 'It's my girlfriend's, sir. I lost my phone yesterday. I had to borrow it. Sorry.' Again, Thor peered warily into the tank. 'Everything all right?'

'Yes.' And Barrington shot him a glance. Thor might be relatively new, but Barrington could read his staff well. He had to. If you worked within a few metres of someone developing a revolutionary explosive you had to understand them and trust them and – perhaps most importantly – realize if something was bothering them. 'Though I suspect you're about to say something that might change my mind?'

Thor took a deep breath. 'It's just the ghost thief reports, sir. Have you seen them?'

'You mean –' and Barrington widened his eyes in mock fright '. . . *Il Fantasma*!'

Thor coloured once more. 'Yes, sir.'

'I don't think we need to worry about ghosts, Thor.'

'I meant –'

'Relax. I know what you meant. It's not a ghost. So what is it?'

Thor nodded.

'Calvino tells me his people are checking it out.'

'And we have to trust in that?'

'I didn't say that.'

'I've been thinking, sir, about what it could be – maybe a projection – while the real thief's in the background.'

'Perhaps.'

'Maybe it's smart dust. Milli-scale robots. Even micro-bots.'

Barrington raised an eyebrow. 'How far would you say we at STASIS are away from developing self-organizing milli-bots?'

'I don't know, sir – six years.'

'Be fair, Thor. I'd give us five.'

Thor sighed. 'Five years, sir.'

'Right. So if we can't do it, who could?'

'I have no idea, sir.'

'Which leads you to believe . . . ?'

'It's not smart dust?'

'Right.'

'– But.'

'It's not smart dust.' Barrington nodded in a way he hoped was reassuring. 'It *can't* be.'

Had he made the right decision? Will had to believe it.

But as he led the way along the damp passageway, feeling Gaia's anger coalescing in the air behind him, he wasn't so sure.

Their target had shifted, that was true. At first it had been to find out what the ghosts really were and if Cristina was all right.

Job done.

But how could they leave it at that? They had to find out what the Master was doing with his volunteers, and what he was planning.

Will pressed a hand to his ear. *'Everything all right,'* had boomed through his jaw.

'Quietly!' he hissed.

It had been Cristina's voice. Checking in. Will had given her the fourth toothphone as they'd left the disused lab.

She'd be fifteen minutes, she said. She'd distract Dino if he asked about Will. In the meantime, Will, Andrew and Gaia would try to find out what lay behind that heavy door. Possibilities spiraled through Will's mind.

He glanced back. Gaia had naturally dark, half-Italian skin. Now she was white as Andrew, Will thought. She'd been silent all the way from the lab, to this spot – just past the castle's small side entrance, through which Will had followed Dino what seemed like days ago.

Will wanted to say something to her. But he didn't know what. She wasn't wrong. There was no right and wrong in this. And he didn't exactly blame her.

'Will, keep going,' Andrew whispered. 'The staircase is along there.'

Will was about to nod. But his inner ear was vibrating. Cristina was speaking.

'. . . *Master?*'

Will froze. Instantly, he registered the alarm on Andrew's face.

The Master was with Cristina?

What had happened to Dino? Was the Master talking?

'I don't know what—' And Cristina stopped. 'Master, no – I have only been exploring. It is such an interesting castle.'

Andrew's eyes narrowed.

'But I am not initiated! How can I?'

Cristina was doing her best to conceal her anxiety. But they could all hear it. It was excruciating, listening to only one side of the conversation. Will clenched his fists.

Whatever was going on, it was *wrong*.

'*Tell us what's happening,*' he whispered.

'No, I swear, I am not a spy! I want to join the cult. I want to – I want to talk to my brother. I miss him. Master, please, you can contact my brother. The others told me you can. *Please.*'

Master. *Master.*

Andrew gritted his teeth. They had to find out who this Master was. Perhaps now was their chance. Cristina was there, with him! Was he wearing his mask? Would he let down his guard?

'Cristina, ask him his name,' Andrew whispered. 'Tell him you revere him, and you must know his name.'

Andrew looked up, saw surprise flashing in Will's eyes. But this Master was powerful. And brilliant. Andrew suspected that, deep down, he wanted the world to know who he was. Perhaps he would tell Cristina. And they could tell the police.

'Master,' Cristina began, her voice steadier now. 'I

admire you so much and I do not even know your name. Please, now I have met you, will you tell me?'

Silence. Or at least, Cristina wasn't speaking.

'Because I am curious, Master, to know the name of the genius who can talk to the dead. Because—'

Again, silence.

Will raised an eyebrow at Andrew, lifted out his toothphone. 'This is dangerous,' he whispered. 'The more she knows –' And he pushed the device back in. It was vibrating. He'd missed her first words. But Andrew and Gaia had not.

'It is an unusual name,' Cristina whispered. '*Caspian Baraban.*'

Caspian Baraban.

Will felt as though he'd been plunged back into Lake 2. He was submerged. Without air. He stared at Andrew and at Gaia. A bomb was going off in his brain. At least, it felt like that. The *voice.* He *had* recognized it, even distorted by the mask. But it had been so unlikely – it had been *impossible* – and his brain had discounted it.

But those tiny robots took genius. And whatever he was, Caspian was that. He was also supposed to be locked in a maximum security psychiatric hospital. Shute Barrington himself had showed them photographs of the facility.

Caspian Baraban.

Ex-STORM.

In-sane.

Will had encountered 'the Master' many times. The last time, he was being hauled into a Tiger helicopter from the roof of an exploding building.

Gaia's mouth had fallen open. 'What?' she stumbled. Disbelief took root in her face. Spread cold branches through her body. 'Caspian *Baraban*?' And she remembered the red-written recipe for the explosive, the lines written in *Russian*, the language of Caspian's parents.

'It can't be,' Andrew said, his voice thick. 'He's in a secure institution. Barrington told us!'

'Then Barrington lied,' Will said. And his mouth felt numb. This was a truth he didn't want to believe. But what he *wanted* was irrelevant. Life had certainly taught him that.

'It can't be . . .' Andrew whispered.

But Will could see, this time, that Andrew *knew* it. And Will thought of the seance. 'Free from time itself', that's what 'the Master' had said. In London, Caspian himself had used an odd phrase: 'only ordinary people are governed by the clock'. And Will had seen him. Dressed in that black cloak and that mask. *Caspian Baraban.*

Reports of a cult on this island, and of the boy's body found washed up on a beach, dated back ten weeks, Will remembered. *If* Caspian really was somehow responsible, that would mean he'd escaped almost immediately after being captured in Russia. Barrington must have known. Yet he'd said nothing. *Why?* And what was Caspian doing here? *How could he have escaped?*

Gaia's face was white. She was shaking her head, trying to shake out the possibility. Memories of St Petersburg were washing through her, a mental tsunami that blasted everything in its path. Caspian Baraban. Andrew's ex-school friend. The most brilliant mind of his generation. Crying. Screaming. The pain through her body. The explosions below. He had betrayed them. He had almost destroyed the world. She let herself fall back against the wall. Her bones and her muscles suddenly weren't enough to support her. 'So now we leave,' she whispered. 'We get *help*.'

Will took in the shock in Gaia's eyes. He, too, was remembering St Petersburg. And he remembered that expression. It had swept across her face the moment she was shot. *Caspian* had been there.

And now he was here, on the Isola delle Fantasme. *Free*. In London, last December, Caspian had been swerving around the tracks of sanity. In St Petersburg, he'd spun right off the road.

Caspian was mad.

He was ruthless.

And now, thanks to his ghostly thieves, he was rich.

Instinctively, Will reached into his jacket pocket. Touched fur. Ratty's head twitched.

'I think,' Gaia said, her voice thick, 'that we should go *and get help*.'

'This time, I agree,' Andrew said. He pulled out his

toothphone, his hand shaking. 'Cristina's in trouble. We don't know what's going on. Barrington lied to us. The *police*.' He turned to Gaia and he flashed her a look that was meant to say: *you were right. I'm sorry*.

But she looked away.

Will glanced at his watch. 3.50 a.m. He had to pull himself together. And he realized, to his shame, that he had forgotten about Cristina. She hadn't spoken again.

'*Cristina . . . ?*'

Nothing.

Gaia met Andrew's alarmed gaze.

'Cristina?' Andrew whispered urgently.

Still nothing.

And then, Cristina's voice: 'Are you there? *Will? Andrew?*'

And Gaia, Gaia thought.

'We're here,' Will said quickly.

'I'm in a cell! I cannot get out. There are three locks. The Master has the keys. He was waiting for me with Rudolfo and Dino. Dino told him he saw me outside Rudolfo's study. He thinks I am some kind of spy.'

'What else did Baraban say?' Will asked.

'. . . *Baraban?* It sounds as though you know him! He said he's going to keep me in this cell until his business is done. And he will use me as a *volunteer*.'

'He didn't say what business?' Andrew said. 'Or what you'll *volunteer* for?'

'No. *Do* you know him?'

'We've met him before,' Will said. 'I'll explain later. What else did he say? *Anything?*'

'I don't know.' A pause. 'Except when he was leaving, he said to Dino: now you must find Shoe Barrington, then kill him.'

'*Shute Barrington?*' Will hissed. '*Are you sure?*'

'You know him too? Who is he?'

But Will did not answer. His heart was pounding. Caspian Baraban was *here. And Barrington was in danger?* But Barrington was on holiday. Or so he had said.

Will saw the astonishment in Andrew's and Gaia's eyes kick up a notch.

'*Barrington,*' Andrew said. 'Is he in Venice?'

Will scowled. 'Cristina, we're going to get the police. We'll be straight back.'

Silence. Then: 'OK. But who is Caspian Baraban? And who's Shute Barrington? Do you know all the bad guys around here?'

'Barrington's not a bad guy,' Will said.

'Just before the Master arrived, Dino was asking about you,' Cristina whispered. 'But then the Master started talking. Dino is very suspicious. Don't get caught. *All right?*'

The castle was fitted with a security system, Cristina had said. But they had no choice. And they had an extremely fast boat. *If* it was still there.

Will's eyes darted around the frame of the narrow door. He couldn't see any wires to an alarm. Nothing for Ratty to get his teeth into. Through a gap where the top right-hand edge of the door was splintered, Will made out a tiny patch of sky beyond. Stars glittered dimly. And Will heard the voice of his mother, telling him that whenever she observed the wonders of the universe, her own problems seemed small. *Rubbish*, Will thought.

Will gripped the metal latch in his hands. 'I think we have to risk it,' he said. 'Are you ready?'

'Yes,' Andrew's voice.

'Yeah.' Gaia. More certain.

He twisted it and pushed.

If an alarm went off, they didn't hear it. Will ran. Gaia's feet slipped behind him. He heard her steady herself. Across the grass, he told himself, down the slope, to the straggly beach . . .

Will hunched as he ran, hoping it would make him less conspicuous. At least the wonders of the universe were not running to a full moon that night, he thought. There was precious little light.

At last, he was at the crest of the slope. Will started to skid down it. And he saw the *Venus*, gleaming darkly in the water, half-smothered in vegetation.

Still there. He glanced back. They seemed to be alone. Will unlooped the mooring rope and with Gaia's help, he pushed the black hull off the dirt-streaked sand. Andrew hopped into the front seat, clearing the branches from the windshield. His shoes soaked in lagoon mud, Will joined him. He grabbed the jetstick.

'Just a second this time,' Andrew murmured, turning his attention to his computer.

Will's eyes jerked back. The castle was hidden. Was Cristina all right, he wondered. Was Caspian still with her?

'Hurry up,' he whispered.

'I'm working on it!' Andrew said. And added: 'Yes, I know – work faster! *I am.*'

Gaia's head shot round.

Shouts.

Someone was yelling. The shouts were moving from the castle towards the shore. But further to the east.

Dino?

'*Andrew,*' Will said.

'Hold on –'

'*Andrew!*'

The engine kicked in. In the corner of Will's eye something flickered. A boy! He'd appeared on the slope. Not Dino. Younger. Red-haired. He locked eyes with Will as he lifted a walkie-talkie to his mouth and called urgently: 'A boat! Three of them!'

'*Go!*' Gaia yelled.

Will didn't need any encouragement. He spun the *Venus* into reverse, and then forwards, nose towards the gap between the sand banks. And his gaze shot towards the west. Something was heading their way.

'What is that?' he yelled.

Andrew lifted his eyepatch. Gradually his eyes made out two distinct figures, on what looked like pogo sticks. They were powering through the water around the curve of the island, heading right for them. '*Hydrofoils?*'

'Yeah!' Will squinted. Two boys, each riding a hydrofoil. They were spraying the lagoon in poisonous jets in the air. Out in front was Dino – already, Will could make out his black hair, his deathly white face. And he was gripping something in his hand.

Andrew blanched. 'It's a *gun*!'

'Will!' Gaia yelled as she was thrown back against the leather seat.

'I see them!' Will was veering away, wishing he could push the engine to full throttle, but dangerous banks of sand beneath the water stopped him. Those banks could beach them – and provide a perfectly stationary target for Dino. He had to keep calm. Easier said than done.

'Stop your engine!' came a yell. *Dino*. Eighty metres away and closing. 'Stop *now*!'

'Will, go faster,' Andrew said urgently.

'I can't!' He looked round again at Dino, who was raising his arm.

Dino's feet were planted firmly on the ski of his hydrofoil. Beneath that single ski, which looked like a snowboard, was a metal shaft that ended in a double anchor-shaped platform. The platform provided lift, while a jet engine ratcheted to the shaft powered the hydrofoil through the water. Another shaft, rising from the back of the ski, was fitted with a moulded seat. Dino was shifting his body weight to control his direction. These hydrofoils looked a bit like water-borne pogo sticks. They were fast, and extremely agile. Will had seen acrobatic competitions involving something similar on cable TV.

'Get down!' Will yelled. He lowered his head. A split second later, the shot rang out.

Either Dino was a bad shot, or he was using his weapon only in warning. Will wasn't going to bet on the latter.

'Gaia, get Blind Spot!' he shouted.

In the back of the *Venus*, Gaia was already unzipping her jacket pocket. The boat was bouncing across the water and she fumbled with the metal tube, anxious not to drop it.

Ahead, she noticed a water taxi arcing from the direction of St Mark's square, heading towards them. Still fifty metres away. Dirty white wake erupted behind it.

'Gaia!'

'*Yeah!*' she yelled.

'Point it at their eyes!'

'Yeah, Will, I've got the idea!'

He met her angry expression. Beside Will, Andrew was keeping a close watch on the hydrofoils. The *Venus* was moving at twenty knots – all Will would dare – and the hydrofoils seemed to be struggling to keep up. But now Dino zigzagged.

'He's catching us!' Andrew called.

'Hold on!' Gaia pressed the switch. A beam sliced through the boat.

Andrew squeezed his eyes shut. 'You're meant to point it at them!'

'Yeah, and they're over there!' she yelled back. 'Unless you spin us so they're right behind, what am I supposed to do?'

Will swung the boat through twenty degrees. In a few more seconds, they'd be clear of the sandbanks, on the home straight back to the Grand Canal. At full speed, there was no way those hydrofoils could catch them.

Gripping the rail of the boat with one hand, Gaia half-stood. She was exposed now. And she could make out Dino's face, as he wiped spray from his eyes, the black gun solid in his hand.

Again, Gaia aimed. Hit the button. A laser beam burst from the weapon – a stream of brilliance penetrating the darkness. She pointed it right at Dino's face. Hit him! In the hideous bleaching light, his features seemed to shrivel. Dino went tumbling forwards, plunging into the water, his hydrofoil staggering.

'Got him!' Andrew yelled.

Gaia cut the beam. Half-standing still, she glanced at Will, who was clearing the last of the sand banks, and at the elegant water taxi which was close now, two middle-aged women with headscarves peering out in surprise. At last, the water taxi zipped past and instantly, a second hydrofoil that had been concealed by the hull came screaming towards them, hitting the dirty wake and using it like a ramp to shoot into the air. The boy on the back soared high, gripping *another black gun*. Gaia could see his angry green eyes, his blond hair.

'*Gaia!*'

Andrew's voice rang loud. She felt a thud into her arm, heard the crack of a bullet. Gaia spun and she lost her balance.

'*Gaia!*' Andrew again. Horror in his voice.

Gaia reached for the rail but her fingers slipped. The *Venus* twisted away. In slow motion, she fell.

Ice. It felt like ice across her freezing skin, slapping her face, her eyes, up her nose. She was under water. Her flesh trembled. She was struggling in darkness. Her long hair was tangling around her neck, her clothes billowing. It felt as though she was moving in mud. Gaia kicked hard, reached up, punching through the water, and she gasped as her head cleared the surface of the lagoon. Her breathing came hard. She hadn't been under for long. It was shock, she told herself. Just shock. She was OK.

But where was the *Venus*? She swung her head. There! Circling. Gaia could make out Andrew, who was holding something against his chest. Will was yelling. Water plugged her ears. But she heard this: an engine, approaching. From the west. A hydrofoil. The blond-haired boy. He was ploughing towards her!

On the boat, Will was shouting: 'Just throw it!'

Andrew's hands were fumbling with Hard Choice. 'Hold on to one end! It's hollow – it'll harden!'

At last, Andrew found the free end. He gripped it – and he heard a hydrofoil, saw their blond-haired pursuer. On their current trajectory, they'd have to pass the *Venus* before they reached Gaia. Gaia was swimming. Her head was above water. She could hold on for one more minute, he decided.

Spinning his body, Andrew hurled the rope out, away from Gaia. It hardened. He rammed the end against a strut in the bow rail.

'*What are you doing?*' Will yelled.

A moment later, he understood. The rope had uncoiled right into the path of the advancing hydrofoil. The blond boy saw it. Too late. Andrew's makeshift trip-wire sent him catapulting forwards, hair flying against the stars, then he was down with a splash, under the lagoon. His hydrofoil circled uselessly.

'Both down!' Andrew yelled, and started to haul in the rope.

'Andrew!' Gaia was shouting.

'Hold on!' he yelled back.

Forty metres away now, Gaia was swimming as hard as she could. She was shivering, and she spluttered as she was hit by the concentric wave created by the falling boy. Water rushed up over her face. She coughed. Her clothes were dragging. Her legs in wet jeans seemed to pull her down. She was stiffening, and her body was racked with shudders. Icy fingers seemed to grip her muscles.

Behind her, she saw the blond-haired boy reaching

for his ski. In the distance, Dino was trying to get back on to his seat. His eyes must be recovering. And *what was that?* A dark silhouette. A third boy! He was speeding out of the darkness. Gaia yelled: 'Andrew!' She coughed hard.

At last, the rope was ready. With all his strength, Andrew hurled it once more, this time towards Gaia. As it unfurled, it stiffened. Until it formed a long rod, cast through the lagoon.

Gaia saw it fall. Her vision was blurry, and her arms felt half-frozen, but she kicked for it. Kicked again, forcing her body to respond, coughing until the last of the lagoon was ejected from her lungs, and she reached it. Felt the synthetic fibre rough in her hands.

'*Hold on!*' Andrew yelled.

'Look!' Gaia tried to yell, and she pointed.

In the *Venus*, Will had already seen it. He reached back with one hand to pick up the dazzle gun. The third hydrofoil was barely fifty metres away. Will aimed his weapon carefully. Out of one corner of his eye, he could see Dino back on his seat. Out of the other, Gaia, holding tight to the rope. *Wait*, Will said to himself. *Wait.*

Forty metres. Thirty . . . Will fired.

Got him.

'Now!' Will yelled. 'Bring her in!'

Andrew was already hauling. As he curled the rope, it softened.

In the water, Gaia kicked as hard as she could. Four metres. Three. Two . . .

And she grabbed Andrew's hand.

The lenses of his glasses were speckled with drops of water, she noticed. Still, she could see the relief in his eyes as he pulled her up and into the back of the boat.

'*Go*,' Andrew yelled.

But Will had been watching. The instant Gaia was in, he shoved the jetstick forward. The thrust was like a fist in his chest. Will felt himself pinioned as at full throttle the *Venus* blistered through the water, her elegant nose raised as though from the stink of the lagoon.

The speed sent thrills through Will's body. It was like being in his father's jet, only here on the water he was in raw contact with the world. Air smacked his face, spray soaked his flesh. He could feel every metre they covered, in the skid and the tremor of the hull. Ahead, he could see the triple bulbs of the lights of the church at the mouth of the Grand Canal. Tiny still. He glanced back. No sign of the hydrofoils. Danger was receding.

'Are you all right?' Andrew was shouting to Gaia.

Gingerly, she touched her arm, which ached. Only ached. No blood, she realized. 'I think so. I don't think I was shot.'

'Maybe that was me. I'm sorry – I was trying to push you down but then the boat spun and –'

'And you pushed me in!'

'Gaia – I –' Andrew faltered. He was holding on to his glasses, to stop them blowing off.

But she smiled faintly. 'It's all right, Andrew, I know it wasn't on purpose.'

And she caught Will's eye as he glanced back. He grinned.

They had lost the hydrofoils. They were free.

'Easy does it,' Andrew said.

Will nodded. He eased back on the throttle, cutting their wake. Here, in the Grand Canal, everything looked peaceful – at least on the surface. Funereal gondolas slept under their black covers. Motorboats bobbed within their berths, marked out by wooden posts. High above, dying candles still flickered on an open balcony.

There was no sign of police boats, which might have had a problem with their speed through the lagoon. Nor any sign of gun-toting cult defenders on personal hydrofoils.

His knuckles still white against the jetstick, Will slowed the *Venus* still more. Gradually, his heart followed suit. His breathing was regular now. The exhilaration was easing.

Andrew was quiet. Thinking, Will guessed. He glanced back. His rucksack had been soaked in the chase, but the devices were waterproof. They'd be all right. Gaia's eyes were tracking the palaces. Her wet hair hung heavily over her shoulders.

And Caspian Baraban reared in his mind. What was Caspian doing, right at that moment? Listening to Dino, as he described the fugitives? Going into hiding? Bringing forward his meeting? And what meeting? What was he *doing here*? And would Caspian realize just who had been in that fleeing boat?

It was possible.

As soon as they arrived back at Cristina's palace, he would call the police, then he would call Barrington. There was an outside possibility that Barrington, if he really was here in Venice, was on holiday, as he'd said. But Will seriously doubted it. If Barrington was here on business, what business? And Barrington would know about Caspian's freedom. No doubt about it. So why hadn't he told them?

Too many questions. Few answers.

'I'm going to try Cristina,' Andrew said suddenly.

He was slotting in his toothphone. 'Cristina . . . ? Hello . . . ? It's Andrew . . . Cristina?'

'We're probably too far away,' Will said. 'In fact, we have to be. The range is only one kilometre.'

Alarm tightened Andrew's voice: 'Then we can't contact her?'

'No.'

'What do you think—'

'I don't know,' Will interrupted. He'd guessed what Andrew had been about to ask. But how could he answer any question about what Caspian was going to do with Cristina, who was hidden inside a castle across the lagoon, behind walls a foot thick.

'*You've missed it.*'

Will turned. Gaia. 'You missed the garage,' she said,

and sat up, pushing her hair back from her face. 'It's back there.'

Will realized she was right. He'd been engrossed in his thoughts, and talking to Andrew. Annoyed with himself, he spun the boat around. The columned entrance of the palace emerged into view. To the left was the narrow side canal, with access to the garage. Will eased the *Venus* along it.

'How do you think we get in?' Andrew murmured. And he noticed a camera mounted on the exterior wall. A moment later, the door began to scroll back, revealing the pale walls of the garage, shadows like black flames against the limestone.

Automatic recognition? Andrew wondered. Had the camera registered a unique feature of the boat? Was a radio-frequency identification tag incorporated into the hull?

But then he saw that someone was waiting for them.

He was sitting on the stone step. And he was scowling.

'In my country,' the boy said, carefully enunciating every syllable, 'taking something without permission is considered theft.'

'And in ours,' Will said. Still inching the *Venus* forward, he threw the mooring rope around its post. He didn't mean to sound facetious. And he *had* just 'borrowed' Angelo's boat. But this boy got under his skin.

'So tell me why I should not take you straight to the police?' Angelo demanded.

'Actually, we'd be rather glad if you would,' Andrew said.

Angelo's eyes flamed. 'I don't—'

And Will jumped on to the landing stage. '*Just listen,*' he interrupted. 'Because we have found your sister. And she's in trouble.'

Will quickly described their discoveries. A cult. Machinery to make ghosts. *Caspian Baraban.* As he described their final conversation with Cristina, the surprise and confusion on Angelo's face turned to concern.

Thirty seconds later, Angelo was on the phone in the reception room, talking in rapid Italian to the police.

'What's he saying?' Andrew whispered.

'He's explaining how important his family is . . .' Gaia said.

At last, Angelo lowered the receiver. 'You say you have video footage of this castle? I am talking to an Inspector Diabolo. He says you must send it. I have an email address. And he wants to talk to one of you.'

'You do it,' Will said to Andrew. 'I need to try Barrington. Give me your mobile.' He glanced at Gaia, who was shivering. 'You should find some dry clothes.'

Will keyed in the number. He listened impatiently to the digital rings.

'You've reached Barrington. Leave a message.'

'It's Will. Call me back on Andrew's mobile. I have to talk to you urgently. Your life is in danger.'

His heart pounding, Will snapped the phone shut. Andrew was still talking, Gaia watching closely. Andrew nodded. 'I will do it now.' He lowered the receiver.

'This Inspector Diabolo sounds serious,' he said. 'He says he's going to conduct another raid – he just wants the footage. I'll send it from Cristina's computer. Angelo, I'll need the keycode to get into her room.'

'Of course!' Angelo scribbled a number on a pad.

'And he wants to talk to you again,' Andrew said.

'Will –'

Gaia. She was still shivering.

'I need Andrew's phone. I want to call my aunt.'

'. . . I told Barrington to call me back on this number. We should try to keep it free.'

Andrew frowned at Will. 'Of course you must call her,' he said to Gaia. 'We'll be in Cristina's room. Join us there.'

Gaia slipped into the room where they had left their bags. She changed into dry clothes, realizing she was delaying the moment. She wished she could somehow discover the answer to her question without having to put in the call. She wanted to know what her aunt had to say, but she didn't want actually to speak to her.

Impossible, of course.

'. . . Amelia?'

'Gaia! I tried to call. I just came home from the hospital –'

'– Is –'

'He is much improved.'

And Gaia closed her eyes. Amelia continued to talk, but Gaia barely heard the rest. Something about further tests, and when was she coming back, and what if her father asked for his daughter? *It wasn't right that* – Gaia ended the call. Feeling warm again with relief, because he was her father, *despite everything*, she headed next door.

Andrew's head was framed by the computer monitor. Beside him, Will was watching.

'Have you sent it?'

Andrew's head shot round. He hadn't heard Gaia come in. Now he studied her expression. 'So it's good news?'

Gaia stiffened. Said nothing.

Andrew sighed. 'Gaia, we are your friends, you know. You can talk to us.'

Gaia blinked at Andrew, who pushed his glasses back up the bridge of his nose.

'. . . I know,' she said. And was silent. Then, quickly, she said: 'He's much better.'

Andrew nodded encouragingly. 'Then that is good news.'

'I need to try Barrington again,' Will said. Out of the corner of his eye, he saw Andrew's smile flicker. But he felt as uncomfortable as Gaia looked in this sort of territory. And he had to get through to Shute. Or, failing that, STASIS HQ. He had to get a message to him.

Again, there was a long pause before the ringing started. And went on. And eventually stopped. A click. 'You've reached Barrington –'

Frustrated, Will turned to Andrew. 'Do you have Spicer's number?'

'No. Shute still isn't answering?'

Will shook his head.

'So what now?' Andrew said.

'I'll try the STASIS front desk.' Will dialled the switchboard for Sutton Hall. A moment later, a polite, unfamiliar voice informed him that Mr Barrington was unavailable. Will asked for Charlie Spicer. Was told Spicer would have to call him back.

'Listen,' Will said, irritation swelling to anger. 'Someone called Caspian Baraban is planning an attack on Barrington's life. Tonight. Get that message to him. Get someone to call me!' The line went dead.

Will scowled at the thick glass of the ancient windowpanes. They reflected the scene within, worsening the sensation that he was trapped, when he should be *acting*.

Behind, he could hear Gaia talking to Andrew about the video, could hear Andrew telling Gaia that he was glad her father was better. What was the point? Will thought. Gaia didn't open up. Except once, on a train to St Petersburg . . . She'd talked to him a little about her mother. And he thought of his blackened cricket ball, at home in London. His fingers almost ached for it. What would Dad think? he wondered. Had they done the right thing?

Perhaps they should have stayed on the island. Perhaps they should have tried to rescue Cristina. The name 'Caspian Baraban' had seemed to paralyze him, he thought, like some foreign poison blow-piped into his veins. He hadn't thought things through. He'd reacted. And Will couldn't help realizing that part of the anger he was feeling now towards Baraban was linked to the cult – to the fake seances. Life after death. He didn't believe in it. But that hadn't stopped a tiny part of him hoping that *just maybe* he was wrong.

Sick of seeing only the interior of Cristina's bedroom, Will pushed open the window. Stuck his head out into the night.

The Grand Canal looked peaceful. The palaces were dark. Heavy drapes drawn. Venice was settled in sleep, rocked on the waters of her black lagoon. Calm reigned. And a twist on an old saying crept into Will's unsettled mind: *the calm before the STORM.*

Darkness.
Cold.
Damp.

Cristina tried to shut out her physical world. She'd been locked alone in the cell for more than half an hour and it was far from pleasant.

Andrew, Will and Gaia must have been captured, she decided. She closed her eyes. Saw Will, with his slim body and Russian cheekbones. Andrew, with his earnest glasses and matching expression. They were both attracted to her, that much was obvious. And Gaia? Gaia had been jealous, of course. What could she do? Most girls were jealous. And when she got out of here, and she told Will and Andrew that she wanted to move to London to join STORM, what would Gaia say then?

Very little, Cristina decided. Will and Andrew would agree. And Gaia would have no choice.

But first she had to concentrate on her escape from this cell. She would have to be more charming to the Master. He was not blind to her beauty, she was sure of that. He was just a little . . . distracted.

Bang.

Something thudded hard against the door.

Christina was sitting on the cold flagstones, and now she lifted her bound legs. Her wrists were tied together with rope. *I will not be afraid,* she resolved.

A moment later, her resolve vanished.

Caspian. He was standing in the doorway. Boring her through with his evidently more-than-distracted eyes. He had a shock of black hair. A red sinewy scar that ran from his cheekbone to his mouth. Eyes blacker than any night-time fear. He was even more intimidating without the mask.

What had she been thinking? He was *insane.* No

doubt about it. Now Cristina swallowed panic. Took it into her stomach, where it knotted and swelled.

'Master –'

He grunted. And he hesitated. He was looking at her . . .

So, she thought, he isn't totally on another planet. She risked a slight smile. His eyelids flickered.

'Master –' she began again. And waited. But he didn't order her to be silent. Taking that as permission to continue, she said: 'Can you tell me what is happening? What will you do with me?'

'You will go down in history,' he said, dangerous black eyes smouldering. 'I told you!' And a wild smile parted his broad mouth. 'My equipment has now arrived. It will not take me long to assemble the new unit. And I will take you somewhere . . . beautiful! I will take *you* on the journey of a death-time!'

Cristina blanched.

And Caspian patted his trousers. A voice was coming from his pocket. He withdrew a communications handset. He pressed it to his ear.

'Master, police boats are approaching the island!' *Rudolfo.*

'*Police!* Are you sure? Where was the warning?'

'Master, yes, I have had the call from the station. I even see the blue, I do not know why this call has come so late. – I –'

'*Enough!*' Caspian's face burned red, his scar flaming. He shook his head violently. The *police*! How could

192

they? Dino had radioed to tell him he had 'dealt with' the occupants of the fleeing boat, and was proceeding as arranged! And the warning system – it was watertight! Or so the idiot Rudolfo had promised.

Caspian's brain seethed. But he would not waste time in defying facts. Assimilate and move on, as his father had told him. *'You know what to do!'* he hissed. *'I will see you there!'*

He reached down. Cristina's white face was inches from his. He grabbed her arm. Strong fingers pinched her flesh. He tried to lift her up.

'No!' she shouted. She flailed, and succeeded in landing a blow with her elbow in Caspian's hard stomach. His grip tightened, a manacle around her arm. Cristina dragged her feet. And she screamed.

Caspian glared at her.

A voice cried out from his pocket: 'They are disembarking, Master! You must come now!'

Cristina summoned all her energy. She met Caspian's furious eyes. And she twisted her body, digging her elbow hard into his right kidney.

'Enough!' he hissed, as his body half-crumpled.

And he dropped her, sending her colliding with the ground. Then Caspian turned, and he ran.

Across the water, in the surveillance annexe of the villa on the Island of the Masks, Shute Barrington was taking a remote control from Thor.

His eyes were fixed on Monitor C. Its split-screen showed the video feeds from Charlie Spicer's creations. They had been deployed successfully and now were engaged in their task of patrolling the murky waters around the island.

Barrington smiled slightly as he recalled the look on The Dog's face as he had opened the holding tank, and declared: 'Now gentleman, welcome to the future of elasmobranch technology!' Even old 'Cane' had looked impressed.

Barrington turned to Thor. 'Ready for a full test of threat-response procedures?'

A glint appeared in Thor's long-lashed eye. 'Yes, sir!'

And Barrington's right leg stiffened. In a moment of affection for old-fashioned technology, he had designed his PDA to convey the identity of a caller through Morse code, in patterns of short and long vibrations. The mechanical wriggling against his leg told him that the caller was at MI6 operations central control.

Irritated by the disruption, Barrington tossed the remote to Thor.

'Barrington?' came the polite female voice.

'What can I do for you?'

'We've just had an anonymous call from someone claiming to have knowledge of a serious threat to the meeting. They asked for you to meet them in the Shield Room of the Doge's Palace in Piazza San Marco in half an hour.'

'*Me?*'

'They asked for you by name, sir. They used a recognized communications code.'

'So it was one of our regular sources?'

'Yes, sir.'

'They wouldn't give their name?'

'We think you should attend at once. Do you require field officer assistance?'

'. . . No,' Barrington said. The local MI6 field officers were busy, he knew that well enough. Practically every officer stationed in Italy was, at that moment, in the villa behind him. Right where they should be. But if this was intelligence from a regular MI6 informant, he was obliged to take it seriously. 'It's all right,' he said. 'I'll be fine.'

Easter Saturday. 06.00

The canal was still dark.

Things didn't feel right, Will thought. What was Diabolo doing? Where was Shute Barrington? Why had no one called him?

He'd tried Barrington's number again, without luck. And the STASIS switchboard – only to be assured that the message was being passed on. Will burned with impatience. He was here, in the lavish reception room of Cristina's louche palace, and somewhere out there in the harsh, real world were Barrington and Caspian Baraban.

He was trapped. Like a rat in a cage. Will plunged a hand into his pocket. Ratty twitched in response. I know, he thought. I hate it too.

The reception room stank of fish. Andrew had gone to the kitchen in search of food. He'd returned with a jar of truffles, roasted artichokes in oil, sardines and some day-old bread. The butler had gone to his mother's for the holiday, Angelo had explained. No restaurant would be open.

Andrew had drooled with thoughts of veal *al limone* or even *risi e bisi*, a peasant risotto broth with peas. But they would have to make do. He ate it hungrily, Gaia beside him on the sofa, refusing even a taste.

At least, she looked more *normal* than before, Will thought. He'd told her as much, when Andrew had left to explore the kitchen. Maybe he should try to talk to her about her Dad. He could at least *try*. And he forbade himself from accepting that a part of him *wanted* to talk to her. Deep down, he wanted to talk to her about *his* father. He'd set up a solid wall around the topic but sometimes that wall seemed to close in on him.

'By before, you mean when people were trying to shoot us and I'd just been pushed into freezing water?' Gaia said.

'. . . Yeah.'

And she bit her lip. 'Dad's not well, I told you. But I spoke to my aunt. She says he's doing a bit better. *I told you.*'

Will had kept his eyes fixed on hers. Gaia's expression held his tongue. She didn't want to talk. At least not at that moment. Fair enough.

Now, Will started to pace. Andrew slapped artichokes on to bread. The ticking of the second hand of the mantel clock sliced at Will's brain. The hand was black. Ebony. Stark against the ivory face. Counting down the seconds they were wasting. But as Will was about to try Barrington one more time, the door burst open.

Angelo. Face flushed. 'They are at the island. They went without us! They have raided the castle!'

'What?' Will said. *'Already?'*

'Cristina?' Andrew asked.

Angelo nodded. 'They have her.' He pressed his phone to his ear: 'Yes, yes, you will bring her straight home! Make sure of it, inspector!'

And Andrew grinned. 'That's good news!'

Will held out his hand to Angelo. Yes, that was good news. But in reality he was more interested in somebody else. 'Can I.' Not a question, an order.

Flushing deeper, Angelo handed over the phone.

'Diabolo? My name is Will Knight. I'm a friend of Angelo della Corte. There is a boy on that island. His name is Caspian Baraban. He has a scar across his right cheek. Black hair. Have you found him?'

'A scar, you say?' The Inspector's accent was thick.

And Will recalled the stark photograph from the psychiatric hospital. That scar had been inflicted in St Petersburg. Caspian had brought it on himself.

'From his right cheek almost to his mouth. He's fourteen. Tall.'

A pause. 'We have the children arranged here. Wait. There are many. But black hair?'

'Yes, black.'

'. . . There are eight. They look Italian. Six are girls.'

'The *scar*?'

'No – there is no one like this.'

'What about the man? Caspian's relation – Rudolfo?'

'. . . There is no man.'

'But—'

'I have them here, and we have searched every room. No boy with a scar, no man.'

'*Every* room?'

'My men have penetrated the castle. Any door that was locked, we broke down. We found microscopes. Some beakers. Things like that. Later, we will return to investigate more. But there were no other people. This Master, he must have fled. Do you think I don't want to rescue these children? This Caspian—'

'*No*,' Will said. 'He ran the cult. He *is* the Master.'

'– Ran it? A *boy*?'

'Yeah. And you haven't found him.'

'. . . If he was here, young man, now he has gone.'

'Are you *sure*?'

A tight laugh. 'I am an officer of the Venezia police! When I state a thing, it is true. Now I must go. There are children here. They need our attention. There are some . . .' The Inspector's voice trailed off.

And the chill in his voice was transmitted to Will. The strange noises, he thought. 'What do you mean?' he said quickly. 'Are they injured?'

'. . . Injured? I don't know. I must consult the doctors at the university.' Concern tinged the joy in the inspector's voice.

'What happened to them?' Will said.

'I must go, young man.'

'But—'

'Ask him about the explosive,' Gaia urged.

'But—'

'*I must go.* As soon as Cristina has talked with us, she can speak to her brother. I will deliver her safely.'

And the line was cut. *I must consult the doctors at the university* . . . the sentence spiked shivers through Will's chest. What did Diabolo mean? What had Caspian done?

'So no Caspian?' Gaia said, her voice flat.

Will shook his head.

Andrew blinked. The smile had vanished. 'What was Diabolo saying about injuries?'

'I don't know,' Will said. 'He didn't explain. He said he had to consult doctors.'

Andrew glanced at Gaia. Will knew what they were thinking. What they were remembering. Andrew had described the 'fretting' sound. Will couldn't help thinking that the *injuries* to these children were somehow a vital clue to what Caspian was doing there on the island.

'So this Caspian has *escaped*?' Angelo said.

'Diabolo says they searched every room,' Will replied. 'They knocked down every door that was closed. So they said.'

'Where would he have gone?' Gaia asked.

Will thought. Caspian had been waiting for equipment. He was arrogant. He was confident in his own superiority. Surely he would not have fled. And Will pictured the castle. Ghosts. Hauntings. Seances. Cults. Artifice upon artifice. 'I think Caspian's still in there,' he said suddenly.

'*Why?*' Gaia said.

'I don't think we can take the chance that he's not,' Will amended.

'But the police—' Andrew protested.

'I do not trust the police,' Angelo announced.

'They found your sister,' Andrew said – and failed even to convince himself.

'Still,' Angelo said, 'now, I do not trust them. When the island was raided last time, the newspapers said the cult was warned. That was why they found no one. So where did they go? Did they *hide*? I said the newspapers lied. But now – where is your friend? If this cult master is powerful, he could buy the police. That is a fact. They should have taken me with them!'

Will considered. For once, Angelo was saying something at least partly worth listening to.

'You really think he could still be there?' Gaia said.

And Will rubbed a hand across his face. He had to trust his instincts. Too much was at stake. Caspian was still at large. He was planning something. And he had already sent someone to kill Barrington, who was AWOL. At least, as far as Will was concerned.

His head shot up. Andrew's phone was ringing.

As he read the screen, Andrew's blue eyes flooded with light. 'Shute Barrington!'

Will grabbed Andrew's phone with relief. *'Barrington.'*

'Will?'

'. . . I thought I'd dialled Shute –'

'You did. He's on a job. Calls to this regular number are forwarding to me.'

Will had recognized the dry voice at once. Charlie Spicer. Barrington's deputy. 'Is he there? Did you get my message? Caspian—'

'Hold on, Will. Slow down. I just got your message. Switch left one for me too.'

'But I told them to contact Barrington! I—'

'Will, what's going on? Where are you? What do you mean Caspian Baraban is after Barrington?'

As Will tried to order his thoughts, a siren from a police boat on the Grand Canal blasted through the window.

'Will, are you in *Venice*?'

'You know the police sirens of the world?' Will said, surprised but not entirely amazed.

'No! I just got a triangulation of your position from your phone signal. According to this, you're in Venice. What are you doing there?'

'Is Shute *here*?' And impatience boiled. 'I saw Caspian tonight! He's out of the hospital. Which I guess you already know. And he has sent someone to find Barrington and to kill him.'

'Slow down, Will. *Where* did you see Baraban? Are you sure that's what he said? He's sending someone to *kill* Barrington? Where's Baraban now?'

'Just call Barrington, Charlie! Tell him what's happening.'

'Yeah, I'm trying now, Will. He isn't answering. Where is Baraban now?'

Will hesitated. He had information that was worth something to Spicer. He wasn't going to give that away freely. He had to regain control of events. It felt as though they were careering away from him, and Will hated that feeling.

He would not risk Barrington's life, and he would tell Spicer about Caspian, but he wanted something in return. 'Is Barrington here? If he is, where is he? Tell me that, and I'll tell you about Caspian.'

'Will – I don't think—'

'Isn't this how it works?' Will said fiercely. 'Tell me about Barrington and I will tell you about Baraban.'

A pause. When Spicer spoke again, his voice was cold. 'Barrington's in Venice.'

'Where in Venice?'

'Dammit, Will, what does it matter? St Mark's Square, as it happens! He's on a *job*. Now where is Baraban?'

Will had his information – if Spicer wasn't lying. 'I don't know. Earlier tonight, he was on an island in the lagoon. The local police just raided it. But they didn't find him. He might still be there, but I don't know. He was running a cult. And he's planning something. But we don't know what. And I don't know how he knows Barrington's here, or why he wants to kill him. What are you going to do?'

'. . . I'm going to get a message to Barrington. What are you going to do?'

'I'm going to find him.'

'No, Will, I wouldn't advise it. Barrington can take care of himself and—'

And Will cut the connection. Spicer didn't have to like it. And Will felt his heart race. This was how *he* liked it. Setting the course of his own life.

Gaia and Andrew were looking at him uncertainly, Angelo in the background. 'What did he say about Caspian?' Andrew said.

'Not much. But Barrington's on a job, and he's in St Mark's Square. Spicer said he was trying to get through to him. He wasn't answering.'

Andrew paled. He pulled off his glasses and started to rub the lenses with a sleeve.

'Who is this Barrington?' Angelo asked.

Will ignored him.

'So, if Barrington isn't already dead, what do we do?' Gaia said.

'He isn't dead,' Will said quickly.

'He isn't answering his phone.'

Will considered their options. They had to find Barrington, who *couldn't* be dead. And they had to stop

Caspian from carrying out whatever twisted plan he had in mind. They'd have to split up.

'Someone has to go back to the island,' Will said. 'I'm going to find Shute.'

6.20 a.m. Dino slunk through the still-silent streets.

He was wet. His eyes ached. And he had lied to the Master about obliterating the occupants of the fleeing boat. But what else could he do? Either way, the Master would be furious. And *this* way, he got to complete his mission. The last thing Dino wanted was to be recalled and replaced.

He had been on the way to his hydrofoil when Bruno, the red-haired watch boy, had alerted him to the silent alarm, indicating a flight from the castle. Dino had already tied his waterproof bag beneath the seat of his vehicle, and he was all set to head for the city, when he had been embroiled in the dangerous chase! A laser! What sort of *boy* had access to a laser?

Dino shook his head. It did not matter now. He made his way across the grey flagstones, dark-streaked with pigeon feathers. Past cafe chairs, piled and tottering, ready to be spread across the vast square. The weight on his back bore down through his body. And he slipped inside the grand arched entrance to the Duke's Palace.

A perfect setting, Dino thought, to release his Master's creation. Only this time, *Il Fantasma* would steal the most valuable object of all. At least, in his Master's eyes. Dino would have argued for more paintings or jewels. But Dino was not allowed to argue. In the presence of the Master, Dino was barely allowed to speak.

The Master treated him almost like an animal. So be it. He was a successful animal. And he enjoyed the superiority that he possessed by association over men, over journalists, even the police.

Whatever the Master wanted . . . And Dino suppressed his speculations. Right now, this morning, the Master wanted Dino to follow his orders precisely. It was enough.

Dino slipped up the lavish Golden Staircase, sticking a couple of wide-angle miniature cameras under the banisters as he went, and headed to the right, into the oblong Shield Room. Maps describing the contours of the world were richly painted on the walls. But it was sparsely furnished. Two enormous browning globes dominated the room. A low, red sofa was positioned beneath the far window. A plain wooden desk, topped with a ceramic vase painted with peacocks, was pushed up against a door to a separate staircase leading to other rooms.

Retrieving three of the tiny wireless cameras from his pocket, Dino slapped one on each of the globes and the third beneath the lip of the desk. He hid the extra smart phone. Then he eased the damp bag from his back.

This job required maximum components. The Master needed strength, and solidity. Dino pushed the mouth of the bag behind the sofa. Very carefully, he emptied out a shimmering mound of high-tech dust.

The roof flickered. Wavelets reflected.

Angelo had led the way to the *Venus* on one condition: he would accompany Andrew, and he would explore for himself the Isola delle Fantasme. His sister was safe now.

'And perhaps I would like to be an adventurer? Why not?' he told them. 'I want to go to castles. My friends do nothing like this.'

Will had raised an eyebrow at Andrew. If Angelo was keen – if he could help – they could use him. Gaia would go with Will. When Cristina returned, Will would use his toothphone to arrange to meet her.

Now, Will lowered his rucksack to the ground beside the boats. He was impatient to look for Shute, but first they had to divide up the technology.

'I should take your phone – you can use Angelo's. I'll transfer the files with the plans for the castle,' Will said to Andrew. 'And we should keep the jacket, then I can keep track of you.'

Andrew nodded. He gently peeled off his jacket, passed it over. In truth, he'd wondered how long he was going to be able to hold on to it. But this was business.

Will reached into his rucksack. His fingers closed on the box that contained Grabber. 'You might be able to use this,' he said.

From her own jacket pocket, Gaia produced Blind Spot. 'Here,' she said.

'You should keep that,' Andrew said.

'You'll be in more danger,' Will said simply.

Then why don't you offer to search the castle, Andrew thought. But he knew the answer. There was, in fact, a good chance Caspian would not be there. And Will wanted action, which was practically guaranteed in the search for Shute Barrington. If he wasn't already dead.

'This is a weapon?' Angelo said, as he crouched down beside Andrew. 'I can use it?'

'Yes, it's a weapon. No, you can't use it,' Andrew said firmly, as he pushed the dazzle gun into one of the many pockets of his trousers. He still wasn't entirely convinced about the need to take Angelo along with him. But it would be good simply to have company, he admitted to himself. Even Angelo's.

'Hard Choice is still in there,' Will said. 'I'll give you the rucksack – you can take the lot. This might come in useful.'

Will was heaving out the helmet with its strip of orange plastic and trailing cables. Memories of

Research Lake 2 flooded back. Confusion. Fear. Barrington's refusal to reveal the truth. His shoulder and his thigh still ached, Will realized. 'I was working on this with Shute.' He held out the contraption to Andrew.

'The tongue kit?'

'Yes. This equipment on the helmet is a sonar scanner. It links to this electrode patch, which creates a map of your surroundings on your tongue. It takes a little getting used to – but your brain quickly works it out. I designed it for use under water. But it would work anywhere in the dark.'

Andrew took the kit thoughtfully. 'I wasn't actually thinking of searching the entire lagoon.'

Will nodded. It was meant to be encouraging. 'You'll be all right,' Will said.

'Yes,' Angelo said, nonchalantly. 'This Caspian, he is probably not even there. Vanished like a ghost.'

'Like a ghost,' Andrew repeated softly. A ghost from the past. A ghost back not from the dead but from a maximum security psychiatric hospital, which in practice should mean almost the same thing! Andrew sighed. He took the rucksack from Will, swinging it on to his shoulder.

'That's it,' Will said. 'We have to get going.'

'Yes! All aboard!' Angelo said, glad the talking was over. He slipped into the driving seat of the shimmering *Venus*, and raised the key tag. At once, the engine kicked into life. 'So much easier,' he said, 'when you don't need to break into my computer.' He smiled at what he thought was his joke, and he ran his eyes over his precious boat. His gaze stumbled at the back seat, which was damp and speckled with sand. 'But she is dirty,' he complained.

'I don't think *she* minds,' Gaia said.

'She is a lady,' Angelo said, glancing meaningfully at Gaia, who still bore a trace of lagoon grime on her forehead. 'She likes to be clean.'

For a moment, Gaia was stunned. Then, to Angelo's astonishment, she laughed. Pleased, he smiled. She might be a little rough around the edges, but Gaia was really quite unusually beautiful, he decided.

Now Andrew turned to Will. And to Gaia. 'Good luck,' he said quickly. And he jumped in awkwardly beside Angelo, lifting the rucksack to the dirty back seat.

'You too,' Gaia called.

They were an odd couple, Will thought. One tall and bronzed, the other skinny and pale. One worth a dozen of the other.

Andrew reached for the green button. As the garage door scrolled open, dim dawn light drifted in. It was a foggy morning. Vague pink and shifting grey. The canal itself was barely visible, smothered in vapour.

Carefully, Angelo eased the *Venus* backwards. As they cleared the garage, Andrew suddenly looked back. 'Will, one question,' he called. 'This tongue kit – what's it called?'

'. . . It doesn't have a name,' he replied.

'You do know that I'm aware of your superstition,'

Andrew said. His voice was wavering slightly. 'Devices don't get named until a test mission has been successfully completed.'

That's true, Will thought. But he couldn't really call the test mission a success, because he hadn't got the box. Though that wasn't exactly his fault.

Angelo was nosing the *Venus* in the direction of the Grand Canal. 'You are ready?' he asked.

From five metres, Will could easily read the uncertainty in Andrew's eyes. He understood it. 'It'll work, Andrew,' he said, because this was all the reassurance he could offer. 'If you use it, you can name it.'

The land-side entrance of the Palazzo della Corte. 06.40

Angelo and Andrew had left. Will and Gaia were on the street, Gaia crouching on her haunches, Will looming above. Across the flagstones, flashes of red geraniums in a window box provided the only colour.

Gaia had slipped on Andrew's jacket and the finger rings, so she could control the in-built computer. She connected to the internet.

'Have you got it?' Will said. 'We need the fastest route.'

'Just a second . . .' And Gaia scrolled through the search results. There it was – a map of downtown

Venice. In moments, she had the location. She stood up.
'It's not too bad. Follow me.'

Gaia led the way, along the canal and up the
shallow, wooden steps of the Ponte Accademia, across
the green water to the other side. After the bridge, they
raced through a small square with lush gardens and on,
past a statue of a man in his greatcoat, then right down
a narrow side street where there was barely enough
room for two people to pass. Quickly, Gaia checked the
map. The Calle dell Spazier. This was right. And she
glanced up, saw a jagged strip of grey sky.

'Which way?' Will demanded.

'This is right,' she said. 'It's not far.'

Three minutes later, after what seemed like countless
tiny humpbacked stone bridges and shuttered alleys,
they emerged at last on to St Mark's Square.

Pigeons flew up, scattering. Gaia stared. This was
huge. Dead ahead was a lavish church with glittering
domes and marble columns of every hue. On either side
of the square ran covered stone colonnades, lined with
shops. To their right, a tower soared into the sky, topped
with a gilded angel. The Campanile. There were few
people. A couple of nuns. A small group of elderly
tourists.

'I'm glad you don't read maps like a girl,' Will said.

Gaia shot him a look. 'If you're not careful, I won't
punch like one either . . . So, where is he?'

In sections, now, Will took in the scene. Most of the
shops were still shuttered. Others were opening. A

jeweller, bright with gold. A display of coloured glass. A dive shop, hung with flabby wetsuits, neon pink snorkels screaming in the window.

His eyes were darting: 'St Mark's Square . . . I don't know. He could be anywhere.'

'You think we should split up?'

Will nodded. 'I'll try Spicer again – see if he's got through to Shute. You've got your toothphone?'

Gaia felt in her pocket. 'Yeah.'

'OK.' And Will hesitated. Before turning away, he said quickly: 'Be careful.' And then he was gone, behind a broad column.

For a moment, surprise rooted Gaia to the spot. She had waited for those words, or something like them, before, in a lab in St Petersburg. Now, here in Venice, they had come.

Focus, she told herself. Will had headed off on a clockwise trajectory. Now, Gaia turned to the right. *Where are you*, she thought. *Shute Barrington, where are you?*

'That is it!'

Angelo's cashmere-clad arm was aiming right at the Isola delle Fantasme.

Andrew nodded, one hand clutched tight to his seat. Angelo was showing a total disregard for the speed limit, Andrew noted, but in the circumstances of course he could hardly blame him. 'That is it,' he echoed grimly.

He shut his eyes. Concentrated on the motion. And he couldn't help wishing they hadn't split up. STORM was a team. His team. They should overcome every challenge *together*.

No, that wasn't it . . . He couldn't lie to himself, and the true reasons for his feelings weren't quite so idealistic. He missed the presence of Will and Gaia – that was all.

Suddenly, Andrew's hair began to flatten down across his head. Their pace had slowed. He took off his glasses, wiped the lenses of dried spray and replaced them. And they were close. Twenty metres. Ahead, the bush-edged beach showed grey in the morning gloom.

'Watch out,' Andrew whispered urgently. 'There are sandbanks!'

'My eyes are open,' Angelo replied. Skilfully, he was navigating through them. Once they were out the other side, he killed the engine and the momentum of the boat carried them to the shore.

With only a moment's hesitation, Angelo leapt into the shallow water. 'Come,' he whispered. 'Get out. We must pull her in.'

Andrew clambered out behind Angelo, the rucksack heavy on his back. Together, they heaved the nose of the *Venus* on to the beach, and Andrew watched as Angelo secured the mooring line around the same tree Will had used earlier that morning.

'We are ready,' Angelo whispered cheerfully. 'Come!'

'I will lead the way,' Andrew insisted. His voice was stiff. 'Stay quiet. And follow me.'

Cautiously now, Andrew made his way across the debris of the beach and up the slope, through the bushes, to the crest of the low hill. The castle reared. It seemed to fill his field of view.

Andrew glanced around. And he listened. But what was there to see – apart from the mottled stone walls. And what was there to hear? Nothing. Apart from the faint rustle of the breeze in the grass. The plaintive call of a black-headed gull, high up in the grey sky.

This island *felt* deserted, Andrew thought. Inspector Diabolo had been convinced of it.

But Andrew, like Will, felt that something was wrong. It wasn't a feeling he could *analyze* scientifically. His psychiatrist father believed that hunches deserved attention. Gut feelings meant something, he'd said once. *Your conscious mind is not everything, Andrew. Trust your sub-conscious. Listen when it speaks.*

Right now, it was telling him that danger lay behind those grim walls. But rather than run from it, he had to face it.

Andrew was aware that Angelo was watching him.

'Is everything all right?' Angelo's expression suggested he had been waiting while Andrew's obviously impressive brain assessed the situation. Now he was impatient to learn the result.

'Yes,' Andrew said. And he pushed his glasses further up along the bridge of his nose.

'. . . We go in?'

'Yes.'

'Good.'

'Good?'

'Yes, good, it is freezing out here.'

Was Angelo being brave? No, Andrew decided reluctantly. He was just lacking in imagination. Cold, warm. Hungry, satiated. Angelo's brain operated in black and white.

Living. Dead. Would that be monochrome enough for him?

But he was being unfair, Andrew thought. Angelo was here, with him on the island. He was not a coward. There was even a chance he might be useful.

Cautiously, Andrew led the way across the damp grass to the castle wall. He edged along it, taking care not to stumble, until he found the side entrance. It was standing open, the lock smashed by Inspector Diabolo's men, Andrew guessed. He took a deep breath.

Stepped inside.

At once, he was hit by the smell. Musty and damp. Unpleasantly familiar sensations washed through him. He remembered that fretting noise. 'Stay close,' Andrew whispered to Angelo, blinking as his eyes grew accustomed to the dim light. 'And don't talk unless you absolutely have to. All right?'

'Yes,' Angelo said. He was peering at the moisture glistening on the walls. '. . . Yes.'

The first decision Andrew had to make was on their direction.

The mysterious inhuman noises had come from away down the stairs to the right. The study, the main chamber and the room with the dusty ghost-making equipment were off to the left. If he was designing a lab complex, Andrew thought, he would put the functional rooms close together. He would put anything he wanted to forget about in a far-flung corner. If Caspian was still here – if he'd been in hiding and emerged to complete his task, whatever it was – he'd be in a functional room. He'd have to be.

For a few minutes, they walked in silence. Andrew could sense Angelo's excitement. It made a change from boredom or anger. But Andrew didn't exactly welcome it. Angelo was looking about him almost as though he was in a theme park, thrilling at the glistening passages and the ominous black chandeliers.

Andrew stopped. They had rounded a corner. Dead ahead, a door stood open. Yellow light was pouring into the passage. If Caspian had decided the police had gone, he might risk working in one of these rooms . . . Andrew held up a warning hand to Angelo. Then, very gently, he removed Grabber from his pocket.

'Good octopus,' he breathed, wishing he had Ratty.

He set the robot down on the cold stone. Andrew gripped the remote in one hand and the screen in the other. To Angelo's amazement, he sent Grabber scurrying forwards, his composite legs scraping loudly, making Andrew's spine twitch, and Grabber was inside . . .

'What *is* that?' Angelo whispered.

Andrew was too busy concentrating on the screen to reply. The twin tentacles waved. And the image flickered. But the room seemed to be empty, apart from a couple of wooden tables. No Caspian.

'This belongs to you?' Angelo said.

'Will made him.'

Angelo raised an eyebrow. Peered at the screen. 'I see no one . . . We go on?'

Andrew nodded reluctantly. Perhaps it would be easier and quieter – and even less risky – if they investigated any open doors themselves. '. . . Yes.'

Together, they found five more doors flung back on their hinges. Five empty rooms. And they entered the passageway with the portrait of the masked Contessa. Angelo was glancing up at the roof, and then suddenly behind him, Andrew noticed. He had the jitters now, that was much was plain.

'Everything all right?' he said innocently.

Angelo jumped. 'It feels . . . *strange.*'

'Haunted?'

Angelo's black eyes widened. '. . . Yes.'

And Andrew silently reprimanded himself. There was

no time for toying with Angelo, however appealing the prospect might be. 'That'll be the infrasound,' he said, matter of fact. 'And maybe a breeze generator. Don't worry about it. Trust me.'

'Don't worry?'

'That's right. Don't worry. Come on.'

Andrew led the way around another corner. Again, the passage right-angled. They reached yet another open door. Diabolo's men had been thorough, it seemed. Andrew approached cautiously. No light this time. And he shivered. Perhaps it was the infrasound, getting to him even though he knew of its presence. But he felt distinctly uneasy.

Andrew plunged a hand into his pocket, feeling for Blind Spot. As he approached the door, he flicked it on and aimed it right inside.

In a sudden, blinding flash, he saw that the room was empty. Though in fact, the flash hadn't been quite as blinding as he'd expected. Andrew shook the device. Surely . . . Surely the batteries weren't running out?

But this thought vanished, as he flicked on the over-head light, and his attention was seized by something else. This room was evidently the study that Will had described. Andrew noticed the ceramic phrenologist's head, the damask-covered sofa. And a pile of boxes, pushed against the wall.

Cautiously, Andrew crept to them. He touched the cardboard. Still damp. The largest box bore a delivery stamp. It had been couriered from an address in

Switzerland. On a plastic-wrapped consignment form, stuck below the word 'FRAGILE', were the addresses of the castle and of the sender: *Institut für Quantum Physik*. Institute for Quantum Physics.

'Come,' said Angelo. 'We should go. There is no one here.'

'Hold on.' Andrew pushed the dazzle gun into his pocket. What would Caspian want with an Institute for Quantum Physics? Could these boxes contain the *equipment* that both Will and Cristina had overheard being ordered? What equipment? And equipment *for what*?

Andrew tapped his knuckles against each box in turn. Empty. Perhaps Caspian had had time to escape the island with their contents. Gingerly, Andrew pulled open the flaps of the nearest box.

'What are you doing?' Angelo whispered.

Andrew peered in. Nothing.

'What are you looking for?' Angelo persisted.

But Andrew wasn't sure. Anything, he thought. And his eye was caught once more by the consignment form. It looked thick. Andrew picked at the sellotape that held the form to the box. He pulled it out, unfolded it. On the front were the address details. The name of the courier. The date and time of collection. Andrew flicked the sheet over. And he stared.

Someone at the institute had written a note in black fountain pen. It was addressed to Caspian – who clearly had not read it. But that was irrelevant. What was desperately relevant were its contents.

For a moment, even Andrew's mind struggled to make sense of it. And then he remembered the red lines on the paper from the safe! The algorithm!

Impossible, he thought at once.

No. It could not be done.

'What is it?' Angelo said.

But Andrew could not speak. Could not move. He was burning up. The red notation seared through his mind. It seemed to bleed.

'*What?*' Angelo said, with urgency. 'What does this mean?'

Andrew's ears felt full. He couldn't hear Angelo. The boy was talking through wool.

'Andrew?' And Angelo grabbed him suddenly. Shook his arm. 'Andrew, what is wrong? Talk! I ask you! Talk!'

Monstrous comprehension took form in Andrew's consciousness. Moments passed.

Very slowly, he lifted his head.

19

Einstein. Newton. Bohr.

To the list of the world's physics geniuses, should one more name be added, Andrew wondered. Carved in burning gold in a Nobel hall of fame? *Caspian Baraban.*

Conflicting emotions fought inside Andrew. On the one hand, he was overwhelmed with awe. On the other, if this was right – if this really was possible – then he had to feel horror. The world as he knew it would never be the same. On the other – and he stopped himself. He was getting carried away. Soon, he would have as many arms as Grabber.

'Angelo, do we have a signal?'

'What signal?'

'Your phone! Do we have a signal?'

Angelo checked it. Shook his head.

Andrew took it, his brow knotted. No signal, and they were too far away to use the toothphone! He had to let Will and Gaia know! He had to tell them! He had to—

'*Andrew?*'

Andrew blinked at Angelo but he did not really see him. They had the plans for the castle. And Caspian was still here on the island, Andrew felt sure of it now. But *where*?

His mind trembling, Andrew scrolled through the black and white images. The east wing. Yes, the room with the strange noises. Passages that led like veins through the cold, decayed body of the castle. The study, where he was now. The dining hall. *Where are you?* he thought. In none of *these* rooms. Behind none of *these* open doors.

The police had been thorough, Diabolo had sworn. And Andrew could believe they'd believed it, because they'd had good reason to be. Find the missing children, and they'd be heroes. Leave some behind only to be discovered later, and they'd be blasted as incompetent idiots. Again.

But what had they missed?

Andrew came to the last page of the plans. At first, he wasn't really sure what he was looking at. '. . . But how?' he said, out loud.

'How what?' Angelo said. He was doing his best to keep the anxiety from his voice. Andrew was behaving extremely oddly. And he was explaining nothing, which made everything worse.

Andrew frowned at the screen. 'According to this, there are cellars. Dungeons.'

'Dungeons!' Angelo grasped at a fact he could understand, even if it was a little unpalatable.

'Yes – at the back of the castle. But look –'

Andrew held up the screen. Angelo did his best to give the impression he comprehended.

'Yes . . . ?'

'According to this, the dungeons are underwater,' Andrew said impatiently. 'They've been flooded for years – since these plans were drawn up. At least, they're below sea level . . .' Submerged, like half of Venice, he thought. But could they be inhabitable? Or could they provide access to other, hidden rooms within the castle?

It wasn't impossible. And it wasn't anywhere near as unlikely as the contents of the note hastily scrawled on the back of the consignment letter. Caspian hadn't invented an invisibility device. And he still had a body. He had mass. He occupied a space in the world. And that space had to be *somewhere* in this castle. Somewhere it would never have occurred to the police even to look.

'So if it is below sea level, your friend cannot be down there,' Angelo said.

Andrew concentrated on the plans. 'Well, maybe he could. If—'

'If what?'

Andrew flicked to the penultimate page. He held up the screen. It glowed, pale and ghostly in the half-light. 'If he could swim.'

7 a.m. Dawn had well and truly broken. Very soon, the 'garden party' would be getting underway, Barrington reflected. Closely observed by Spicer's creations, the delegates would be arriving in the mirror-windowed Multi-Role Tactical Platform patrol boats, then making their way into the ballroom, through a series of security checks that he, Shute Barrington, had devised.

'Cane' Calvino would be lapping up the occasion. Meanwhile, he was hanging around in the Duke's lavish palace, in a room richly painted with, to be fair, slightly wonky maps.

The window was open an inch. Through it, Barrington could hear the distant siren of an ambulance boat. He could see a jumble of red-tiled roofs and TV antennas. Dim rays drifted down behind him, through a skylight.

Barrington's PDA vibrated. Charlie Spicer. Again. *Not now*, Barrington thought. Spicer had called half a dozen times in the night, to check up on his precious *devices*. Barrington had had enough.

He let the phone ring off. Instantly, the world fell silent. Barrington felt the comforting weight of the STASIS-issue transmitting gun, slotted into the holster concealed by his leather jacket.

He glanced at his watch. *Five more minutes*, he thought. *Then I'm back on a launch to the island.*

Barrington leaned against the wooden panelling fixed below the maps. Using his PDA, he tapped into the feeds from Spicer's creations. Saw murk. And the unmistakable hull of a patrol boat. He enjoyed peering in on other people's lives. Only professionally, of course.

Barrington did not know it, but the spy was also being spied upon.

Three miniature video cameras were tracking his every move.

On the Island of the Ghosts, in a distant room known to its present inhabitants as 'Laboratory B', images streaming from those miniature cameras settled on a screen.

Three metres from Barrington, hidden from sight, a smart phone had already connected to the Internet.

Ten metres from Barrington, in the great courtyard and around the back of the Giant's Stairway, Dino was lying in wait. He was to take receipt of the item, then transmit its contents to Laboratory B!

Softly, Caspian Baraban whispered, safe in his remote location. *Softly, softly.*

He had been infuriated when the police had arrived before he'd had a chance to shift the girl, Cristina. Before he'd had a chance to test the ultimate technology with her. The cult members had been captured, he presumed, but that meant nothing to him now. He had no further use for them. And they wouldn't be able to give away the secret of his current location, he was perfectly sure of that.

Now he had to get over the loss of the girl. Move on. Keep moving, so no one could ever catch him . . . .

Caspian glanced down at his motorized roller skates, which allowed him to move his ghost through its distant world.

'Lights!' he shouted.

At once the dungeon blazed with white.

'Cameras!'

And Caspian's pulse soared. This morning, he would send shockwaves through the city of Venice. It would go down in history – for more than soaring palaces, rich desserts and a rising lagoon. In the final story of the greatest achievements of science and technology, Venice would be the setting for *Chapter One* . . . But that would come later. This was only Step One. Or Part A? Or a Prologue? Caspian couldn't quite decide.

'Are you ready, Master?' came Rudolfo's voice, from behind the red curtain.

Caspian was inclined to reply: *What do you think, imbecile?* But he didn't want the moronity of others to mar the occasion. So he restricted himself to commanding:

'*And action!*'

Back in the Shield Room, Shute Barrington swivelled his head.

He had been focusing on his PDA. Now his attention was seized by a sound emanating from . . . emanating from *what?* It seemed to be coming from behind the red sofa. A slithering.

Barrington was fast.

Two kilometres away and watching Barrington's every move, Caspian was faster.

Before Shute Barrington had the chance to take more than a step, the *thing* materialized. Hazy, growing, swelling in thin air!

Barrington froze. His eyes popped.

'*No*,' he murmured. And then, under his breath: 'Thor, my deepest apologies. You were right.'

It looked like a human. It had *assumed* human shape. But its face! Its eyes seemed fused, skin translucent, like a fetus. What skin! It gleamed. Shimmered, silver and pink. This was astonishing, Barrington found himself thinking. But was this really supposed to look like a *man*? Or rather . . . a *boy*? And what was it? A *ghost*?

No. It was clear to Barrington that these *were* self-assembling milli-bots. And this was certainly '*Il Fantasma*'! It had the form, he observed, of a tall, muscular boy.

And if he had to bet his life on the identity of that boy, Barrington suddenly realized where he'd stake it.

Baraban. It had to be. Baraban was free. After fleeing from the hospital, he had vanished! Could he be here now, in Venice? But where was the informant who had called MI6? Had *Caspian* somehow summoned him here to the Shield Room? But *how*?

And a tide of cooling answers suddenly washed through Barrington's simmering brain. In January, someone had hacked into the STASIS network. It had looked like the work of an amateur who'd got lucky – or so the IT department had said. No critical files had been touched. Or rather, it hadn't *appeared* they had been touched, Barrington thought now. What if Caspian had somehow managed to steal secure communications codes, and conceal his tracks? It wasn't impossible. He had to consider it.

But there was little time to consider anything – even if he was using only a small portion of his brain to do it. He was right in the middle of what his field colleagues at MI6 might call a *situation*.

The *ghost* was standing and it was staring blindly, its chest heaving. It gave the impression of breathing. Barrington knew the theory. He'd read about it, most recently in the *Annals of Micro-Engineering*. Somewhere, in a remote location, cameras were focused on a human – if you could call Baraban that. They were recording his every move in three dimensions and that data was being used to recreate those movements *here*.

But why? What did Caspian want with him? And Barrington could think of only one, screamingly obvious, answer. Something to do with the *meeting*. The 'garden party', as he was supposed to call it.

Meanwhile, another part of his cortex had been occupied in deliberating on a plan. His gun would be useless, he realized. If he shot a hole through the 'ghost', the body of tiny robots would automatically reassemble. He'd need a grenade to cause any real damage, and he had only six puny nine-millimetre shots.

'Caspian?' Barrington called now, trying to disguise his surprise. 'Caspian Baraban! Is that you? Can you hear me?' Barrington's eyes darted around the room. Cameras had to be concealed somewhere, he knew. And Barrington caught a spark of light reflected from one of the globes! That could be a camera. If he could get to the cameras, he could blind the machine.

Slowly now, as if moving in confusion, Barrington started to head for the globe.

The *thing* was still motionless, he noticed. What was Baraban doing, he wondered.

As if in answer, the ghost-machine moved.

It came fast, and it came right at him, flashing through the dusty air. Before he could respond, Barrington found himself shoved back against the wall by a solid hand. This *thing* had real substance. And now the head of the *ghost* bent close to his. Unseeing eyes peered at him. It was a desperately unnerving experience.

Barrington mustered his own strength. He had to respond. As the camera wasn't close enough to reach, he did all he could think of. He clenched a fist. And he punched.

His fist collided with the head – and pounded right on through it. Barrington watched, mouth falling open, as the head separated like a swarm of bees only instantly to re-organize itself into an other-worldly image of *Baraban*.

Instantly, Barrington felt the powerlessness of his own vulnerable flesh and blood. And he felt sudden pain in his wrist as the hand of the *machine* grabbed him.

The PDA.

It had happened too quickly.

Barrington had still been clutching the PDA as he'd moved to investigate the slithering. Now the device was in the ghost-machine's hand.

Barrington cursed. He'd been out-manouevred. He was stunned, yes, but he should have come up with something better than a punch! He punched again, still flailing for a solution. But the machine recovered instantly and as Barrington turned, it shoved its shimmering hand inside his jacket and jerked from his tight leather holster the STASIS-issue smart gun.

Caspian's machine backed away. Barrington's brain stumbled. And anger tore like barbed wire through his chest. What had he done? He had to get that PDA back. Stop it reaching Caspian.

Barrington dived forwards, concentrating on one thought only: if he used his entire weight, could this *ghost* be tackled? Could he, Shute Barrington, take it down?

A moment later, his question was answered. As Barrington launched into his leap, the ghost-machine levelled the gun. And it fired.

'Gotcha!'

Charlie Spicer leapt from his desk. *Come on*, he urged the Global Positioning System of satellites. *Get a fix. Get a fix!*

A purple starburst was flashing on his monitor. The STASIS network was configured to register the firing of a STASIS smart gun immediately.

As Spicer's fingers fumbled to dial Thor over in Venice, he got a GPS location. He'd found Shute Barrington! And he stopped himself from thinking any further – about what the shot might actually *mean*.

Out of the corner of his eye, Spicer saw the purple starbust suddenly double in size. *Two* shots. Instantly, he put in a twenty-second call to Thor, ordering him to deal with the situation. And he dialled another number.

The digital rings ceased.

'Will? If you're in that Piazza, get out. Barrington's smart-gun has just been fired!'

'Where?' Will yelled.

Spicer hesitated. Will didn't have a death wish. If he told him the truth, he might keep Will out of danger. If he didn't, Will might stumble into a serious situation. 'The Duke's Palace. So *stay away*.'

In Venice, Will reacted immediately.

'*Gaia!* The Duke's Palace! Next to the Basilica – Barrington's in there!'

Will ran as he hissed into his toothphone. It was early, but still he managed to collide with a yawning waiter, who was starting to set out chairs, and a rag-tag party of English tourists in socks and sandals. Will staggered out of the other side of his human obstacles and ran on, indignant shouts stinging his ears. And Gaia's voice: 'I'm at the back of the square. But I can see it!'

At last he emerged from the row of shops, into open territory, the lagoon to his right – and there it was. Pink. Irregular. The palace. For a split second, Will hesitated. Barrington had fired his gun. Which meant he was either out of danger, or right in the middle of it. Then Will ran through the arched entrance – straight into an empty courtyard.

Statues loomed. Where was Barrington? And Will glanced back. Echoing down the staircase to his right had come what sounded like a groan.

He ran. Up the staircase, its vaulted ceiling glittering with gold, and he was on the loggia, with a view of the courtyard and its twin wells. Will hesitated. Listened hard. Pulled out his toothphone. Listened again. Another groan! He headed up, to the right once more, through the Scarlet room – and there he was.

Barrington.

On the floor, just inside the door, face pale. Clutching his leg. Wincing as he tried to get up and failed. Will took in the maps. The globes. The desk, the sofa, the blood. It was trickling from Barrington's shoulder, oozing from his calf.

'*Will!*' Barrington's blue eyes burned with astonishment. 'What the hell are you doing here?'

'You've been shot!'

'Full marks. The Observation badge is all yours. Oh wait, we're not boy scouts. *What the hell are you doing here?*'

'Caspian?' Will asked.

Barrington's eyes narrowed. What did Will know about Caspian?

'I saw him,' Will explained. Anger at why Barrington hadn't told them about Caspian's escape could come later.

'Where?' Barrington demanded.

Quickly, Will pulled off his jacket, and started to tie the arms tightly around Barrington's leg, above the blood.

'On the Isola delle Fantasme. A girl called us in – Caspian's *ghost* stole something from her house. We found the equipment on the island to make them. I was there last night. This girl overheard him sending someone to find you and kill you. And he's planning something but we don't know what. The police raided the island an hour ago. Caspian wasn't there.'

Barrington absorbed this blizzard of information. First St Petersburg. Now Venice. Encountering STORM was becoming something of a habit. And Barrington winced.

At the time, the shots had felt more like solid blows than metal searing through his flesh. Now, the wounds were starting seriously to hurt. But Will's words were almost more startling. So he knew about the milli-bots, and Caspian's location, even the fact that Caspian wanted to kill him. Will was well up on him, Barrington realized.

'You need to get to a hospital,' Will said.

Using his good arm to ease his leg into a marginally less tortuous position, Barrington shook his head. 'I can't. Not yet. That machine has just taken my PDA. There's vital data on it. I have to get it back!'

'But why are you here? What happened to the *ghost*?' Will said. 'You fired your gun?'

'Correction. It fired my gun at me. It shot me – and it ran off. I have to stop it.' Barrington took a deep breath. He rolled his body forward, and he peered past Will, around the corner of the doorframe.

'Don't move!' Will said. 'You'll lose more blood. What's in your PDA? Why are you here? What's Caspian doing here?'

Barrington said only: 'Ow!' Then, his voice an octave lower: 'Will – hide! *Now!*' He yanked his head back inside the room. 'It's back!'

Will shoved in his toothphone. 'Gaia, stay away,' Will hissed through the toothphone. 'We're in a room with maps. The ghost is coming back. It's got Shute's gun. Stay back!' Will was already running to the far end of the oblong room – and slamming down hard against the

236

far side of the desk. It would provide only limited protection. He peered out. He had to.

A microsecond later, a gleaming figure appeared in the doorway. Will recognized it at once. *Il Fantasma*. Caspian Baraban's inhuman slave. And now it was here, in this room, barely ten metres from him. Incredible technology. Brilliant, and deadly.

The machine had only one thing gripped in its glittering hand, Will realized. Not the PDA. *Barrington's gun. Il Fantasma* faced Barrington.

'Shute—' Will started to whisper, in alarm. Stopped himself. And he watched, helpless, as Barrington began to drag himself up along the wall to a standing position. Will's jacket wasn't an ideal tourniquet. Blood was dripping to the polished floor. Barrington was badly injured. But he wasn't dead – was that why the ghost was back?

I have to stop it, Will thought. But *how*?

'Baraban, can you hear me?' Barrington called now. 'This machine is genius. We should talk!'

The ghost's head twitched. Its blind eyes shifted their focus. *Right to Will*. Fused eyes. Will stared back at them. Could Caspian actually *see* him?

Suddenly, he remembered Andrew scrabbling under the sofa in Cristina's palace. This ghost was controlled by a wireless network. Somewhere in this room, there had to be a PDA or a smart phone, to provide that wireless connection. But it was empty, apart from the globes, the sofa, this simple desk, and the vase above his head.

From here, Will could see underneath the sofa. It looked clear. A phone could be shoved down behind a cushion on the sofa. Or it could be in the vase.

The ghost was edging forwards now, waving its gun in a broad semi-circle, as though unsure which of them to take first. Barrington was talking again. But Will did not hear him, because Gaia's voice erupted in his ear, whispering urgently: 'Will, I'm on a back staircase. I can hear Shute. I must be just outside. What's going on?'

And Will realized he could hear Gaia's voice not only through his jaw, but through the air – from behind a door just the other side of the desk. The machine had him in his sights. If he moved, it would see him instantly. Was Gaia outside Caspian's field of view? Will had to hope so.

'If you open the door, you'll see a vase on a desk,' he whispered hard. 'It's just inside the room. If there's a phone in there, *turn it off*.'

In the background, Will heard Barrington still trying to talk their way out of danger: 'Caspian! This is ridiculous! I could help you! You are the greatest mind of your generation – do you think I want you locked up?'

But if Caspian could hear Barrington, his words had no effect.

Will's head shot round. The *ghost* was moving. Its gleaming feet were skidding lightly across the stone floor, as if on rollers, and it was aiming the gun *right at him*.

'*Will!*' Barrington's voice, in horror.

Time slowed. Out of the corner of his eye, Will saw a flash of black as Gaia appeared through the door and reached into the vase. He half-rose, and she locked her burning gaze with his, gripped the phone and pressed a button.

Time returned to normal.

Barrington was clutching his leg, his pale face expressing astonishment *in real time*. Gaia was still by the door, clutching the phone, eyes on Will.

Barrington stared at her. '*Gaia*. What the hell did you just do?' His eyes shot from her to the floor. It was scattered with thousands of tiny grey granules. With *smart dust*.

Awkwardly, Barrington hobbled across the room. He reached down to collect his gun from the mess. With his good leg, he couldn't resist grinding some of the robots into the floor.

Gaia was looking at Will. Her brown eyes were sparkling.

She did it, he was thinking. His heart was racing. He felt light-headed. Another minute, and he could have been killed. The ghost could have murdered him and Barrington both. Will forced his breathing back under control.

'Talk!' Barrington ordered. 'Tell me what just happened!'

Will broke Gaia's gaze. 'Caspian uses PDAs or smart

phones to provide the wireless connection to control the ghost,' Will explained. 'There was only one likely place in this room where he could have hidden it.' And he jerked his head towards the vase.

'I turned it off,' Gaia said.

Barrington's eyes widened. 'Of course,' he murmured. 'Ingenious.' His head swivelled. The cameras. Baraban was still watching them. But what did it matter? Baraban was powerless now. Without his connection, he had no *ghost*.

'What happened to your leg?' Gaia said suddenly. 'And your shoulder?'

'What does it look like?' Barrington said, and he slumped inelegantly to the ground. 'Nurse Knight here kindly applied a tourniquet. But my leg is not priority number one. Before coming back, evidently to attempt to finish me off, Caspian's ghost disappeared with my PDA. Right now, I imagine that the PDA, or at least the data inside it, will be on its way to the hands of our young Russian friend.'

'And?' Gaia said. She crouched, inspecting Barrington's leg. She tried to touch it but he batted her hand away.

'. . . And that is a bad thing,' Barrington finished.

'Because?' Will said.

Barrington considered. Perhaps now wasn't a time for respecting the official secrets act. But it was possible that Caspian had planted mikes in the room. 'If Caspian can hear us—' he started.

Instantly, Will checked his watch. 'It's all right,' he said. 'Dad gave me this watch. It can pick up bugs. There's nothing here.'

'You're sure?'

'There's nothing here.'

Barrington nodded. He took a deep breath. 'You've been to the Island of the Ghosts, as it's known. Did you happen to notice a rather charming little island to the east? On that island, right at this moment, a top secret meeting is taking place. And when I say top secret, I mean with all the bells and whistles. The heads of intelligence for each of the Group of Eight countries, plus representatives from Syria, Iran, Iraq, Afghanistan – you name it, they're there.'

'This is unprecedented,' he continued. 'The aim is to do real deals before the G8 meeting this week. If the G8 gets it right, we could get our hands on some of the world's most notorious terrorists. Like the ones who set off that bomb in Paris. If the meeting goes badly, the stability of our entire world will be at risk. If anything *happens* to those sixteen people, we will have *anarchy*. Global turmoil. War. Without doubt. Like nothing we've seen before. It would be the excuse certain nations have been waiting for – assassinations on European soil! At a meeting supposedly protected by the G8!'

Could this be the meeting Caspian had talked about, Will wondered, his blood running cold. Caspian needed 'equipment' for a 'meeting'. This could be no coincidence. He meant to target the intelligence chiefs?

'Caspian talked about a meeting,' Will said. 'He was ordering "equipment" for it. We don't know what.'

'But why would Caspian want to disrupt it?' Gaia asked, glancing uncertainly at Will.

Barrington moved his leg. Flinched. 'I have a few theories. But right now, "why" isn't the most pressing question. It's "how".'

'I found aluminium and iron oxide on the island,' Gaia said suddenly.

Barrington regarded her grimly, lowering one hand to his injured leg. 'Right. But look – and this is what I've been telling myself – even if Caspian does have a bomb, and even if he does have my PDA, I can't see there's *any* way he's getting close to that island. We're talking about a security system that *I* designed. Now do either of you have a phone? Preferably before I bleed to death!'

Inconceivable.

This was *inconceivable*. And yet Caspian Baraban had not been without suspicions. When Dino had reported his chase of two boys and a girl in an unidentifiable boat, Baraban had thought at once of Will, Andrew, of Gaia – of *STORM*. Dino had lied about destroying the boat!

Caspian's scalding black eyes fixed on an image frozen from the interior of the Duke's Palace. It showed Will Knight, his face deadly white as the STASIS smart gun was aimed right at his chest. And Caspian pursed his lips.

His gaze flicked to the monitor hanging from the stone wall. Dino had called a few minutes ago with the news that he would be transmitting the contents of Barrington's PDA. Caspian had cursed him for his mendaciousness – and stopped. Like it or not – and he didn't – right at that moment, he needed Dino.

Now, Caspian watched as a stream of data swept across the screen.

'The Island of the Masks,' he almost spat. 'Now, I have all your secrets. STORM cannot stop me.'

And at once, he put STORM out of his mind. There was much work to be done. He had to use the data from Barrington's PDA to get precise geographical coordinates for the location of the meeting room. He had to test the equipment. And he had to change the world. It would be a busy morning.

First, there was one vital task to complete.

Contrary to his plans, Barrington was not dead. Caspian wanted revenge on the man who, he believed, had led the action that had killed his father – and what sweeter way than at the hands of a ghost-machine, with his own gun? But there was another vital reason for desiring Barrington's demise: if Caspian didn't put him out of action, he could warn the meeting. He could thwart everything!

In just seconds, Caspian had an idea.

Three weeks after escaping from his psychiatric prison, he had succeeded in breaking into the STASIS computer network. He had managed to get in via a virus attached to an email he had sent to one of Barrington's assistants – a woman who had visited him in hospital. According to plan, the idiot had read it on her PDA, and the virus was unknown to the STASIS mail scanners. Access to the network had been his!

Caspian had stolen every access code he came

across, and he had probed the network for *useful* information. In this way, he had found out about the 'garden party' in Venice. He had taken what he wanted, and he had left, very carefully concealing his tracks.

He could not disguise the fact that he had penetrated the network's defences, but he could make himself look like an amateur hacker. And he could make it appear that various regions of the network had gone untouched.

Now, Caspian signed on to the network using the login and identity code of a STASIS officer with fifteen years' service, currently on assignment with MI6 field officers in Moscow. He brought up the Red List window.

Red List alerts triggered a defined response, as Caspian knew from his probing. Proper procedures had to be followed. And proper procedures would put Shute Barrington out of action for at least one hour . . .

His fingers flying, Caspian typed: 'ALERT: Evidence Shute Barrington paid by Russian government. Double-agent. High threat.'

A bitter smile playing across his lips, Caspian hit *Enter*.

Three seconds later, on STASIS computers around the world, Red List stars began flashing.

'I don't understand,' Angelo said.

'I'm not sure there's much to understand,' Andrew replied grimly. And he coughed.

The air stank. They were in a low, flooded room, in the bowels of the far north-west corner of the castle. A series of steps, crusted with barnacles covered in slime, led down into the dank water. Drilled into the wall beside Andrew, a line of rusting metal loops disappeared beneath the surface. Beside them, a larger, new loop was shining. Clearly, something was usually tethered to it. Andrew suspected he knew what that was: a miniature submarine.

According to the plans, this flooded room was linked to a network of dungeons. Yes, they were below sea level. But these were the only unexplored rooms on the island. If Caspian was still here, he could be down there, Andrew guessed. In a room pumped out and air-sealed. Or in a chamber somehow accessed by those dungeons.

It wouldn't be beyond Caspian's means to buy a submarine. These things were relatively cheap. And, of course, Caspian was now extremely rich. And if you did want to hide on the island, where better? Down underneath the murky, green waters, no one would ever know you were there . . .

'You think he is under the water?' Angelo said doubtfully.

'I think he might be,' Andrew said. 'At least, access to a laboratory might be under water. But I have no idea how we'd get to it except—'

'. . . Except?'

'It would seem we will need to go underwater.'

'But how?'

Andrew bit his lip. That had been the question he had spent the past minute deliberating.

Here, the water looked black. He could take the laser gun with him, to provide light. It was waterproof. But he risked blinding himself.

There was the sonar 'vision' kit, of course. *Theoretically*, he could use that to search for a *theoretical* underwater entrance to this *theoretical* lab. Naturally, he didn't exactly want to. But *want* wasn't his main consideration right now. Will and Gaia were depending on him. He had to do whatever he could to find Caspian – and stop him. Though how he would do that, even if he did find him, was another matter . . .

Stop, he told himself. Concentrate on the immediate.

He could swim well enough, so that wasn't a problem. He could take the tongue kit and swim down there, to search for an entrance. But there was another minor question.

'I don't know how I'd breathe,' he murmured.

Angelo's eyes brightened. 'How you would breathe?'

There had been a very slight emphasis on the word 'you', Andrew realized. So Angelo was relieved he wouldn't be required to make the exploratory swim.

'Let me think,' Angelo said keenly. 'How you would breathe?' He glanced around the tiny, flooded room, as though he might find an answer in the bacteria-ridden water or the unhealthy air.

Andrew lifted the rucksack to the top step. Mentally,

he ran through its contents. Grabber? No use for breathing. Though he might come in handy later. And Andrew zipped Grabber into his pocket.

. . . *Of course*, he thought.

Quickly, he hauled out Will's rope.

'Rope?' Angelo said. 'You cannot breathe with rope!'

'This isn't ordinary rope,' Andrew replied. He pulled his penknife from the bag and sliced off about a metre. Then he took off his shoes and his socks. The slimy steps made him flinch.

Andrew was wearing just a T-shirt and his lightweight trousers, with their multiple useful zip pockets. He had Grabber, Blind Spot, the sonar kit – and he slipped on the helmet. Then he picked up the length of Hard Choice.

'This is hollow,' he explained to Angelo. 'And when it's straight it stiffens. I can use it as a snorkel.' Andrew slid the rope through the strap of the helmet to hold it in place. 'Any questions?'

'. . . Only one. If you find an underwater lab, if you find this Caspian, what will you do?'

Andrew nodded. 'Good question.' He sat down on the wet step and lowered his legs into the water. It was colder than he'd hoped.

'. . . And the answer?' Angelo ventured.

Andrew took off his glasses and placed them on dry ground behind him. He blinked. The world was blurry.

But it wasn't too bad. 'I belong to STORM. I'll think of something,' he said.

Will put a hand to his ear. Barrington was talking into Andrew's phone. But through his jaw, he could hear someone else.

'Will, Andrew, can you hear me?'

'*Cristina?*'

Beside him, Gaia scowled. Cristina della Corte was the last thing they needed.

Cristina was still talking: 'At last, I am out of the police station! Where are you?'

'. . . St Mark's Square,' Will said.

'Why?' she said. 'What is happening?'

'We're with a friend,' Will whispered. 'What happened at the station?'

'Not very much. I talked, and I demanded they answer a few questions. They didn't find your friend Caspian. They said they searched the whole island. Diabolo would have told me.'

'What about the kids?' Will said. 'They were in the cult! They must know where he is!'

'Maybe. But they weren't talking. None of them. They would not speak. Not to me. Not to Diabolo. Maybe eventually the police can get something useful from them. I saw them, without their cloaks, and their hoods. They looked *sick*. But two – I didn't even get to see them – they were taken straight to *hospital*.'

'You don't know what happened to them?'

'No!'

And Will's attention was seized suddenly by Barrington, who had just yelled into his phone and dropped it in his lap. Barrington's lips were blue now. He looked exhausted.

'Cristina, I have to go. Come to us. Get in touch when you're close.'

Will turned his full attention to Barrington. And he didn't have to wait long to learn what was wrong. Grimacing as pain cut through his shoulder, Barrington ejected: '*Someone* has Red-Listed me!'

Gaia glanced at Will. 'What does that mean?' she said.

'It means,' Barrington continued, fury pinching his white cheeks, 'that someone in our security family has claimed I have been compromised, and my actions cannot be trusted. I have lost all clearances, until the alert can be investigated. None of my people are allowed even to talk to me.' He ran a blood-streaked hand through his thinning hair. 'I just called "Cane" Calvino, a man who by some inexcusable *idiocy* is actually in charge of security for the meeting, to try to warn him about Baraban. And he tells me he will not listen to me, and that my presence will not be tolerated on the island, and if I try to approach, I will be turned away, *with all necessary force.*'

'But that's crazy!' Gaia said.

Barrington scowled. 'Usually – no. Alerts have to be taken seriously. This time – yeah, I agree.'

'But who put the alert out on you?' Will said.

'I am not privy to that information. But let's think. Presuming for the moment I'm not in fact a double agent and this purported evidence does not actually exist and bearing in mind the timing of the announcement—'

'*Caspian?*' Will said.

'Not long ago, we had an intrusion on the STASIS network,' Barringon said. 'I guess *Caspian Baraban* somehow got the information he needed to get a coded call in to get me to come to meet him, to get me on the Red List – even to find out about the meeting . . .'

'But can't you call Spicer – you tell him about Caspian – he'll back you up!' Will said.

Barrington shook his head angrily. 'I told you: red alert means my access to STASIS personnel, bar the investigating officer, is blocked. Spicer would lose his job if he talked to me. Though of course I did try.'

'And?' Will asked.

'I got as far as saying 'Caspian' and my voice pattern was automatically detected by the phone system. The line was remotely cut.'

'But you said the heads of G8 intelligence are out there,' Will said. 'The director of MI6 must be there – surely he'd listen to you, if you told him about Caspian—'

'Told him that a fourteen-year-old Russian boy was about to sabotage the most tightly protected meeting of the year? While I'm supposed to be in the pay of the Russians?'

'Isn't it worth *trying*?' Gaia said, incredulous.

'I don't have my PDA,' Barrington said. 'Without that, I can't get a secure line through to the chief. I'd have to go through Spicer—'

'But you're the head of STASIS!' Will exclaimed. 'They have to listen to you!'

'Not when one of our own is claiming to have evidence that I'm a double agent! Getting the meeting abandoned could be just what the Russians would like, for all they know. This will be cleared up. But it will take *time*.'

Gaia shook her head in disbelief. 'So what are we going to do?'

'*I* worked on this security detail,' Barrington said. 'I insisted on extreme measures. There is no way Caspian or his *ghosts* can get on that island. But—' he said, as both Gaia and Will opened their mouths to protest '—no, you're right, we have to act.'

'How?' Will said.

Barrington said meaningfully: 'I don't think I can even walk.'

And Will looked at Gaia. He understood what Barrington was asking.

'What can we do?' Gaia said.

Barrington took a deep breath. 'There would be serious dangers, of course. I have to warn you—'

'*What can we do?*' Will said.

'No, listen, because this is important: there would be dangers. You are kids.'

'So do you want us to help you, or do you want anarchy?' Will said. 'Or global turmoil? It looks like we're all you've got!'

Barrington fixed his piercing blue gaze on Will and then Gaia. Will could see right through to the steel core of the man.

'. . . You need to get to the island,' he said. 'You have to find C, the quaintly-named chief of MI6. And you have to insist on an evacuation.'

'What about the security?' Gaia said, her heart starting to race. 'They won't even let us anywhere near the island.'

But Barrington was picturing something he'd spotted on his way to the Palace, hanging in a window in St Mark's Square.

It was a crazy plan, he thought at once. Only a desperate lunatic would even consider it.

'They can only stop you if they *see* you,' he said.

Dark. Confusing. Freezing cold.

There wasn't much that was appealing about his current situation, Andrew thought. But he had no choice.

For a few minutes, he trod water with his eyes closed, letting his brain get used to the patterns of sonar data being written across his tongue. At first, the sparks felt random. But as Andrew slowly turned his head, they began to make more sense. He found he could picture the scene around him. He could make out the steps. He could actually sense the outlines of the rusting loops. He could even detect Angelo's upright form.

Andrew raised a thumb. He hoped Angelo would translate: *All OK. I'm going down.*

It was awkward, kicking with the rope clenched in his mouth. But – for now – the makeshift snorkel seemed to be working. His best bet, he'd decided, was to hunt for an exit from this cellar and, if he found one, to follow the exterior wall, in search of another entrance to the castle.

That could mean entering the open lagoon. What would live in there? Aside from bacteria, of course. Andrew tried his best not to think about it.

Andrew kicked. His flesh tingled. He was breathing too quickly. He forced his lungs to slow down – and his brain to concentrate on the sonar data. Now, very slowly, Andrew panned his head. Solid wall. He kicked. Still solid.

And he turned his unseeing eyes towards the east. *Hold on*, he thought.

The crackles had shifted. Something peculiar was happening on the rear right-hand side of his tongue. In a moment, he realized what it meant: open space.

An exit. *The* exit. It had to be.

Breathing hard, Andrew kicked again. With his thin arms he swept the water away, and he descended towards the hole, holding his breath. Three more kicks, and he was through. He exhaled hard, blasting the water from his snorkel.

Now, Andrew's pulse started to speed. He was out of the castle, in open water, but heavy cloud meant his eyes were still next to useless.

Breathe, he told himself. Breathe! He panned his head, to read his surroundings. The wall was to his left. To his right, he received mixed signals. Something was close. Weed? A sandbank? And then there was nothing – the sonar pulses shot horizontally through the lagoon, towards the neighbouring island. But it was too far away, or the returning signals were too weak. Andrew's tongue registered nothing.

He turned, so he could touch the wall with one hand. And he kicked, harder this time, feeling his lungs strain. It had to be there. Another entrance. A way to Caspian.

A moment later, his legs stopped.

Something strange was happening across his tongue.

Andrew bit down harder on the snorkel. What was that? A rapid sequence of signals. Getting stronger.

And now panic rose in his chest. Something was coming. Not one thing. Two. Or more.

Coming fast.

Thor shook his head. For the moment, he was alone in the surveillance annexe. The goons were making another sweep of the island, after the bizarre news about Shute Barrington . . .

That had to be a mistake, Thor decided. It had to be.

And Barrington's gun had been fired! Spicer had called, and one of the MI6 field officers had set off to investigate.

But other things were also on his mind.

Cameras J and K showed the sixteen delegates taking their seats in the ballroom.

The feeds displayed on Monitor C were steady. Images from the cameras fixed to the heads of Charlie

Spicer's creations had been flooding back, as the units made their inspection of the waters around the island.

These units had been designed for underwater patrol and elimination. Buoys marked an exclusion zone around the private island. If the units spotted a potential threat to the meeting – a diver who shouldn't be in the zone, or an underwater vehicle – Thor could use the remote to move them in for a closer view, or he could fire their weapons.

'Thor!'

His head shot round. One of the Italian security detail.

'Signor Calvino wants to talk to you about Barrington.'

'But—'

'Now.'

Thor glanced uncertainly at his monitors. 'All right. I'll be there in a minute.'

He got up to leave the annexe – and so he didn't see the images from the three head-mounted cameras start to shift. They were no longer steady. The units were darting. The video feed was rushing. They were veering away and barrelling back, homing in on a strange sonar signal.

If Thor had seen these images, he'd have been faced with a decision:

Should he operate the sonar guns mounted on their backs? Or should he order them to make a more *instinctive* response to this intruder?

For 'instinctive', read 'bloody'.

Because these 'units' were at the forefront of animal cyborg research. Spicer himself had selected the species.

Latin name: *Carcharhinus leucas.*

Size: Females: to 3.5 metres and 230 kilograms. Males: to 2.1 metres and 90 kilograms.

Appearance: Grey on top, white below. Rounded snout. Triangular, serrated teeth.

Behaviour: Solitary hunter

Common name: The bull shark. Why? Because they like to ram their prey to stun it before moving in for the kill.

Danger to man: The bull shark is rated in the top three, along with the great white and the tiger.

But these units were subservient to him. They were cyborgs. Part beast, part machine. Electrodes inserted into their brains by Charlie Spicer and his team meant they could be remote-controlled. They were tamed. At least, in theory.

Thor left the annexe. And he jumped. His phone. He didn't recognize the caller's number.

'Hello, Thor.'

'*Sir?* I'm not supposed to talk to you. . . .What's going on?'

Barrington tried to focus. His head was starting to swim. Thor had borrowed his girlfriend's phone, he remembered. It wasn't STASIS-chipped. Which meant he might have a chance of a conversation.

And he glanced up. Will was at the door, talking on his toothphone to some Italian girl. Gaia didn't look impressed, he noticed.

Barrington steeled himself. 'Thor, I know you're not supposed to talk to me. But I am not a double agent. Remember: the STASIS network was hacked. Someone could have got access to login codes—'

'That's impossible,' Thor interrupted.

'*No*, just unlikely. What's more likely – that codes have been stolen, or that I'm a traitor?' Barrington waited for an immediate agreement. None came. 'Thor, you have to trust me. Now listen: *Caspian Baraban* is planning to blow up this meeting. The kid from St Petersburg – you remember. You have to try to convince C to evacuate. I'm sending some of my people to the island.'

'Sir, you *can't*. I'm not even supposed to talk to you. I'll lose my job! And they'll see you. Sir, they'll intercept the boat – which *people*?'

'Associates. I'm not planning on sending them in a *boat*, Thor.' Barrington waited for his words to take effect. But Thor didn't quite grasp his meaning. 'The *units*!' Barrington exclaimed irritably. 'You'll have to send units.'

Gaia turned, Will beside her. They were both listening now, Barrington realized. Good. 'They're fitted with harnesses, right? For the sonar guns. They can hold on to the back—'

'Sir, that is madness!'

'They can hold on to the back. They can approach the island with stealth. No one but you will see them coming. I can get hold of re-breathers. They have to try, Thor. You have to trust me.'

'But, *sir*—'

'If I could, I would come. But I've been shot! I could hold on, but the blood would have an impact, wouldn't it? Remote control doesn't suppress that sort of thing!'

'They'd go into a feeding frenzy, sir! I'd have to terminate them!'

'Right. So listen, Thor, this is your chance to be brave. Bravery isn't all about facing bullets or swimming on the damn backs of sharks. You have to have the courage to make big decisions. You have to trust me. If you won't go to C, let my people. You know how important this meeting is. The fate of millions rests on it. Will you risk that for *regulations*?'

For a moment, there was silence.

Back on the Island of the Masks, Thor wrestled with his conscience, and with what he believed.

'To send units, I will need a position for them, sir,' he said quietly.

Relief flooded through Barrington's injured body. 'Get the sharks to St Mark's. I'll give them my gun. They'll shoot it into the lagoon. You can get a fix on that.'

Andrew trembled.

Whatever these things were, they were circling. And they were inspecting him! They dominated the gloom. Andrew felt desperately vulnerable. The sonar data across his tongue was going insane. Rippling, faster and faster as, again, something large approached. *Large* wasn't good, he thought. Large was dangerous. And then there was a second *object* – was it diving?

It felt as though his pulse was going to burst his neck. He didn't know whether to remain still or to try to flee. He had to do something. He'd swim! He'd take his chance. Better that than waiting blindly.

Andrew's lungs palpitated. But he clung to his resolve. If he was going to die in a polluted lagoon trying to find a crazy Russian with possibly the greatest invention of the past two hundred years, so be it. His teeth clamped so hard against the snorkel that his cheeks swelled and ached, Andrew turned his back to the things. Kicked. Felt his body slide through the water.

And then, as he turned his head, felt something else.

An *absence* of something.

The sonar traces. They were becoming softer. The objects were suddenly *receding*!

Andrew held his breath. Counted.

One. Two. Three. Softer still.

Four. Five. Six. Barely a touch against his tongue.

Seven. Eight. Nine . . .

They were gone.

And, as Andrew turned his head, he detected

something else. A change in the density of the structure to his left. Not just a change. A *hole*.

A submerged entrance to the castle. *Another way in.*

Will crouched. Barrington was looking even paler. He had to get to a hospital.

But Barrington was insisting on talking. He wanted to explain everything, before the paramedics with their sedatives took him away.

'What *units*?' Gaia said.

Barrington took a deep breath. He wasn't in a mood to prepare them gently. And time was short. 'They are bull sharks. With brain implants. So they're remote-controlled.'

Gaia's mouth fell open. 'You mean like *Ratty*?'

'Pretty much *exactly* like the rat,' Barrington replied, with a trace of sarcasm – or was it just pain? 'Only bigger and with sharper teeth. And weapons.'

Gaia glanced at Will. 'What weapons?' she said uncertainly.

'Sonar guns. They shoot ultrasound. And they're attached to the animals with harnesses. Which you will hold on to, as they whisk you underwater across the lagoon, to the Island of the Masks.'

Barrington looked at Will. So far, he hadn't said a word.

But the implications of Barrington's words were clear to Will. Now, he understood what had happened at

Sutton Hall. 'When I was in Lake 2,' he said quietly, 'they were the things in the water. They were in the water, with me. But that was a lake – it was fresh water. They couldn't have been sharks. And no one was controlling them—'

'Bull sharks, Will,' Barrington said. 'That's one reason we chose them. They can tolerate salt *and* fresh water. And if they weren't being controlled, you wouldn't be here today. Spicer pulled them off.'

'But only at the end,' Will said. 'Only when you realized I was in there.' And his mind was flooded with sensations from that night. Fear. Terror. The cold metal of the tubular frame in his hand as he'd gripped it, hoping for protection.

'You were our guest,' Barrington said, touching his shoulder again and wincing. 'I gave you rules for your own safety. I treated you like an adult. And you broke the rules. But that is past. You weren't hurt, so get over it. Move on.'

'What are these sharks even doing here?' Gaia said.

'We're using them for underwater surveillance. It's part of the security package for the meeting.'

And Barrington was trying to be as matter-of-fact as he could, Will realized. Matter-of-fact about riding on the back of a dangerous predator. Was he trying to stem their fear? Or make the risks plain.

'And these sharks won't attack us?' Gaia said.

Barrington fixed her in his gaze. 'Do you want the truth or patronizing reassurance?'

'. . . The truth,' Gaia stumbled.

'Then, no, I don't *think* they will attack you. At least, not if Charlie Spicer has done his job properly. But I can't guarantee it.' *Kids.* But he was badly injured. He was barred access to MI6 field officers. And if they did get caught, they were *kids.* They'd be OK. In theory. And then he'd be cleared, and he'd sort out the mess. Was this what it came down to? Two fourteen-year-olds?

'When we get there,' Gaia said. 'What exactly are we supposed to do? How will we get to this C?'

Barrington rubbed his head, as though trying to polish his intelligence. It was a good question. He could get them so far – but access to the ballroom while the conference was in progress would in practice be impossible, even if Thor was prepared to help.

But Will's brain was racing. 'Do we have to *see* him? There must be protocols. If we can't get to C, is there some other way we could get the meeting abandoned? What if they thought they were being attacked? Then what? Would they evacuate?'

'. . . Maybe,' Barrington said. 'Or they might just lock down. It would depend on the scale of the attack.' He hesitated. But they were short on plans. Even if this wasn't perfect, at least it was an *idea.* He said to Gaia: 'I'm presuming you're not packing anything useful?'

She shook her head.

'Right,' Barrington said. 'When you get to the units, look at the harnesses. You'll see black packs at the base of the skulls. They're filled with explosive. It's a safety measure. If the sharks freak out for some reason, we can blow a hole in their brainstems and terminate them.'

Gaia flinched at the gruesome image. 'Plastic explosive?'

Barrington nodded. 'C4. Nothing fancy. A last minute addition, after some of our *trials* in England suggested they might be useful.' He glanced meaningfully at Will. 'The detonators for that explosive have to be set off with a remote. I'll give you mine. If you could find a way of making an impact with that explosive, at least it would sound the alarm. Meanwhile I'll get myself cleared, and we'll try to locate Baraban.'

'We can do it,' Will said. He felt his blood start to rush. 'We can use the C4 – we'll make them think they're being attacked. They'll evacuate.'

'If they don't lock down,' Gaia said.

Flinching, Barrington glanced at his watch. 'I think we have to try it. I give MI6 another half an hour, then the procedures will have been followed, and if I'm not on a slab, I'll be there – at least, I'll be on the other end of a secure, accepted line. Thor might refuse to help you, but I'll try to scare him into it. But you run a real risk. Don't let anyone catch you *with* the explosive. Or you'll be classed as posing a material threat.'

'And we'll be terminated?' Will said.

Barrington glowered. 'If this wasn't so critically important, I wouldn't even suggest it. Look: you're kids. If you get caught, they're not going to take you out – unless you're in the act of placing the explosive. They'll hold you for questioning and when I get cleared, I'll get you free. If there's even a chance that Caspian has a way to blow these people up, we have to try to stop him. We absolutely have to. Prepare for the cliché: it's more important than all of us.'

Gaia's face showed an expression of developing resolve. She wanted Caspian too. Will saw it. He met Barrington's gaze. Nodded.

'Then listen,' Barrington said. 'I have to tell you about the layout. And I guess there's something I should give you.' From around his neck, Barrington pulled a silver-coloured tag on a chain. It flashed, the metal forming the word 'STASIS'. 'And there's something else you would do well to remember: that old Latin caution "*Cave canem*". Beware of The Dog.'

22

Will skidded. He was with Gaia, running from the Duke's Palace. In his ears were the echoes of a man's shout: *'Shute Barrington? Are you in here?'* coming up the Golden Staircase.

An MI6 field officer, dispatched by Thor on Charlie Spicer's orders, Will had guessed. He and Gaia had taken the back staircase.

Now Will watched as Gaia dodged behind a stand selling striped gondoliers' T-shirts and Italian flags. And a voice burst into his ear:

'What is happening? Will – are you there?'

Cristina.

Over the toothphones, Will had explained the situation to Cristina before he had left the Shield Room. She wanted to help.

'My family is important,' she'd said. 'If we get into trouble, I can get us out!'

Barrington had asked Thor to send all three units.

'It's Cristina,' Will said to Gaia now. 'Can you get the re-breathers and the bag? I'll see you by the bridge?'

Gaia's eyes narrowed. 'Will – I don't think—' I don't think we need Cristina, Gaia had been going to say.

But Will turned his head. Prickling, Gaia slipped away, towards the dive shop and its neon kit, Barrington's wad of euros damp in her hand.

'I'm almost there!' Cristina said. 'Where are you exactly?'

'Round the side of the palace. Down from the Bridge of Sighs. At the entrance to the lagoon. There's a little humpbacked bridge.'

'I know it. I'll be there.'

Will crouched. It was quiet here. Just the sound of water lapping against the steps.

Two minutes later, Gaia re-appeared, clutching a carrier bag.

'Did they have everything?'

She nodded.

Will wanted to take Ratty. So long as he filled a waterproof dive bag with air, the animal should be able to tolerate the short journey through the lagoon. He hoped.

'And you got a re-breather for Cristina?' he asked.

'. . . Yeah.'

'She might be able to help,' Will said. 'And Barrington agreed.'

'Barrington's half out of it,' Gaia said. 'He's barely got

enough blood going round to move his mouth, let alone power his brain.'

'Barrington *agreed*,' Will said tightly.

And he turned. They'd both heard the low shout. Cristina. Her black hair swinging as she made her way down the side of the Duke's Palace. She dropped to a crouch beside Will. Grinned.

'So!' she said. 'We are together again. Where's Andrew?'

'. . . Looking for Caspian.' Will explained why they had split up.

'And *Angelo* went with him . . . ? I can't believe it! So now we go to this other island? We save this important meeting?'

Gaia was checking her watch. 'It's time,' she said stiffly.

Will nodded. Barrington had told him to give Thor ten minutes to get the sharks across the lagoon. Now Will reached into his pocket and pulled out Barrington's gun.

Cristina's perfect eyebrows arched. '*What are you doing?*'

She watched, astonished, as Will knelt at the very edge of the limestone steps and plunged the weapon into the water. It felt heavy. Apart from an air rifle back in Dorset, this was the first gun he had ever held. Barrington had showed him the safety catch, and how to switch it off. He'd described the stealth modifications. Yes, there will be a slight noise, Barrington had said. But if you are lucky, no one but you will hear . . .

Now, after glancing around to make sure no one could see them, Will fired.

The bullet rocketed through the water. Spray blasted from the surface in a murky plume. It soaked Will's T-shirt. He staggered back, surprised at the kickback through his arm.

Gaia checked over her shoulder. Saw no one. Just tourists in the distance, shielding their eyes from the developing sun. The fog was lifting.

'Will, what are you doing?' Cristina demanded again.

'When it's fired, this gun transmits its location,' Will explained quietly. 'The officer on the island who controls the sharks can get a fix on it, so he knows exactly where to send them.'

'And these sharks . . .' Cristina said. 'They won't attack us?'

Gaia, who had been checking over the re-breathers, spoke quickly. 'Do you want patronizing reassurance? Or the truth?'

'*No,*' Will interjected, shooting a frown at Gaia. 'They won't attack us. They're going to take us straight to the island.'

Will fixed his gaze on the haze that still concealed the Island of the Masks. He tried to picture the villa, and the ballroom, which Barrington had described. And he tracked to the west. Towards the Isola delle Fantasme, where right at that moment, Andrew was trying to find Caspian Baraban.

The world was racing at top speed, Will felt. Each

minute, their ground moved. And now Barrington was badly injured and STORM had been split. Andrew was out there, alone. And though they knew that Caspian wanted to sabotage this secret meeting, they still didn't really know how. Yes, he had explosive. But he'd also created milli-bot machines to steal, to pay for equipment – *what* equipment? Aluminium and iron oxide wouldn't cost much.

'Look!'

Will's head jerked. Cristina was jabbing a bronzed finger towards the water washing under the bridge.

'You see them?' Will called.

In answer, something appeared above the wavelets. It was grey. Pointed.

A fin.

Maelstrom. They were tumbling through a vortex, sparks coursing through Will's veins. He was aware of three things:

The sandpaper scrape of the shark's skin against his flesh.

The tug of the Kevlar straps of the harness, which were wrapped tight around his wrists.

The second bull shark, speeding to his right. Carrying Gaia, who was flat against the solid back of the fish.

Cristina followed, the animals assuming a reverse pyramid formation as they shot towards the Island of the Masks.

Shot on the back of what felt like pure muscle. The shark controlled the water, dominating the gloom. Tiny bubbles streamed from Will's re-breather. They came in bursts. He was *holding on to a shark*! If it shook him free, it could kill him. Ram his body, tear his flesh to shreds.

And Will tried to concentrate on his breathing. His lungs were powering, his pulse racing.

Yet here, rocketing through the chill semi-darkness, he began to feel a strange sort of peace.

Was it the adrenalin, he wondered. Had his father felt like this? Was it this feeling that had kept him in the field, that had taken him to China, that had led to his death? What would his father think now, Will wondered. Would he be proud?

And Will tried to banish the thought from his mind. His father was gone.

Will tried to let his muscles relax, to let his body shift at the whim of the shark. He saw the sharp outline of its menacing head, an occasional fish darting and fleeing. Will had no idea how much time had passed.

But ten seconds later, his shark abruptly swerved and slowed. The water above Will's head rippled. Dull sunshine made Will blink. Through the refractive lens of the lagoon, he made out the dirty yellow haze of a steep beach. And the body of a man. Crouched low. Peering at him.

'*Gaia*,' Will said.

Two words vibrated back through the toothphone.

'I'm here.' As the turbulence settled, Will made out Gaia's shark, swerving close to his, Cristina's beyond.

Followed immediately by: '*Will!*' *Andrew's voice.* He must have come into toothphone range! 'I think I know where he is! I think I know what he's going to do!'

Three minutes earlier, Andrew had swum up through the underwater entrance and emerged into another silent, glistening room. It was also half-flooded. And it was edged with stone ledges topped with metal boxes, the ledges meeting at a set of slimy steps, which led up to a wooden door. Beside those steps, tethered to a gleaming metal hoop, was a silver two-man submarine.

Caspian, Andrew thought at once. So he *was* here.

For a moment, Andrew just held on to the ledge. Then he wedged the snorkel under one of the metal boxes and he pulled the strip of plastic from his tongue, letting it dangle. He hauled himself out of the water. His legs trembled from exertion. But they held.

Caspian was here, somewhere. Through that wooden door? In a hidden room?

Had the boxes been used to ferry his equipment? Probably. Was this where Caspian had hidden with his acolytes when the police first raided the island? It was possible. Was this where he'd holed up while Inspector Diabolo conducted his second raid? Undoubtedly.

As Andrew steadied himself, his jawbone vibrated. *Will.* Asking for Gaia.

Andrew heard Gaia's response. *I'm here.* So they were close! At least, they were less than one kilometre away. But where? And he couldn't stop himself: 'Will! I think I know where he is! I think I know what he's going to do!'

One second later, came Will's whispered, urgent response. 'Andrew, hold on.'

At that moment, Will was unwrapping the Kevlar straps from his reddened wrists.

He rolled off his shark, into the shallows. The animal seemed to hover. Will caught a glimpse of a cold eye. It flicked like something mechanical. And he noticed that Gaia was already hurrying across the beach, explosive in her hand, as Thor beckoned them on towards the relative protection of a large bush. His blond hair was like a siren in the rising sun.

Will's fingers fumbled with the Velcro tabs that held the plastic explosive in place. At last, he released the package, pushed it gently into his pocket. He undid the waterproof seal on the bag secured to his belt and he peered inside. Beady black eyes focused on his.

'Good rat,' Will said, slipping Ratty into his pocket, then running after Gaia and Cristina.

Christina was squeezing out her long hair, sending droplets flying to the sand. 'That was incredible—' she started. But she fell silent as she noticed Thor's black expression.

'I don't know what you're smiling about!' he exclaimed quietly, as they reached him, and he put the remote in his pocket. 'Shute must be mad.' Huge blue eyes blinked at Will and Gaia. He pulled out a hand-kerchief and blew his crooked nose. 'But good to see you.'

'You know each other?' Cristina said.

'I met Will and Gaia in St Petersburg last Christmas,' Thor said. 'Now listen, I don't have long. I managed to cut the video signal from the units, and I'm supposed to be in the hardware depot investigating what is wrong. If I'm not back soon, they will send someone out to find me. I don't know what you're going to do—'

'—We have a plan,' Gaia interrupted.

'I see,' Thor said, momentarily thrown.

'Yeah,' Will said. 'We're OK.'

'You're going to tell me what the plan is?'

Will rubbed a hand across his mouth. Spat lagoon water on to the sand. 'Just get us through the sensors to the terrace.'

'The terrace?'

'*Yes,*' Will said firmly. Did this man have to question everything they said?

He looked up. Pictured the scene, as Barrington had described it.

This small island was home to a short landing strip and a villa, plus its outbuildings. The villa was roughly square in shape, three storeys tall, with a series of full-length glass doors that opened on to a broad terrace at the ground-floor level. This terrace faced the sea. The meeting was taking place in the ballroom, behind the central set of doors.

The security monitors were housed in a Security Annexe – a converted old gondola-construction shed, positioned some way behind the villa, and reached via a path through maple trees. The hardware depot was in another converted shed, just along the path from the annexe.

In a series of rooms attached to the hardware depot, the translators, the assistants, and the other members of the delegates' entourages would be working and waiting, while the meeting was in progress.

It would be impossible for them to approach the ballroom from the land-side. They'd have to get on to the terrace, and gain access that way. This would mean climbing a scrubby hill from their beach and passing through two primary security systems.

First, a field of infrared movement and heat sensors, designed to spot intruders, dotted across the hill. Second, a line of smart security posts fitted along the high stone balustrades that formed the outer perimeter of the terrace. Snake-branched bushes grew between the balustrades, concealing the posts.

Anyone trying to access the terrace had to transmit an authorized radio-frequency code to the posts – or the armed response would be instant.

Thor listened quietly as Will explained their intended route in.

'There is a small problem.' Thor said. 'Barrington asked me to disarm the movement sensors—'

'*But?*' Gaia said.

'*But* I had to cut the sharks' video feed, so you could come in, and they wouldn't get suspicious! I've been kicked into the hardware depot, where most of the hardware is, and where I'm supposed to be fixing the shark equipment. But in the hardware depot—'

'—You don't have access to the sensor network,' Will guessed.

Thor nodded. Gaia glanced at Will. They needed Andrew, she thought. He was the computer systems genius.

Cristina's tanned arm shot out. 'Let me see your phone,' she said to Thor.

Raising an eyebrow, he handed it over.

Cristina flicked through the menus. 'This sensor forest – the nodes are linked by a wireless network? They gather data and they transmit it wirelessly to each other, and on to a central computer? So if we interfere with the wireless network, the system goes down?'

'. . . I imagine so.'

'Then give me a little time,' Cristina said. 'I can use this phone. But it might take a few minutes. I should be able to send a jamming signal. But I don't have access to all my tools.'

'You think you can do it?' Will said.

Cristina's black eyes flashed. 'When it comes to computers, I am a genius. Did Andrew not tell you that?'

'Andrew managed to get into your deleted files,' Gaia observed. 'Didn't Will tell you?'

'Andrew? How?'

'I'll explain later,' Will interrupted. 'Cristina, right now you have to get to work.'

Cristina shot a final defiant glance at Gaia then bent her head over the screen, using her hair to blot out the brightening sun.

'Right,' Thor said, though he didn't look particularly convinced. 'If you succeed, I will try to assure Cane Calvino that the temporary network problem is *somehow* down to my work in the depot . . . But then there are the security posts in the balustrades – Shute must have told you about those. And I don't have clearance to get through those. I just can't help you.'

Will nodded. 'It's OK. We have this.' He pulled Barrington's silver-white metal tag from his pocket.

'Barrington *gave* that to you?' Thor sounded astonished.

Inside Barrington's tag was a radio-frequency transmitter. It broadcast a sample of Barrington's own genetic code, a code that would be accepted by the posts.

And in his mind, Will saw Barrington's face, white with apprehension – and perhaps a little blood loss – as he'd handed it over.

'But you're on the Red List,' Will had said. 'Surely they'll have stopped your access.'

'*I* designed the system,' Barrington had replied. 'I'm

the only one who knows how it works. I'm the only one who could change it. That tag will let you through.'

Now, on the beach, Will swallowed hard. Beyond the dune, beyond the sensors, the bushes and the sweeping terrace, in a villa that for centuries had hosted political violence and intrigue, the critical meeting would be in full swing.

Baraban meant to destroy it. To throw the world into turmoil. And they had promised Barrington. They would stop him. *Somehow*, STORM had to stop him.

Now Thor glanced at the phone in Cristina's hands. 'You still need that?'

She was concentrating hard and didn't respond.

'Look, I'm sorry I can't do more,' Thor said. 'But I really can't. I couldn't get access to C anyway. And if I did, he wouldn't believe me – I'd have to tell him my information came from Barrington. And I'd get fired. I really have to go. They'll miss me.'

'Thanks,' Will replied. 'You've been very helpful.'

Thor half-opened his mouth to say 'thanks' – then held his tongue. Was Will being serious? Or sarcastic? It was hard to tell. He nodded quickly and he headed for the path that led north, from the dune towards the hardware depot.

Just less than one kilometre away, Andrew listened impatiently to this long – and, in his opinion, frustrating – exchange.

He was glad to hear Will's voice, and Gaia's, but he'd made urgent discoveries. At least, he thought he had. And he pictured the scrawled hand on the back of the consignment note. The algorithm he and Gaia had discovered in the safe. There could be no doubt. Everything pointed in the same direction. And he was logical. He couldn't stop himself recognizing a truth just because he didn't like it.

Andrew was hunched on the steps behind the submarine. The door to his right separated him from genius – and from madness. Andrew started to imagine what might lay behind, and stopped himself. Speculation is a waste of time, his father used to say. Gather the facts, *then* deal with a situation. Only Andrew wasn't sure he was going to like his facts.

He had to stop Caspian. He had no idea how. At least in St Petersburg, he'd had Will and Gaia, and Ratty. Here, he was alone, in the half-flooded dungeons of a remote castle. And how could you stop a person who could vanish into *thin air* . . . ? *If* he was right. No, he *had to be*.

'*Thanks,*' Will replied. '*You've been very helpful.*'

At last, the conversation was over! 'So what's going on?' Andrew said. 'Where are you?'

Quickly, Will filled him in. He described the meeting – and its importance. 'We're close,' he said. 'It's the next island.'

Andrew's blood chilled.

'We're going in,' Gaia whispered. 'We're going to try to get to the head of MI6 and get him to get everybody out. But Barrington says security is tight. He doesn't think Caspian will even be able to get to the island.'

'Well, he doesn't have to!' Andrew exclaimed.

'What do you mean?' Will whispered.

'I found boxes. They contained imaging equipment. And a *quantum computer* – delivered from an institute I've never heard of in Switzerland. That must have been what he needed the money for. A computer like that would be hugely expensive. And there was a note, from the director of the institute. He knows what Caspian's doing!'

'Andrew,' Will interrupted, 'what is he doing?'

A pause. When Andrew spoke again, his voice was very quiet: 'Caspian has developed equipment for . . .'

'For *what*?' Gaia demanded.

'Breaking a body down into pure information. Working out the type and position of every atom in a body – and transporting them. For *teleportation*.'

'That is impossible,' Will hissed at once. He ran through his knowledge on the field. A group in Austria had teleported light across the Danube River. Scientists in Australia had sent light from one side of a laboratory to the other. 'No one is close to teleporting people!' Will said.

'I don't care what other people have done,' Andrew exclaimed, and glanced anxiously at the door. 'This is *Caspian*. And this is what he's planning. I am sure of it. Gaia – those strange noises we heard in the castle, remember? Think. What would happen if you were experimenting with teleporting people. If you didn't have the necessary processing power, you might not get a perfect copy.'

'The *noises*,' Cristina breathed. She'd glanced up from Thor's PDA. Was half-listening to Andrew.

Will's brain throbbed. The cult, which supplied willing 'volunteers' for experiments. The ghosts, used to steal valuable items to sell for quick money. The inhuman noises. Inspector Diabolo's description of 'injured' children. The theft of Shute's PDA, which contained the layout of the villa, and the location of the meeting . . .

To teleport somewhere, Caspian would have to possess precise geographical coordinates for his destination. Otherwise he would risk appearing in the middle of a desk. Or between floors.

It *seemed* impossible. And yet it made an awful kind of sense.

Will took a deep breath. '*If* you're right. *If* he really has done this, what do we think – he's planning to teleport in with a bomb?'

'Teleport in, set off that bomb, and instantly teleport out,' Andrew whispered. 'Or just teleport the bomb.'

'Where exactly are you?' Gaia asked.

'In the old dungeons. I'm close to Caspian. There's a submarine. I'm sure he's here.'

'Then nothing changes,' Will said. 'We'll try to get the island evacuated. Andrew, you have to try to find Caspian and destroy the equipment.'

'. . . Yes.'

Will could hear the trepidation in Andrew's voice. But they had no alternative. There was no Plan B. And Andrew knew it.

Suddenly Cristina held up the pink phone. She nodded at Will.

He understood. 'Right,' he said. 'We have no idea how much time we've got. We all have to move fast!'

Caspian Baraban permitted himself a smile.

Here, in his laboratory in the ancient bowels of the miserable castle, he would make history. Not with the beautiful Italian girl, unfortunately. The blockhead of a policeman in the Venezia station had issued his warning of the second raid far too late for that. Instead, the honour would be given to his uncle.

His uncle, who now knew rather too much.

Caspian's gaze wandered approvingly over his desk with its new computer, and hit Dino, who was awaiting instructions.

Andrew had been oblivious to Dino's return. He had been busy investigating empty rooms when Dino had arrived back from St Mark's Square on his hydrofoil, slipped through the castle, and been collected in the submarine by Rudolfo.

Caspian glared at Dino (punishment for the lies could come later, he had decided – right now, he needed him) and moved on. Beyond the desk, the scanning/

transmission chamber and the associated entrails of equipment stood waiting in the corner of the dungeon.

In essence, the theory of teleportation was simple: break down an object into its constituent blocks and reassemble it at another location. But when it came to teleporting a person, that theory, simple on the outside, was Tardis-like. Coiled inside was a vast, seething mass of a problem.

To teleport a person, it was vital first to map the precise location of every single atom in their body. That required an incredibly fine body-scanner, and a computer capable of dealing with the almost incomprehensibly enormous amount of resulting information.

Fail to capture all that data properly, and the 'copy' of the person wouldn't come out quite right . . . and Caspian's mind flickered to the earlier experiments. The girl he had sent to the other side of the laboratory – and who ended up with a vertical mouth that ran up to her forehead. The boy who unfortunately, but not entirely unexpectedly, died. After all, half of his liver had become lodged in his skull.

But now, thanks to his ghosts and to the Institute for Quantum Research, Caspian had the fastest computer that vast amounts of ill-obtained money could buy. This computer could deal with the data. Caspian was sure of that. The director of the institute had gone so far as to assure it. And if Caspian would be so good as to include his name as a co-author of the journal paper . . .

The director was irrelevant! Caspian blasted him from his mind.

With this invention, he would gain his revenge! His father had died because of MI6 and because of the Russian intelligence agency! If Barrington and his three fourteen-year-old stooges hadn't gone to St Petersburg, his father would still be alive!

In the Tiger helicopter, rising over the disintegrating remains of the exploding laboratory, Caspian had sworn vengeance. And what better vengeance than to wipe them all out? The chiefs of every intelligence agency! Show them up for the imbeciles they truly were. If they could not protect themselves, if they had so little *intelligence*, how could they protect the world? The world needed its eyes opening. He would do it.

When Earth was in chaos, they would come back to him. They would *need* him.

'Uncle,' Caspian said, his voice wavering with pride in his achievements and disdain for Rudolfo, 'I shall grant you the honour. You shall go first. Take the seat.'

Rudolfo had been standing warily in the corner of the lab. Now, in his state of sudden startlement, he looked especially stupid, Caspian thought. Rudolfo's slit-like eyes and his thin mouth made him look like some archaic reptile. He was primitive.

Caspian turned his attention to Dino. 'Start the program,' he ordered.

'But where will you send me?' Rudolfo stuttered. 'Where will I go?'

Caspian sought a convincing reply. 'A beautiful square,' he lied. 'I will send you to Red Square – to Russia, my dear uncle! You will see it at last, with your own eyes!'

'. . . And you will bring me back?'

'Naturally!' Caspian exclaimed. 'What do you take me for?'

Don't answer that, Rudolfo said to himself – and he realized he was too afraid to defy Caspian Baraban. Caspian would kill him if he refused, Rudolfo decided. This was a psychopath. He felt nothing. No guilt. No empathy. No fear.

Limbs dragging, Rudolfo slowly made his way into the hideous scanning/transmission chamber. Walled in a white composite material, there was a single transparent screen mounted at head height. His hands trembling, he shut himself in.

Now Caspian crossed to Dino. Whispered something in his ear. A stunned look pierced the boy's eyes. His pupils dilated.

'Just do it!' Caspian hissed.

Taking a deep breath, Dino bent over the computer. Typed rapidly. The destination coordinates were locked in. He turned, awaiting the final command.

'Transmit!'

At that instant, before their eyes, Rudolfo vanished. There was no apparent disassociation of cells. No blurring of bodily fluids and fats. One moment Rudolfo was there. The next he was gone.

'. . . Master?'

But Caspian was temporarily deaf. He could hear only the self-congratulation that was trumpeting through his mind. He was basking in the enormity of what he had just done. The new quantum computer had worked. He was sure of it.

'Master, I thought the purpose of this test was to make sure someone could be safely brought back . . .' Dino stuttered. 'How is that possible, when you have just sent Rudolfo into *outer space*? The cold, the loss of pressure – he will be dead!'

'Silence!' Caspian thundered. 'The machine works! Though perhaps you are suggesting I should be sending you to the island?' And the thought fluttered in Caspian's mind. No. After all, he *could* just teleport the bomb. But he wanted to see the admiring *and* terrified looks on the faces of those 'intelligence' chiefs for himself. The plan for their imminent obliteration impressed even him.

'No, Master,' Dino stumbled. 'That honour is yours.'

'Make the final preparations,' Caspian hissed. 'We proceed in –' and he checked his watch. Eight o'clock seemed a neat, auspicious time – 'ten minutes.'

'Ready?' Will asked.

He was crouching, Gaia and Cristina close up beside him. The fog had lifted, and the lagoon glowed bottle green. Will could smell salt and a bitter stench from barnacles clustered on the roots of bushes growing against the shore.

'We'll only have a few minutes,' Cristina warned.

'That's OK,' Will said. And he ran through their immediate plans once more. 'So we head to below the eastern edge of the terrace? We scramble up. Then we go through the posts together, and we hide in the bushes. Agreed?'

Two nods.

Cristina's slender finger hovered above the *Enter* key. Once she pressed it, the sensor field would go down. It would not detect them. At least, that was the idea. *This will work*, she said to herself. There was no room for failure. Holding her breath, she hit the key.

Instantly, Will ran.

Around the bush, over the dune and immediately to the west, towards a thicket of pine trees. As Will crossed the dark ground, he scanned it. And he glimpsed a sensor in a patch of shade, beneath a twist of ivy. The size of a golf tee, it gleamed white. And then another. Will noticed a tiny LED set in the side, glowing red. It was not transmitting. *The network was down.*

Thirty seconds later, Will hit the thicket. He could hear Gaia and Cristina close behind, their shoes snapping fragile twigs of pine. Will pressed his back to a coarse trunk and his T-shirt chilled his skin. He was still soaking wet and it was cool here, in the shade.

Now Will gazed up. He could see no one. There were guards, Barrington had said, but perhaps they relied heavily on the security technology. *Barrington's* technology, which right now, they were probably cursing. Will hoped Thor could be convincing in his claim that *he* had caused the network outage.

And still, Will's brain toyed with their plan. Trying the explosives was risky, he thought. What if the meeting simply went into lockdown, while security hunted down the 'attackers'? And if security found them, no one would believe their story. Thor would deny everything. Or even if he backed them up, and explained Shute's version of events, Shute was on the Red List. They'd be locked up, and Caspian would be free.

If Andrew was right – if Caspian really had perfected teleportation – none of Shute's sophisticated security systems could stop him. It wasn't just the lives of the intelligence chiefs that were on the line. If Caspian got a bomb to the island, they risked being caught up in it.

He had Ratty, Will thought. Could he use him to somehow get into the ballroom, and get a message to C? No chance. The rat would be noticed. If only he'd brought Fly Spy, his remote-controlled, flying robot insect. It would have been far less conspicuous.

Gaia and Cristina were peering up through the trees. Will touched Gaia's arm.

'How much C4 do we have in total?' he asked. 'What exactly could it do?'

Cristina looked surprised at the question. 'What is she?' she whispered archly. 'An *explosives expert*?' Cristina was feeling a little put out. There had been no congratulations, she had observed. She had successfully rendered the sensors temporarily useless – and where were the thanks?

But Will ignored her. His gaze was fixed on Gaia.

'There isn't much,' she whispered, after a moment. 'It might be enough to blow serious holes in shark skulls, but if we put it against a wall, we might get through a layer of plaster and brick . . . and that's it. Or we could blast out a door. Though we might hurt someone. The glass could fly anywhere.'

This wasn't ideal, Will thought. Perhaps, if they could get closer to the ballroom, a better option might present itself.

Once more, he faced the electronic barrier of green posts. He gripped Barrington's STASIS tag. They would have to go through in a tight formation. Will reached for Christina. Took her arm. 'Stay close,' he whispered. Gaia moved in. Arms linked, Will gripping Barrington's tag, they edged forwards. Twenty seconds later, they reached the balustrade – and the line of posts. They did not stop.

And they were in, among the bushes. Woody smells filled Will's nostrils. He waited, his senses on edge.

No alarm. *No armed response.*

He breathed again. Shute's tag had worked.

Now Will peered dead ahead, through the loose knots of branches, towards the ballroom.

The villa was square. Painted pink, edged in cream around the doors and windows, shutters secured back.

Six four-metre high doors provided lofty exits to the marble-chipped terrace. It stretched thirty metres, its white-veined cladding glittering in the sun.

At the far end of the terrace, a lone guard had his back to them. He was dressed in black. A black leather holster was strapped across his broad chest.

The central pair of doors led into the ballroom, Barrington had said. If they could get a glimpse inside, it might help them choose a site for the explosive that would do maximum damage, without risking anyone's life. Or perhaps give clues to an alternative plan.

Will lifted his eyes to the roof. There, next to an iron weather vane, he found what he'd hoped for. A chimney. Gleaming white.

'I'm going to use Ratty to take a look in,' he whispered. Gaia and Cristina leaning over the video screen, he sent the animal scampering across the terrace and up the sheer wall. Ratty's paws were silent. The guard hadn't even turned. Ratty scaled the chimney, and vanished. The tiny head-mounted microphone relayed the scraping of his gecko-padded feet against the brick.

'He won't slip?' Cristina breathed.

'Actually, that's how we got into your room, and into your computer,' Will murmured. 'We sent Ratty up through the chimney in our room. Down through yours.'

Now, once more, he needed Ratty's agility, and his electronic eyes and ears. If he could get Ratty into the fireplace without him being noticed, the rat could reveal exactly what was going on inside the ballroom.

A flash of light suddenly splintered across the screen. The image settled. It was patterned. Ratty was peering through a grate, Will guessed. Then he was looking up at a vast chandelier. The animal's head shifted. The camera skipped over three oil paintings, caught the glint of crystal glasses, and hit faces.

Slow down, Will breathed. He brushed the touch-screen, using the remote to adjust Ratty's head movements, to make him scan those faces properly.

Around an oval polished table, Will counted thirteen men and three women. Most were uniformed in dark suits, a few with military medals bristling on khaki jackets. Behind the table, lined up against the wall, were four security officers. Like the guard on the terrace, they were dressed in black. Black sunglasses. Black holsters. Black handguns.

Will focused on the delegate closest to the fireplace. From the moustache, tanned skin and black hair, Will guessed he was South American. A wire was dangling from his ear. His head was cocked and he was focusing not on the stout, elderly woman who at that moment was talking, but on something in mid-air . . .

He was listening to the translation, Will realized. The delegates spoke different languages. The stout woman in a blue blouse who looked east European was still talking. Somewhere, in a room in that villa complex, a team was providing simultaneous translations of her words. The implication wasn't lost on Will. Those translators had the ear of every single delegate in that room.

Will turned to Gaia and Cristina. 'The *translations*,' he whispered. 'If I could get on the channel for C, I could talk to him. I could try to get him to evacuate.'

Gaia screwed up her face. 'How will you do that?'

'Thor,' he said. 'Maybe. Or at least he could help.'

Cristina's eyes brightened. 'I could go with you. I know about computers, you have seen that. If Thor will not help, perhaps I can get you on that line – perhaps I could connect you.'

Gaia looked uncertain. 'Barrington said to let off the explosive. That's what we should do.'

Will hesitated. 'Barrington said it *might* force an evacuation. Or they might just lock down. Which would make things worse. If I can get to C—'

'But what if you get caught?' Gaia interrupted. 'They could shoot you. And Barrington's on the Red List. Why should C believe you? Why should he listen to anything you say?'

'But I won't be talking for Barrington,' Will whispered. 'Andrew knows what Caspian is planning. MI6 doesn't. C must have heard of us, after St Petersburg. I'll be talking for STORM. It's worth a chance. If he doesn't believe me, you can still blow the C4.'

Will was determined. Gaia could see that. And she could hardly fail to notice Cristina's excitement. So be it. But Cristina wasn't a member of STORM. She – Gaia – should be going with Will. Except that she knew only the basics about computers, and she knew a great deal about explosives.

But if she had to stay behind, she wouldn't give Cristina the satisfaction of seeing her annoyance. 'I'll try to find a place where the C4 could have the biggest impact,' she said. 'Stay in touch.'

Cristina had already started to edge towards the slope that led back towards the hardware depot. Now, as Will turned to follow her, Gaia blurted out in a whisper: 'Don't take any unnecessary risks.' And she bit her lip. Her words had been stilted. She hadn't meant to sound so formal.

But Will smiled faintly. 'You heard Barrington: the security of our world is at stake. What could be unnecessary?'

'Dying,' Gaia said quietly.

Will's smile faded. He shook his head. 'No one is going to die.'

'Slowly now,' Andrew breathed to himself.

He was making his way along the passage that swerved left from the half-flooded room with its tethered submarine. The tongue strip dangled from the helmet, and he pushed it back, out of the way. He could take the helmet off, of course. But it felt comforting, as though it might offer some protection. Self-delusion, Andrew realized. And decided to give himself a break.

Here, the walls and the floor were rough. Zigzag

mineral trails shot through the rock. This seemed natural, Andrew thought. Was it a *cave*? Perhaps an architect wouldn't map out *natural* rooms.

Andrew stopped. He'd taken out the toothphone, so he could focus entirely on his surroundings. And he'd heard a voice. But from where?

Andrew peered along the passage. Without his glasses, this wasn't easy. But inset several metres further along, cut high in the wall, was what appeared to be a niche. Andrew hurried closer. Craned his neck. Saw a grille. Dull light and subdued voices were drifting through it. And Andrew caught an accent. *Caspian*. He swallowed hard. *Once upon a time*, Caspian had been his friend. But that fairytale was well and truly over.

And Andrew froze. The voices had been dull, but now three clear words had rung through the grille. A boy's voice. Raised. Dino's? Announcing: '*Five minutes, Master!*'

Five minutes until teleportation, Andrew guessed. Is that what he'd meant? Suddenly, at that moment, Andrew didn't care about the delegates or world security. *Gaia. Will. Cristina.* They were on that island. He had to do something!

Fingers trembling, Andrew slotted in his toothphone. 'Five minutes until teleportation!' he whispered hard. 'Tell me you're on your way out of there!' And he gripped his fist hard around Blind Spot.

Gaia responded at once. She'd been placing the explosive and trigger for the detonator on the ground beside her. Now she tensed as she heard Andrew's urgent announcement. 'No!' she whispered. 'Andrew, we're still here. Can you stop him?'

'Gaia. I don't know.'

'Will?' she said.

No answer. What was Will doing?

'Andrew,' Gaia whispered, 'we just can't get them out in five minutes. If you're sure, you have to stop him!'

'Gaia . . . Acknowledged. Roger.'

Andrew's voice was wavering. He was reverting to faux-military speak.

'It's OK,' she whispered. 'You can do it, Andrew.'

'I don't even have a real *weapon*,' he breathed.

'. . . You've got your brain.'

'Yeah. If only it fired bullets, it might be more useful right at this moment. Stand by. I'll do what I can.'

'Roger,' Gaia said, hoping the word would be reassuring. '*Over.*'

Five minutes. Gaia's blood chilled. She focused on the guard at the far end of the terrace. Until two minutes ago, he'd been pacing his corner. But now he was at the stone balcony, peering out between the bushes, towards the horizon beyond the beach. She'd have to take her chance.

Gaia gathered the explosive together and pressed it into a ball. She ran. Four seconds, and she was at the villa wall. She turned her back hard against the plaster and immediately she edged sideways, towards the elegant wooden frames of the central set of doors. If she could blow out the glass, that would trigger an alarm, *surely*. She'd have to risk injuring someone. Better that than everyone dying.

'Will, if you can hear me, say something,' she breathed.

No response. *What was he doing?*

Gaia crouched, one eye on the broad back of the guard. She pressed the soft putty hard against the wooden frame. Quickly, she inserted Barrington's fuse. Her heart pounding, Gaia dashed across the terrace, back to the relative safety of the trees.

The guard hadn't even turned. Now Gaia's gaze shot from the doors, via her watch, back through the bushes, and the trees beyond. *'Where are you, Will?'* she whispered. Still no response.

Should she stay here at the terrace, or go back to the beach. It would be safer there, if Caspian appeared, if he – and she stopped herself.

Will might need her here, on the terrace. He must have heard Andrew. She had to trust him.

Will and Cristina had been lucky.

Down the hill, through the cypresses, the white-washed Surveillance Annexe and the hardware depot beyond were easy to spot. They had run, slipping between trunks and jumping branches. And they had found the door of the depot standing open, Thor – alone – inside.

'What –?' Thor's mouth dropped open. 'What's going on?'

Will explained quickly. While he talked, Cristina's eyes scanned the room. She took in the twin computer displays. Optic fibre was roped in the corner, like a high-tech lasso. A wireless communications headset had been dumped on the desk.

Cristina pulled up a chair and grabbed a keyboard. Her fingers ran over the keys, as she probed the system. 'You said you didn't have access to the field sensors!' And she swung round.

Thor's mouth was still open. 'I—' he began, colouring.

'Don't you trust us?' she said angrily. 'Don't you trust your own boss?'

Thor looked at Will. There was shame in his eyes. 'You don't understand. I've been with STASIS six months. This is all I ever wanted to do. I have to follow procedure. I would *lose my job.*'

'How long, Cristina?' Will said tightly.

'Wait . . . He has a headset. If he can communicate . . . if I can find the path of the translation transmissions. Ah! The password?' she demanded. 'Come on! *Forza*, Thor. Have strength! I cannot guess this, you must tell me!'

A split second later, before Thor had chance to

respond, Will and Cristina heard Andrew's voice in their ears: 'Five minutes until teleportation!'

Will yanked the toothphone from his mouth. He grabbed the headset. And he faced Thor. 'In five minutes, there is going to be an attack on this meeting! You're in the security detail. You *must* know the password. Or how to get it.'

Thor's blue eyes blinked. He took a deep breath. Without looking at Will or Cristina, he reached over, grabbed the keyboard, typed rapidly. Hit Enter.

Instantly, icons for channels to each of the delegates appeared on the screen.

'There!' Cristina said. And she beamed at Will: 'You see, Will, you need me! First the sensor networks, now—'

'—Which is C?' Will demanded, interrupting her. '*Which is C?*'

'Here.' Thor pointed. Closed his eyes.

'I presume you would now like me to re-route the connection from the translation office?' Cristina said coolly.

'There's no time for congratulations,' Will said. 'Just do it.'

Biting her lip, Cristina transferred the connection to the headset in the hardware depot.

Will's eyes shot to Ratty's video screen. The image showed that the South American was holding the delegates' attention. And, as Ratty's head moved, it revealed a frown splitting the brow of a grey-haired, moon-faced man in a dark grey suit. This man turned to a blond-haired guard standing behind. He had his hand on his earphone. He was wondering why the translation had stopped, Will realized. So *that* was C. The MI6 chief. Grey hair, grey eyes. *Nondescript.* Apart from that round face and a trace of ruddiness in his broad cheeks.

Will held the mike close to his lips. What he said now would be critical. His mouth was dry as cardboard. The room around him blanked out.

'I know you are C. And I think you can hear me. My name is Will Knight. I belong to an organization called STORM. In three and a half minutes, someone is going to *teleport* into that room with a bomb. You have to evacuate *now* . . . If you can hear me, raise your hand.'

Will took in the barely concealed astonishment on C's moon face. But why wasn't he reacting? Why wasn't he raising his hand?

'I work with Barrington. He is no traitor. I am deadly serious. You must evacuate everyone *now*.'

Instantly, C's eyes flickered around the room. What was he looking for, Will wondered? *Video cameras?* The guard posted behind C's chair bent over, and murmured something. His blond hair was highlighted with grey. Black sunglasses reflected a crystal water glass – and the water that suddenly spilled across the polished table. C was standing up. He was interrupting the South American delegate—

'He's going to do it!' Will exclaimed. 'He's going to get them out!'

Andrew took a deep breath. Melodramatic lines were whirling through his mind.

Your time is up, Baraban.

And: I'm too young to die.

Would Caspian kill him? If he stood in Caspian's way – yes. The answer was inescapable.

But there was nothing for it. Raising the dazzle gun, Andrew prepared to kick open the door. For Gaia's sake, and for Will's, he had to try to be aggressive. Caspian had changed. Maybe so could he. Andrew took a deep breath.

He kicked, and instantly the scene inside was unleashed.

Dark scenes. Andrew's brain staggered. He saw Caspian, all in black, face as inhuman as his high-tech ghost. Dino, turning in amazement from a computer. Behind them, a unit that resembled a decontamination cubicle.

On the ground beside Caspian's feet was a black silk bag, containing – and there was no room for doubt – the *explosive*. The images bombarded Andrew's mind. He took the blows. And he did not waver. He could not.

Now, Andrew aimed the useless weapon at Caspian's stunned face. It was the face of a true genius, Andrew had time to reflect. And he was aware that his breathing was coming in shallow waves. He had to say something. 'No one move,' came out. *Stupid*, he thought. He swallowed hard.

Caspian had been staring. Now Andrew's voice acted like an emotional switch. The fuse went. Fury started to twist Caspian's blanched features. '*Andrew Minkel.* What are you doing here?'

'What do you think?' Andrew said, trying his best to keep his voice even.

Caspian's eyes narrowed to black slits. 'Maybe you have come to steal my invention – is that it? You know what this is, Andrew?' And he jabbed a finger towards the white chamber. 'Where I am, the world changes. But you—' he spat. '*You* spend your life in pursuit of me!'

Suddenly, Caspian's eyelids retracted. The whites gleamed. His face seemed to have hollowed, baring the structure beneath. Andrew became strangely aware of the bones that supported that flesh and skin. Caspian *was* human. He was vulnerable.

'I can't let you,' Andrew said quietly. 'You *can't* do it, Caspian.'

And Caspian barked a hard laugh. 'Why? Because you say so? Because Shute Barrington has sent you once more to do his work! To kill me, like you killed my father!'

'No—' Andrew started. But arguing would get nowhere. He could only try cold logic. 'No one wants to kill you,' he said. 'But I must stop you.'

303

Caspian's nostrils flared. 'And how do you think you could stop me?'

'With this,' Andrew said simply. One last time, he aimed Blind Spot. His finger hesitated above the button. It had to work. It was all he had.

Caspian's defiance wavered.

Andrew closed his eyes. And he pressed.

He knew what he'd hoped for: that the weak batteries, given a chance to rest, just might in their dying moments produce a blinding flash of light. Enough to disorient Caspian and Dino, while he collected the bomb, and somehow—

Andrew stopped picturing the scene. Because what he got was this: a dull gleam.

Caspian's black eyes stared. 'With *that*?'

'. . . That is the laser finder,' Andrew stumbled, his brain searching for lies Caspian just might believe. 'This is an experimental weapon—'

'Ah, one of *Will's* gadgets!' Caspian scoffed. 'You have too much faith in him. He is *nothing*, Andrew, compared to me.'

Caspian took a menacing step across the floor of the cave. He was an animal, Andrew thought. He should have been inscribed in Neolithic ochre on the pre-historic walls. 'But it is not too late, Andrew. Now you are a slave. You follow orders. Come with me. *Join me.* Imagine, together, what we could achieve . . .'

Imagine, together, what we could achieve.

Four months ago, in his house in Bloomsbury,

Andrew had used those words exactly. Caspian had bought them. He'd willingly joined STORM. But STORM was for good. Caspian was for himself. Unfamiliar anger caught again at Andrew's veins.

Caspian's gaze remained skewered through him. 'I am generous, so I will give you one last chance to join me,' he said darkly. 'Or you may do your worst.'

Andrew's thoughts scrambled. *What could he do*? He had *nothing*. A useless weapon. Thin arms. Weak legs.

And Caspian laughed. The sound sent nausea charging through Andrew's stomach. He'd come so far. He had to do *something*.

'Dino!' Caspian bellowed. 'Use the cable!'

The boy rose. From his belt, he suddenly produced a handgun. The gun he'd tried to shoot them with from the hydrofoil, Andrew guessed. Brandishing his weapon, Dino gathered up a cable lying loose beside the computer. He advanced on Andrew, moving so rapidly that Andrew felt his arms pinioned almost before he could react.

He tried to struggle, but it was a token effort. Dino was much taller and the gun was pressed into his back. Andrew could feel it jabbing towards his kidneys.

Andrew squeezed his eyes shut, as he felt the cable wrap around his wrists. And Dino bent, looping it around Andrew's legs. He tied a knot and pushed him to the ground. Andrew fell heavily. His arm rang through with pain. The helmet had been pushed askew, down over his right eye. But he could make out Caspian, who was heading for the back of the cave, clutching his silk bag, slipping inside his gleaming machine.

'Where is Will now?' Caspian cried, his voice almost joyful. 'Is he there, with Gaia, on the Island of the Masks? Your *friends*?' Caspian slid the door shut. He shook his head at Andrew, who was struggling to sit up. 'Then they too will *die*.'

Dino headed back to the computer. He bent over the keyboard.

A white light clouded Andrew's vision. His stomach felt sick with failure. And he whispered for the benefit of the other toothphones: '*Now*! He is going to teleport now!'

Gaia's brain pulsed. *Now. He is going to teleport now*. She hissed into her toothphone: 'Will, did you hear him? What's going on?'

Simultaneously, in the hardware depot, Cristina responded to Andrew's urgent voice. 'Now!' she shouted to Will, sending Gaia's hand to her aching ear. 'Andrew – he says he is going to teleport now!'

Thor stared at her. '*Teleport?*'

But she wasn't listening. Neither was Will. Instantly, he ordered Ratty up over the grate, out of the fireplace. He had to see exactly what was going on in that ball-room. And Will saw C with his hand still raised, irritation on the face of the South American delegate – and he heard shouts! Ratty's mike was close to the table now. It was picking up voices. Cries of astonishment. *Warning*. The delegates were turning as one to stare at something. C was pointing, turning to the blond security officer.

There. In the corner. It had been empty. *Not any more.*

There, on the video screen, was Caspian Baraban! A black silk bag was clasped in his hand. Ratty's camera showed Baraban place the bag on the floor. Showed him take a step forwards, as a dozen guns of different technologies bristled into the air.

C started to edge around the table, towards Caspian.

Caspian raised his arms. But he wasn't indicating surrender. Rather, supremacy.

The bag, Will thought.

'Are we too late?' Cristina whispered, blanching at the face of the Master.

On the terrace outside, Gaia could hear the commotion. A man inside was shouting. The guard suddenly began to skid across the marble, his gun clasped in both hands. He disappeared inside the ballroom, slamming the door shut behind him. Gaia ran to the window. She had to see what was going on.

What she saw was this: Baraban, arms raised, guns pointing at him.

A blond security officer was shouting in Welsh-accented English: 'Stand still. Stay where you are!'

The man took a few steps towards him and Caspian spoke: 'I would not advise it.'

Gaia had a side-on view of Caspian. She could see his pale face, his hideous scar, the shock of black hair. Delegates were moving back, to the rear of the room. But none was leaving. They were *watching*, she realized. This was a *boy*.

She saw the cool eyes of the blond security officer shoot down to the bag. 'Who are you?' he shouted. 'What's in there?' And he called: 'Get everyone out of here!'

There was movement, but sixteen pairs of eyes were still *watching*. They *had* to. Caspian seemed to glow.

'You wonder who I am? My name is Caspian Baraban.

'You wonder why I come? I come to exact vengeance.

'You wonder what I want? I want this: that you salute me – and *die*!'

No.

That same word was still echoing through Andrew's skull. But this time he meant it. He would not let Caspian kill those people and take his friends.

Dino had slotted in an earpiece and was listening hard. Behind him, the computer screen had turned black. Screen-saver mode. Dino was monitoring Caspian, Andrew guessed. Waiting for the signal to bring him back. The signal that would mean Caspian had succeeded, and Will and Gaia were dead.

Andrew struggled. The cable was biting into his

wrists, but around his legs it seemed looser. As Dino turned away, eyes on the teleportation machine, one hand at his earpiece, the gun resting behind him on the desk, Andrew started to struggle against the cabling that twisted around his ankles. He wriggled his right leg and at last, he managed to push a loop of the cable down from around his foot. His helmet kept slipping, and he had to push it back with his shoulder so he could see.

Again, Andrew pushed at the cable. And he got his right foot free! His arms were bound. Dino could reach for the gun in a split-second. But he had to chance it. Andrew scanned the walls, the room, for anything that might help. And he saw the *light switch*.

Twisting his neck, and using his shoulder, Andrew managed to get his teeth around the strip of plastic with its microprocessors. Gently, he used his tongue to pull it into his mouth. He pressed the plastic hard against the roof of his mouth, securing it against his tongue. At once, he felt the sonar kick in. A representation of the cave fired into his brain. The *cave*. There was no natural light. Once he hit that switch, the room would be pitch black.

His hands aching in their bonds, Andrew stumbled up. Dino's head shot round. Eyes widened in anger. He started to reach for the gun. But Andrew was quick. He dashed along the wall and with his shoulder, he flicked the switch, plunging the room into blackness.

'You!'

Dino! An angry shout. Andrew heard something fall, as Dino scrabbled on the desk for the gun.

'You? *What are you doing?*'

Dino started to stagger towards the light switch, gun raised, one hand waving, as though trying to push the darkness out of the way. Andrew could 'see' him clearly. This was exactly what he wanted. He backed against the wall, and he waited until Dino was close. Then Andrew launched himself at the boy with all his strength. Andrew felt his shoulder collide with Dino, his bruised arm aching – and he heard the gun clatter to the floor.

Dino was flailing. He reached blindly for Andrew but Andrew managed to dart away, and he made instantly for the small, irregular outline that had skidded across his tongue – across the ground towards the desk. Andrew slipped. Righted himself. Reached out, his bound arms straining. At the instant that Dino at last made it to the light switch, Andrew's trembling hand gripped the gun.

'. . . *Salute me, and die!*'

In the hardware depot, Thor had activated a video feed from the security cameras in the ballroom. Cristina's eyes were fixed on Caspian's manic face. He had just finished his little speech!

Will was focusing hard on Ratty's video screen. He knew what was inside that silk bag. Aluminium and iron oxide. Enough, he presumed, to explode that ballroom. Somehow, he had to get the bag out.

He hissed: 'Gaia, blast the door. I'm going to use Ratty to drag the bomb out! Andrew?' No answer. And Will instructed Ratty to scurry past the fireplace, towards the corner of the room, to Caspian and his bomb.

'Will!' Cristina exclaimed. 'Will – look!'

She was pointing to the monitor.

Caspian had finished speaking. And his raised arms were wavering. He glanced down. His eyes started to dart across the weapons bristling into his face. He was looking mildly surprised. Suddenly Andrew's voice cut through Will's ear:

'I've got Dino! Caspian's not coming back!'

Will glanced at Cristina. Her quartz eyes sparkled.

'Andrew – well done! Keep him there!' And Will took in Caspian's increasingly puzzled expression. He smiled grimly. *You're wondering what you're still doing there,* Will realized. *Keep wondering . . .*

'The bomb!' Andrew called.

'I'm on it,' Gaia replied. Outside the window, she had the detonator hot in her hand.

In the hardware depot, Will kept his eyes fixed on the surveillance footage. He watched as the blond security officer slowly advanced towards Caspian – and as the scene turned white!

Gaia's voice: 'I've blasted the doors!'

And Will hissed back. 'But now I can't see!'

Outside, Gaia coughed. Dust was pouring out of the blast hole. Wood had splintered, and glass was shattering, smashing to the ground. Shouts were going up in the ballroom. As the first wave of dust began to settle, Gaia made out Caspian in the near corner, dishevelled but standing – and the blond guard, his hair now thick with white dust. She glimpsed something else: the small silk bag.

Gaia made a decision. *She* had to act. She slipped in through the demolished doors, stepping on to a carpet of glass, hearing it crunch beneath her trainers. People were shouting and coughing.

Blinking hard, Gaia bent down, reached out. Her fingers touched silk. Then fur. *Ratty*. Will must have got him back to the bag! She tugged. Met resistance. Ratty had his teeth through the fabric. And Gaia dragged at the bag, the rat clinging on. She edged backwards, and she was on to the terrace. Dust and sunshine made her eyes water. She would throw it down the scrubby hill, towards the sea.

In the hardware depot, the image from Ratty's camera became a little clearer. Will saw sky. Marble. The terrace! And a flash of curly brown hair. He hissed angrily into his toothphone: 'Gaia, what are you doing! I have Ratty on the bomb!'

Suddenly his eyes squeezed shut. Pain had rocked through his skull.

Beside Will, Cristina screamed.

Eight hundred metres away, on the Isola delle

Fantasme, Andrew crumpled in two, slamming a hand to his ringing ear.

The noise had been horrendous.

Will staggered out of the hut. A vast plume of dust was turning the sky yellow. The air itself seemed to echo.

He understood at once.

Caspian's bomb.

24

Will didn't think. He couldn't. He could only run, through the trees, towards the ballroom. Fragments of thoughts caught his brain like shrapnel. *What if . . . ? Gaia was going back . . . ?*

Will skidded on a fallen branch, reached wildly for a slippery trunk, almost fell. And he stumbled on, coughing as the dust began to soak into his lungs, up the narrow path, through the bushes, on to the terrace.

Will's stunned eyes took in the smashed doors. And the blond-haired guard, who was emerging through them, propelling in front of him a moon-faced man in a dust-spattered grey suit.

Will tracked the scene. The far end of the terrace had been obliterated. Trees had been levelled. Smashed stone balustrade littered the cracked marble. Half the wall beside it had been blasted through. One corner of the ballroom was missing. It gaped unsteadily. And Will's own words echoed through him: *No one is going to die.*

A voice. From behind. Cristina's. '*Will.*' She'd run after him.

He barely heard her. Called: 'Gaia!'

Heard an unearthly silence. Will ran to the edge of the blasted terrace. The blond officer yelled something that Will did not hear.

Will peered down. Crumbled lumps of stone littered the slope. He could see down through the trees and scrub, to the top of the dune, way below.

'*Will!*'

He turned for an instant. Cristina again. Behind her, people were emerging on to the terrace. Guns were waving. He heard Thor's voice. It seemed faint. Thor was pointing at him.

'*Gaia,*' Will said again, willing her to answer him. Silence.

And then: 'Will.'

Gaia!

'He's here! Will, get down to the beach!'

Gaia. She was all right. His heart thudding hard against his ribs, Will glanced back. Cristina was being grabbed by the blond guard, Thor standing to one side, looking on. But *Gaia was alive.*

Will turned, and ran. He skidded off the terrace, falling hard against a tree. He stumbled up and raced across the scrub, towards the dune, and the beach. His legs were loose. He could hardly even feel them as they moved automatically, carrying him on. Shouts from behind him faded to nothing. They did not exist.

He reached the crest of the dune. And he saw Gaia. Covered in yellow and white dust, as though made of marble. She was standing on the beach, and there, beyond her, starting to wade into the green water, was *Caspian.*

Will yanked out his toothphone. 'Gaia!'

She turned, for an instant. Baraban's head shot up. He was clasping his arm. Ruby blood dripped to the sand. Caspian's face blackened.

Will ran to Gaia, feet heavy on the sand. *'Are you all right?'*

She nodded quickly. 'I got the bomb off the terrace – I saw Caspian run!'

'Caspian!' Will called now.

Caspian's face was wild. Anger and arrogance were ejecting in poisonous bursts from his eyes. 'Too late, Will! This is Caspian Baraban! And I am free!'

'This place is full of guards,' Will shouted. 'You're not going anywhere.'

'I will take my excellent chances. I will swim!' And Caspian bared his teeth, lips blood red against white enamel. He swerved, and waded deeper into the water.

Will started towards him. Gaia grabbed his arm. 'Will,' she said in a low voice.

Will had seen it. A flash of motion.

A fin.

'Hey!'

The shout had come from behind. Will looked back. The blond guard was making his way over the dune, ten metres down the beach. His handgun was raised, dull black.

'Do not move!' he yelled. 'Do you hear me? *Do not move.*'

'Is he talking to us?' Gaia whispered. She wiped her mouth, streaked dust from her lips. And her gaze shot back to the water. Caspian had struck out. He was buoyant now, his arms pulling his sturdy body through the water. His hair was black against the wavelets. Caspian was strong. He was moving fast.

'He's *bleeding,*' Gaia said.

Will glanced back at the security officer, who had run to the water's edge.

'Hey!' the officer shouted to Caspian. 'Return to the beach!' He lifted his gun. Aimed. 'I *will* shoot. Return to the beach!'

Caspian was a good fifteen metres off-shore. He turned his head briefly. Will saw the arrogance fixed in his eyes. Then, in an instant, Caspian's expression changed.

Will knew what it meant. He'd seen the dark shadow zigzag below the surface.

Will's body flinched. He'd almost felt it.

Caspian had been *hit.*

The blond guard was lowering his weapon. He was trying to peer into the lagoon.

Will took Gaia's arm, and made for the shallows. His chest was tight. He was remembering Research Lake 2 and the *impacts.* Remote control couldn't totally suppress an animal's most instinctive behaviours. He knew that as well as anyone. And sharks had an incredible sensitivity to *blood*.

'Caspian!' Will shouted. Despite everything, he had to try to warn him. 'That is a bull shark! It's probing you before it attacks. Swim back!'

Will watched as Caspian slipped on to his side, arms flailing.

'Caspian!' Will yelled.

And the blond officer called: 'Will Knight?'

Will's head shot round. C must have passed on his name, he thought. And he turned back – just in time to see the shadow barrel out of nowhere, right at Caspian, fin slicing through the waterline. The fin vanished, taking Caspian with it.

Gaia shuddered. The collision had sent water droplets spurting high, casting a thousand dark rainbows through the sky.

The lagoon had been green. Now it was stained with red.

'I don't care what Calvino says, get the launch here!' The grey-haired man with the moon face was shouting.

Will and Gaia were on the terrace. People were milling around them. Dusty uniforms, white-stained suits. Guns still waved in all directions. Cristina seemed to have vanished. Down the terrace, the blond guard was touching C's shoulder. Pointing at Will. Whispering something.

They had been ordered to stay where they were. C wanted to speak to them, when he was ready. Andrew had contacted them via the toothphone. He said Angelo had the gun trained on Dino. They were on the beach, waiting for a pick-up. He asked what had happened. Will told him they were OK. Told him about Caspian.

'Are you sure? He's . . . dead?'

'He has to be,' Will replied. '. . . Andrew, I don't know what you did yet. But well done.'

'Thanks. Um. You too.'

Will glanced uncertainly at Gaia. 'Andrew, he would

have killed everyone here. Including us. *We stopped him.*'

'I know.' The voice was quiet. 'It's a shock, that's all. I know. We did it. Again.'

And Will smiled slightly. '*Again.*'

'I need water!' A female shout. The stout eastern European woman. Beyond her, a red-haired man was leaning over the balcony and spitting out dust. Others were shouting, some yelling into mobile phones. The terrace was packed. After the explosion, security officers had swarmed out like bugs from the villa's woodwork.

Tiredness was beginning to seep into Will's body, along with relief. But it still felt as though his blood had been replaced with coffee.

And he stiffened. He'd heard a small noise, almost lost in the commotion. But he had recognized it at once. '*Ratty!*'

The animal was trotting towards him, skirting the crowd. He was grey, his brown fur thick with dust. Will crouched. Grabbed him by the belly. Met his beady black eyes. Whiskers flickered.

'Ratty!' Gaia exclaimed. 'You're all right!' She touched the animal's head. Smiled. 'He must have let go. Will, I meant to tell you. He was biting the bag. I thought—'

And a shadow dappled their eyes. The blond security officer had approached. His large frame was blotting out the sun.

'My name is David Allott,' the officer said. A trace of a Welsh accent lilted his vowels. Rich brown eyes fixed on Will. Lines were etched deep into his forehead. 'I knew your father well.'

Instantly, Will tensed. His smile vanished. *Your father.* These were words he no longer heard.

'I was with him. Just a few hours before he was killed. I'm sorry.' Allott held out his hand.

Will stared. This man had been with his father? But—

But now C was striding towards them, grabbing Allott's arm. His expression was grim. When he spoke, it felt to Will as though he were miles away. The words were drifting vaguely towards him. *Your father.*

C's moon-face loomed. Will could hardly bring himself to look at it. He was remembering. The man in the dark suit. The screech of the tyres as the messenger from MI6 had raced to get away from their grief.

Gaia touched his arm. He barely felt it.

'Will Knight,' C said. His voice was deep. Curt. 'Yes, I had heard about you. You want to tell me your version of what has just happened?'

Will looked as though he hadn't heard. It was because of Allott's mention of his father, Gaia realized. But Will didn't need to talk. She could explain. And the reality of the situation hit her.

They had almost died. *She* had almost died. Caspian was dead. They had risked their lives. She had left her father behind in hospital. And they were being *interrogated.* Treated like suspects.

'I can tell you my version,' she said. 'A boy called Caspian Baraban, who *somehow* escaped from a top security psychiatric prison, just teleported into your meeting and tried to kill you.' She swallowed. Her throat felt tight. 'Shute Barrington, your *traitor*, got us here to the island, so we could try to stop him. Which we did. We are STORM, by the way. You might have heard of us. Though Barrington would have told you – and of course you can't believe anything he says.'

A smile lifted the corners of David Allott's mouth.

But C pursed his lips, as if pondering Gaia's words. His cool grey eyes shifted to Will, who looked up now and nodded slowly in agreement.

'Interesting,' C said. 'Though there were two errors in your statement. One: Shute Barrington is not a traitor. Two: Caspian Baraban did not exactly escape.'

26

Marcelette Street, London, SW1. Easter Sunday.

Bright sunshine reflected off the upper windows of the stucco-fronted mansion block. From the lintel above the blue door, a carved lion and two spiral-horned unicorns commanded the narrow street.

It was cool and silent here, in the shadows. Hard to believe that just fifty metres away was the Mall, and, beyond, the deck-chairs and ducks of St James's Park. Gaia would meet them in the park, she'd said. On the bridge with the fairytale views to the palace of Westminster.

Will glanced at Andrew. Pale blue eyes blinked from behind his heavy glasses. Andrew was dressed in white jeans and a T-shirt embroidered with a stern-eyed Sphinx. A souvenir of one of his parents' trips, Will guessed.

'This is it?' Andrew said.

'Number Twenty,' Will replied. 'That's what he said.'

Will climbed the three steps and lifted the brass knocker, which was shaped like an anchor. Before he'd had a chance to slam it down, a voice burst from a concealed speaker: 'No need for that. Come on in. First floor.'

The heavy door jerked open. It revealed a grey-painted hallway and a staircase carpeted in blue. They could hear nothing. See no one.

At the top of the first flight of stairs, a long landing opened out. Will noticed a door standing ajar. He pointed. Andrew nodded. Even before they reached it, it was thrown open, and Shute Barrington appeared, in familiar black jeans and black T-shirt, his arm in a sling, his right hand resting on a cane. In a faux upper-class English accent, he said: 'Welcome to our London residence. Do come in.'

'You shouldn't be walking,' Andrew said, concerned. 'The doctors said you shouldn't.'

'What are you going to do?' Barrington said. 'Tell on me?'

Andrew frowned and peered into the room beyond. 'You work *here*?'

'Not if I can help it.' Awkwardly, his leg dragging, Barrington led them through into his office and on to a leather Chesterfield sofa. The room was decorated in a Victorian style. Brocade curtains. Brass lamps. Paintings of gutsy clippers on stormy seas.

'This building used to belong to the Navy. We took it over last year. We're supposed to have a London office so government types who don't want to make the trek to Sutton Hall can interrogate us here.' Barrington pulled a chair from behind his oak desk. He stretched out his leg. And he faced Will and Andrew.

Will felt expectancy surge. This was the first time he'd seen Barrington since the Duke's Palace in Venice. Twenty-seven hours since Caspian Baraban's bomb had blown a hole in the corner of the ballroom of the villa on the Island of the Masks.

MI6 field officers had collected Andrew, Angelo and their grimy captive from the beach of the Isola delle Fantasme. At that moment, Dino was locked up, assisting police with their enquiries. Angelo and Cristina, who apparently had been spirited away from the terrace by the Italian delegation to the 'garden party', were undergoing a 'debriefing' at home.

Will, Andrew and Gaia had been put on the C-17 transport plane back to London. They'd been chaperoned by a remorseful Thor, who, after discovering Barrington's integrity was not in doubt, apparently wished he'd done more to help.

'You know, it would have been very difficult to disrupt the sensor field without—' he'd started, as he strapped himself in.

Will had only shaken his head. And Thor had shut up.

On the plane, at last, Will, Andrew and Gaia had a chance to talk about the events. To discuss what had happened in the cellar of the castle, and at the villa.

'You hit Dino?' Gaia said, her jaw dropping.

'Not exactly *hit*. I got in the way, really.' Andrew smiled. 'He sort of fell over me. And that doesn't exactly compare to riding on the back of a shark!'

Will shook his head. 'We did what we had to do,' he said. 'You went further.'

Andrew coloured. 'No – I—'

'*You went further,*' Will said.

'Well, I didn't get rid of the bomb.'

Will glanced at Gaia, the smile still there. 'No. I had Ratty on that job.'

'I fought Ratty for it,' Gaia said, smiling back. 'He *is* determined. But I still won.'

Mid-flight, two JPEGS arrived from Cristina. She'd texted Andrew, explaining that she'd 'obtained' them from Diabolo's computer.

They showed two children. A girl, her mouth twisted across her face like a slash, her nose missing. A boy, his head horribly shrunk, unseeing white eyes staring with inhuman terror. Andrew had retched. Gaia had turned away. Will had forced himself to look. *This* is what Caspian had been doing. Experimenting on people. He'd got what he deserved.

And if it hadn't been for his soaring pride, in wanting to see the looks on the faces of the people he was condemning to death, he just might have got away with it. He could have teleported in that bomb and kept a safe distance. Caspian's own pride and arrogance had killed him.

Now, back in London, Will and Andrew had agreed

to be debriefed by Shute Barrington. Gaia would be 'processed' later.

They had gone through a debriefing after the events of last Christmas in St Petersburg. Will still wasn't clear what it was supposed to involve. In Russia, Barrington had asked lots of questions and answered few. Now Will wanted to get his in first.

'What happened to Caspian? I mean – did you get his body?'

'. . . What was left of it.'

Andrew paled.

Will pressed on. 'On the terrace after the bomb, C told me two things. One, you're not a traitor. Two, Caspian Baraban did not escape.'

Barrington's expression did not flicker. 'Is that a question?' he said at last.

'*How* did Caspian get out of his secure institution?'

'Ah . . . All right. We let him out.'

'*What?*' Andrew exclaimed.

Barrington rolled back in his chair. 'I mean, obviously we didn't let him know that. He thought he was using his genius to outwit us. We left a key code lying around somewhere not too obvious. Sent him a "sympathetic" psychiatrist, who could plant a few ideas in his messed-up mind – and who could help him "escape".'

'But *why?*' Andrew said.

'You remember Sir James Parramore? Billionaire British businessman. Shady as you like. Paid for the research in St Petersburg.'

'Of course,' Andrew said tightly.

'Well, we wanted him. And we knew he'd been in touch with Caspian, after he was admitted to hospital. We thought that Caspian would lead us to Parramore.'

'But?' Will said.

'Our psychiatrist picked Caspian up just outside the secure perimeter. He was supposed to keep an eye on Caspian. Caspian was supposed to trust him.'

'*But?*' Will persisted.

'*But* Caspian killed him. He used a syringe from the hospital. Injected air into his carotid.'

Andrew's face twisted. 'Caspian *killed* him?'

'And that surprises you? He just tried to kill sixteen people. More, if you count security. And that boy that washed up . . . So, Caspian vanished. A few days later, someone hacked into the STASIS network. Evidently, Caspian found out about the meeting, and so on. And he plotted revenge. He blamed intelligence agencies for his father's death. Why not wipe them all out? His logic was twisted. Remember that.'

'So it was definitely Caspian who got you Red-Listed?' Andrew said.

'Who else?' Barrington replied. 'It wasn't the agent in Moscow. He had no idea about the whole thing, it turned out, in due course.'

'And who was Rudolfo?' Will said. 'Cristina said he was a relation.'

'A distant relation. Caspian went to his "uncle" seeking refuge, I imagine, and evidently was granted it. I wonder how long it took Rudolfo to realize his mistake . . . Whatever he thought, he's vanished. We've got our people searching all over. No sign of him yet.'

'But he didn't give Caspian up,' Andrew said. 'Why not?'

Barrington shrugged. 'I imagine he was afraid to. And he was a parapsychologist. Perhaps on a certain level, he enjoyed it – the ghosts and the cult and the power. He'd spent years as a recluse. Suddenly he was vice-general of a crazy island empire.'

'OK,' Will said. 'And C knew you weren't a traitor? How did he know that?'

Barrington pushed back his chair. Lifted the blind and pretended to peer outside. 'Yes, well, if my estimates are correct, he made that declaration precisely one minute after I'd been cleared. He followed protocol. He had to.'

'And Cristina?' Andrew asked.

'Her lion has been located,' Barrington said more brightly, letting the blind drop. 'She'll get it back. Eventually.' And he frowned. 'Though apparently she has been crowing about hacking into *my* wireless sensor network, which doesn't exactly encourage me to expedite matters.'

'I meant about *her*,' Andrew said. 'What happens to her?'

'Who knows? A warning not to get involved in secret service business in future. A pat on the back. That's up to The Dog . . . You haven't heard from her?'

Andrew glanced at Will. 'Well, I did get an email—'

'When?' Will said. Andrew hadn't mentioned this.

'Last night.' Andrew hesitated. Cristina had said how much she'd enjoyed working with STORM. She said she'd like to join them in London. She thought STORM should set up cells around the world. They should go global. This was private business, Andrew decided. He'd discuss it with Will later. 'She asked how we were . . .' Andrew stumbled. 'She said she was well.'

'You teenagers have such fascinating conversations,' Barrington observed. And he staggered up from his chair. He yanked open a drawer of the mahogany desk. 'I need to ask you questions, you know that. But first things first.

'You did well. I have to tell you that.' He looked at Will. 'I got you and Gaia and Cristina to the island, but from there on in, it was you all the way. And, Andrew, I want you to show me the manoevre you used on Dino some time. And if you want to take a look at the tele-portation cubicle, as I speak, it's being investigated by our team at Sutton Hall. You're welcome to visit. I can arrange it. Which brings me on to these. I have some-thing for you. For each of you, in fact. You'll have to take Gaia's.'

Barrington held up a metal box. Will recognized it at once.

'Yeah,' Barrington said. 'From Research Lake 2. Will, you did find it, so by all rights, this is yours.'

Families laughed in the afternoon sun. Couples strolled past with prams and Easter eggs. It was a Sunday, so there were no cars on the Mall. Hordes of tourists in sturdy shoes were heading along the wide flag-lined avenue towards Buckingham Palace. People ambled about, as though all London was theirs.

Will was walking with his head down, thinking. Beside him, Andrew's polished shoes kicked up dust. In his pocket, Will had the original contents of the box, plus another for Gaia. Andrew had his own.

A STASIS tag, made from osmiridium. The embedded transmitter would get them only through the barrier at the entrance to the drive to the Sutton Hall HQ and in the front door, Barrington had told them. But they were symbolic more than practical, Will knew that.

STASIS recruits started out with plain plastic passes. Osmiridium tags were awarded to recognize outstanding work. In handing out these tags, Barrington was telling them they belonged. STORM to STASIS.

Should they? Will wasn't sure. He was proud of their independence. And, yes, it was true, he was proud of what they had achieved. Without STORM, C and the other intelligence chiefs would, in all probability, be dead – with all the global fallout that would have ensued.

In the event, the 'incident' in Venice had stopped nothing, Barrington had told them after distributing the tags. The meeting had been rescheduled for two days' time. No, he could not tell them where . . .

331

He should be feeling great, Will knew. But he wasn't sure how to feel about Caspian.

'I was thinking . . .' Andrew stopped. They were in the park now, starting to weave between picnic blankets and footballs, making their way towards the bridge. Will was looking pre-occupied, Andrew thought, and it would do him no good. 'In the light of recent events, I was thinking we should temporarily rename ourselves.' He resumed walking.

Andrew's ploy worked. Will was back in the immediate present. He caught up. 'To what?'

'Maybe: Society To Out-wit Russian Mavericks? What do you think? And while we're talking about names,' Andrew continued, 'you said I could name the tongue device, if it worked.'

Will nodded.

'Good.'

'So . . . ?'

'Andrew.'

'*Andrew?*'

Andrew nodded. 'Is there something wrong with the name?' he said innocently. And he smiled.

'But that's got nothing to do with what it does!' And Will turned. They'd reached the path that led to the bridge, and a voice had called to them, from the direction of the palace.

Gaia.

She hurried closer. She was smiling. She was out of breath, after walking fast. Her hair was scraped back from her face and she looked tired. But she was smiling.

'Good news?' Andrew said quickly.

Gaia nodded. 'He's a lot better.'

'Excellent!' Andrew clapped. 'We have something for you – from Shute. The keys to STASIS headquarters, no less.'

'The front gate, anyway,' Will said, and he smiled now. 'Shute told us to pass on congratulations. If it weren't for us—'

'—The world would be in turmoil?' Gaia finished.

'He wouldn't be here to congratulate us was what he actually said. But I think we can take the turmoil bit as a given.'

'So what did the doctor say exactly—' Andrew began.

But for Will, Andrew's voice suddenly faded into the background. His pocket was vibrating. Will pulled out his new phone. A text. He read:

Just saw you leaving Marcelette office. There are things I should tell you about father's death. Will be at Sutton Hall next week. Find me. D.A.

Instantly, the park vanished. Will's fingers fumbled. He scrolled through the menu, searching out the number of the sender. Found nothing. All details had been withheld. And Will looked up, aware that eyes were on him. 'D.A.' had to be David Allott, the blond guard. But what did he mean: *There are things I should tell you . . . ?* What his father was doing in China? How exactly he died?

Andrew had linked his arm through Gaia's. 'Is something wrong?' he said.

Will hesitated. He should tell them. But this was private. *Later*, he thought. '. . . No.'

'I'm going to escort Gaia back to the hospital,' Andrew said. 'Do you want to come?'

Behind Andrew, a ball sailed overhead. White ducks waddled past, heading for a small girl offering bread. The Earth rolled on.

What did David Allott mean? Suddenly Will had the unpleasant sensation that the world was still shifting and he wasn't sure what to hang on to.

But the answer was right in front of him. Literally.

Deep down, he knew it.

Will met Andrew's steady gaze, and then Gaia's. In his jacket pocket, something twitched, as though spurring him on. *Ratty*. He nodded. 'I'll come.'

Andrew nodded, pleased. 'Oh,' he said, remembering something. 'In honour of our Venetian victory and our reunion here in St James's Park, I think it's time for that handshake.'

'What handshake?' Gaia said, before realization struck. 'You mean the American ball-player handshake?'

'Indeed.' Andrew held out his hand formally to Gaia, who cautiously took it and glanced at Will.

'Andrew, I don't think that's how American ball-players do it,' Will said.

334

'No, but I think we have to face the fact that we're English,' Andrew said, smiling. 'So shake my hand. Go, STORM!'

Author's Note

All the gadgets in this book are based on genuine research and inventions.

1. Will's tongue kit is based on the Brain Port and tongue strip under development at the Florida Institute for Human and Machine Cognition.

2. The STASIS 'I've been shot' gun is based on a patent application by US inventor Kevin Sinha (US patent application 20060042142).

3. A gadget for recording and playing back smells has been created at the Tokyo Institute of Technology in Japan.

4. Andrew's curtain screen, and the screen in his wearable computer jacket, are based on research at the University of Connecticut, US, on woven, conductive plastics.

5. Ratty's patches are based on a super-sticky material inspired by gecko feet, created at BAE Systems in Bristol, UK.

6. Finger rings for wearable computer input have been developed by researchers at the NTT Human Interface Laboratories in Japan.

7. The SmarTruck is built by the US Army's National Automotive Center.

8. Hard Choice is loosely based on a patent by an American inventor, but this rope is inflated with air (WO 2004/092463).

9. Blind Spot is loosely based on a 'green beam designator' device made by B.E. Meyers, based in Redmond, US, for the US military.

10. Grabber is loosely based on a number of different research projects, including work on robotic tentacles at Clemson University in South Carolina.

11. Research on so-called 'sol-gels' of nano-sized particles of aluminium and iron oxide, and other explosive combinations, is taking place at Lawrence Livermore National Laboratory, US.

12. Motorized roller skates, for use in moving around

virtual reality environments, have been developed by a team at the University of Tsukuba in Japan.

Notes on the science

1. **Teleportation.** Scientists have succeeded in teleporting light and aspects of atoms. But, so far, that's it. Teleporting objects is theoretically possible but teleporting even molecules is thought to be decades away. Among the obstacles are current data transmission rates, which are far too slow.

2. **Milli-bot ghosts.** Research on a system of modular robots – which ultimately could resemble Caspian's 'ghost' – is being carried out at Carnegie Mellon University, US. The team calls their system 'claytronics'. I have borrowed their ideas on methods of adhesion and movement of the individual components.

3. **Infrasound and ghosts.** This information is based on genuine findings and theories. Richard Wiseman at the University of Hertfordshire has studied many supposedly haunted sites, including Mary King's Close in Edinburgh. Wiseman thinks environmental factors (such as sources of infrasound and breezes) and psychological factors account for reports of 'hauntings'.

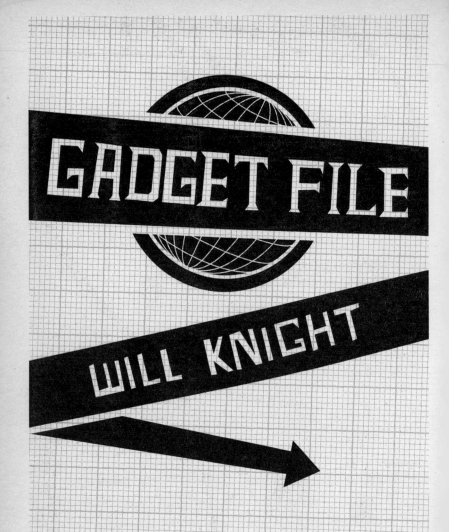

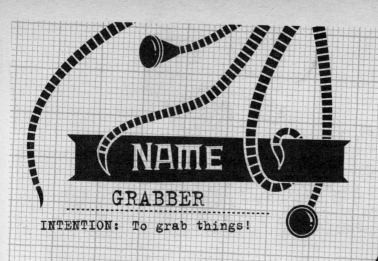

NAME

GRABBER

INTENTION: To grab things!

SPECS:

Carbon-fibre body. Prehensile
tentacles, extendable to
30 centimetres. Miniature
cameras in the tip of the
first pair of tentacles.

30 cm

CREATED:
Garden, Bloomsbury

TESTED:
Dining room,
Sutton Hall
(used tentacles to
covertly retrieve one
green bean and one
cherry from table)

POTENTIAL MODIFICATIONS:

Use sound-absorbing pads?
(Grabber noisy when he walks).

(Get Grabber a dedicated carrying rat?
Ratty has his own work to do! - Andrew)

NAME

UNNAMED

INTENTION:
To see underwater
in the dark

SPECS:
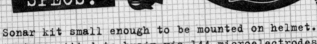

Sonar kit small enough to be mounted on helmet.
Data transmitted to brain via 144 microelectrodes
in strip of plastic stuck to tongue.

CREATED:
Bedroom, Bloomsbury and Lab 5,
Sutton Hall, STASIS Research &
Development HQ, Oxfordshire

TESTED:
Research Lake 2
(test not completed)

(I conducted a successful test and
its name is 'Andrew' - remember?
And under 'intention', shouldn't you
put: 'to allow unarmed colleagues to
triumph over dangerous enemies in pitch
darkness?' - Andrew)

● POTENTIAL MODIFICATIONS:
Add thermal underwater camera - could help indicate
whether approaching objects are living or not??

13

TESTED:
On robotic heads with imitation human sensory systems in Lab 13

NAME

BLIND SPOT

CREATED:
Sutton Hall

INTENTION:

To stop an enemy without causing lasting damage

SPECS:

15 cm long. At 10 metres, has power output of less than 2.56 milliwatts per cm^2 — and should not cause lasting eye damage.

● POTENTIAL MODIFICATIONS:

Improve the safety catch

(Can you look at the batteries? The 'this is actually a laser finder for help in aiming my seriously deadly weapon' line didn't really convince anyone. Andrew)

NAME

WALKABOUT

INTENTION:
To allow hands-free
computer/Internet
access on the move

a n d r e w

SPECS:

Solid-state hard
drive stitched into
pocket. Heads-up virtual
display. Secondary display in
lining made from electrochromic
polymers, which change colour
in response to an electric
field. Finger rings act
as a wireless keyboard.

100GB

TESTED:

Grounds of Sutton
Hall (checked
email while
jogging to wood)

CREATED:

Bloomsbury and
Sutton Hall

POTENTIAL MODIFICATIONS:
(Modify so that only Andrew can use it,
so no one else can borrow it? Andrew)

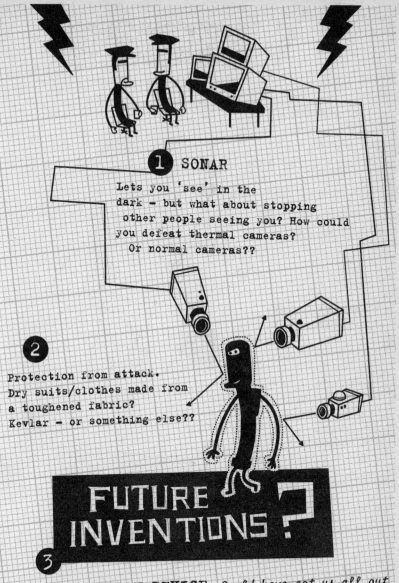

1 SONAR

Lets you 'see' in the
dark - but what about stopping
other people seeing you? How could
you defeat thermal cameras?
Or normal cameras??

2

Protection from attack.
Dry suits/clothes made from
a toughened fabric?
Kevlar - or something else??

FUTURE INVENTIONS?

3

(TELEPORTATION DEVICE. Could have got us all out
of trouble on our various islands. Oh wait, it's already
been invented. So did MI6 make off with the plans as
well as the chamber? Andrew)

Acknowledgements

Thank you to James, for all his comments and VGs. To Harriet Wilson, my editor at Macmillan. To Sarah Molloy, my agent. And to Dr Terry Percival of National ICT Australia.